# MAKE-BELIEVE WITH THE MARQUESS

ANNABELLE ANDERS



IN FOR A PENNY PUBLISHING, LLC

**Make-believe With The Marquess**



*Cover by Barbara Cantor, Forever After Romance Designs.*

❀ Created with Vellum

## WHEN HE MISTAKES YOU FOR A CHAMBERMAID...

### GRUMPY/SUNSHINE, FAKE BETROTHAL, SECRET PAST

The Marquess has something this teacher wants, and, as luck would have it, she has something he needs.

Beatrice Wolcott is desperate to keep her past a secret. She can't afford to make the same mistake other teachers have made—mistakes that have forced them to marry! So when the Marquess asks Beatrice to pose as his temporary fiancée, she would have refused... Until he offered to discover the identity of whoever has been vandalizing the school. How could she not agree to the bargain when the safety of the students is at stake?

In conceding, however, she insists all proprietary be upheld! Chaperone, check. Separate coaches, check. Signed contract, double check.

All this prim teacher lacks is a little self-control—or rather, quite a lot of self-control—as she's having increasing difficulties keeping her hands off this devil of a detective.

Lord Sexton, Chief investigator, and Interim Director of the Society for the Advancement of Ingenuity in London, needs to address one last detail to convince the board to make his position a permanent one: A wife.

In his mind, a temporary betrothed will be just as effective.

And Miss Beatrice Walcott is perfect for the job! As an intelligent woman, she'll understand the practicality of his offer, not yearn for romantic gestures, and most importantly, never expect him to make her his marchioness.

The charade works out perfectly until they surrender to the steamy attraction between them. And to complicate matters, the woman Sexton is inexplicably falling for, seems to be keeping her own secrets. Is his make-believe betrothed as uncomplicated as he'd initially believed, or is she perhaps, the greatest mystery of all?

# FIRST IMPRESSIONS

"You can't wear that to tea," Beatrice's former colleague and tomorrow's bride, frowned at Beatrice's apron. The garment, which had been white earlier this morning, along with her dull gray morning gown, had been soaked by the freshly cut flowers Beatrice had transferred from the orangery to the ballroom. Rather than join Priscilla's guests in assembling the centerpieces, Beatrice had been more than happy to volunteer for the unwanted task.

What with that many women sitting around talking, one could barely hear oneself think in the large ballroom.

Beatrice far preferred to make herself useful, and she alone had kept the tables supplied with flowers. She hadn't cared that she'd been working amongst servants. The wedding and subsequent breakfast were the following day, and Beatrice had done more than her fair share of socializing.

She was exhausted, and not from the performing of

crafts or walking along cliffs or even a few dance lessons, but from...

*All of the talking!*

As friends of the bride, Beatrice and a few other teachers from Miss Primm's had been treated as honored guests. Miss Adelaide Royal shared an expansive chamber with Miss Primm, and Beatrice shared an equally lovely room with Miss Chloe Fortune

Regardless of any of their personal inclinations, Miss Primm had demanded that her teachers participate in all planned events and perform the occasional task with grateful enthusiasm.

... So long as one didn't consider Victoria Shipley. But she didn't count, considering she had also been the assistant director. And considering that the earl she'd married was Miss Primm's brother... Although Miss Collette Jones had done well for herself as well, and as her husband was a duke, she'd have to be included as yet another exception.

Regardless, spinsters rarely married, especially above their stations. So both matches had been quite exceptional.

Beatrice dragged her stare around the various tables, half of which were going to run out of supplies shortly.

She appreciated all the pomp and circumstances, but she'd rather have a tooth pulled than live through another week like this one. It was a reminder of the life she'd once had—of a life gone forever.

These people had shared memories—a shared past. They *belonged* to one another.

"I can't leave yet," she insisted. "Hardwood's servants are already buried in extra tasks." But Priscilla was firmly guiding Beatrice toward the exit.

"Emerson's mother and sisters are perfectly capable of

coping with any catastrophes that might occur without you here to prevent them."

Hardwood Cliffhouse, Priscilla's intended's estate, buzzed with excitement, making an early escape sound positively lovely.

"Are you sure, Priscilla?" But her protest was a feeble one.

Beatrice yearned for the time to herself. She'd promised her brother a letter and once she'd penned that, perhaps she could take a solitary walk, or even a nap before presenting herself in the Sapphire Drawing Room for the next gathering.

"Absolutely." Priscilla gave Beatrice a gentle shove. "Besides," she glanced at the timepiece that hung at her waist. "We're nearly finished here. Just don't be late. There are at least two lords I know of who have asked for an introduction."

"To me?" Beatrice barely stopped herself from rolling her eyes at the idea of such ridiculousness. "I'm not that naïve, Priscilla," she laughed.

Not that she'd welcome such introductions.

In her mind, she'd already slipped away alone. Having most of the afternoon to herself was going to be glorious!

"Send for me if you require my assistance earlier." Beatrice walked backward.

In response, Priscilla held up two fingers. "Two, gentlemen," she said. "So don't be late."

Beatrice shook her head, already wondering if she'd mention the joke to Jasper in her letter.

As she made her way through the seemingly endless foyers, a nap sounded better and better. After she penned her letter, she could lie down in nothing but her shift. She'd be blissfully cool and rested for the remainder of the evening, whereas if she took that walk, she might be accosted and forced to endure more banal conversation.

Contemplating her choices, Beatrice skittered through the empty corridors, anxious already not to waste a single moment.

But then, partway down one hallway, she noticed a very tall, masculine figure ambling toward her.

*Dash it all.*

She ducked and hurried her steps.

So far this week, she'd managed to avoid mingling with the male guests. As friends of Lord Hardwood's, many of them either held titles or were positioned somehow to inherit one.

All in all, precisely the sort of gentlemen she avoided—the type who might have known her parents, or even worse, associate with Aunt Ursula or Uncle Titus.

But before she could pass, a hand reached out and snagged her arm.

"Excuse me." Not a hint of apology sounded in the man's voice.

A cry of surprise caught in her throat. It was quite unexpected for a lady to be manhandled in such a manner. Not at a house party, not at a school, not anywhere.

And at five feet six and a half inches tall, Beatrice rarely needed to look up to meet a person's gaze. This man, however, loomed over her.

Although she'd not been introduced, she was well aware of who he was— Ranulf Winters, the Eighth Marquess of Sexton. He was one of the few lords in London who had taken on a profession—scientific investigations of sorts. And if she was not mistaken, he held one of the higher positions at the King's Society for the Advancement of something or other in England.

But in this moment, he was simply in her way… keeping her from having some precious time to herself.

Beatrice tilted her head back and met his cold, black, unrepentant eyes. His mouth was set in a grim line, his jawline stern, and his nose long and arrogant. Lines of annoyance creased the skin between his brows. Not one aspect of his expression revealed even a hint of kindness.

"I beg your pardon—" she began.

"You'll change the counterpane in my chamber at once." He spoke before she could demand that he release her.

His words were a command, not a request, and being spoken to thusly, left Beatrice speechless.

"Your counterpane…?" She blinked up at him, confused.

Her heart skipped a beat at his unfamiliar spicy scent—earthy, almost like freshly cut wood. She rarely found herself this close to a man except for the few occasions when one of her student's fathers lacked the ability to recognize personal boundaries.

It must have been her failure to jump to perform his bidding that deepened his scowl.

"It's been doused in perfume by some brazen female." His black eyes were cold as onyx. "How is a person to sleep while inhaling such poison?"

What on earth…? Was he suggesting that *she* had been the one to pour perfume on his linens?

"I'm afraid—"

"Go on, now." Having dispatched his orders, he released her. "It's the third door on the left." His eyes flicked past her and then closed for half a second, like he was fighting the urge to fall asleep. Was he unusually pale?

Looking closer, she noticed shadows etched beneath his eyes.

But his next words stole any sympathy she might have had.

"Must I report your insubordination to the housekeeper? I'll have your name, miss." He thought she was one of the servants. Was he going to tell on her—another guest—*for insubordination*?" Beatrice would have giggled if the entire situation wasn't so unnerving.

And humiliating.

"I'm not—I believe you've…" she stammered. "I'm a *guest* here, my lord."

He studied her with narrowed eyes. Did he think she was lying?

"You are mistaken," she added.

She should not have to defend herself to him or to anyone! She cringed at her urge to ease his embarrassment.

That was the worst of it—that he made her feel foolish, as though she was the person in the wrong—apologetic, even, to be pointing out his error.

His gaze slid down her face to the soaked apron covering her less than fashionable gown and then back up to meet her eyes.

"Am I?" But then he dipped his chin.

"I teach with the bride-to-be—with Miss Fellowes." *Or taught, anyhow. And tomorrow Priscilla would become Lady Hardwood.*

"At Miss Primm's."

"Yes."

His resulting grunt made her feel lower than if she had been an actual chambermaid.

Not that Beatrice was below performing the menial

tasks. Teachers, quite often, had no choice but to deal with various bodily fluids.

But those incidents had never demeaned her as much as the insult behind this man's stare. What gave him the right to be so odious?

"So, you see, I am a guest. Just as you are." She lifted her chin.

Lord Sexton glanced over his shoulder and then over hers. When he finally met her gaze again, he failed to utter the apology she expected.

"Where the devil are the maids then?" he asked instead.

Normally, Beatrice would have offered to find one for him, but normally, a person wouldn't have treated her with such rudeness.

She shrugged. "I've no idea, my lord. Now, if you'll excuse me…" She moved to edge around his lordly ill-will, almost hugging the wall to pass him. "Good day."

Two minutes later, after closing the door to her chamber firmly behind her, she caught a glimpse of herself in the looking glass set atop the vanity.

True, the mob cap on her head was similar to those the servants wore, but her gown was greyish blue, not black, and last year she had embroidered tiny bluebells around the neckline.

That beastly marquess had been so caught up in his demands that he'd not bothered to look beyond her cap, beyond her apron.

He'd not seen *her*.

It was the sort of thing her uncle would have done.

She shuddered at the reminder. She'd done everything she could to leave her aunt and uncle in her past—her and her brother's past—and she had succeeded.

*So far, anyhow.*

A shiver ghosted down her spine.

A glance at the mantle clock reminded her that her time was limited and she shifted into action. The Marquess of Sexton may have doused some of her enthusiasm, but she'd not allow him to ruin this beautiful afternoon.

Flicking the cap onto a chair, she then unfastened her gown at the front, stepped out of it, as well as her shoes, and sat down at the small desk near the window.

Jasper was in his last year at Eton, and no doubt found her letters trivial, but she sent them anyway. As she only saw him at Christmastime, she considered it important to keep in touch—to remind him he had a sister who loved and cared for him—and who he was.

After signing her name on the bottom, she stared at her words while the ink dried. She and Jasper had yet to decide what he'd do after his graduation, which was fast upon them, but they would come up with something—they'd done well enough so far.

Mentally filing away her worries, she sealed the letter and tucked it into her small valise. She couldn't give it to Lord Hardwood's butler to post, but she'd mail it from one of the inns on the way between here and the school.

With her letter written, she climbed onto the unusually large bed.

The scent of her counterpane was fresh and lovely. Likely, Lord Sexton had imagined the perfume. Why would anyone purposely waste their perfume in such a manner, anyway?

Lord Sexton was either mad or overly demanding.

Most likely, both.

With a grimace, she rolled over.

She'd do well not to become accustomed to such a grand bed, but for now, she'd take full advantage.

WHEN SHE OPENED HER EYES, she blinked, frozen.

Not only was the room unfamiliar but judging by the light filtering through the windows from outside, the sun was low on the horizon.

"I didn't mean to awaken you," Chloe Fortune, the teacher with whom Beatrice shared this beautiful room, spoke softly. "You have a full hour before we need to be downstairs. If I'd realized napping was an option, I'd have volunteered to help with the flowers too."

Beatrice sat up and stared at the other woman, immediately noticing her pallor. Was that green tinge simply a result of her delicate condition, or from the stress of not yet having informed Captain Edgeworth?

"How are you feeling?" she asked.

Chloe had gotten herself into an extremely difficult situation, and if that hadn't been enough, had felt ill for most of the house party. It was mind-boggling that the most independent Miss Fortune had acted with such little regard to her future—it was the one thing a lady did her best to prevent.

But to make matters worse, Chloe didn't seem to grasp the gravity of her circumstances. She'd had all week to speak to the man responsible, but had failed to do so!

Chloe grimaced, her face tight with uncertainty, or sickness, or both. "As well as can be expected, given the--ah—the circumstances."

Beatrice shook her head. "You're running out of time."

"I know what I'm doing." Chloe's nostrils flared and a hint of pink flooded her cheeks.

She was too proud for her own good! Beatrice pinched her mouth together. She and Chloe had discussed this a thousand times, and yet still, the other teacher's future had not been settled.

But it would have to be, and soon. If the thickening of Chloe's waistline was any indication, people were going to start suspecting her condition…

Rather than embark on that particular argument again, however, Beatrice removed her prettiest day dress, a jonquil muslin—from her trunk. Her mother had once told her the color suited her best, and ever since then, it had been her favorite.

Following the encounter with that nasty gentleman, she needed a little extra confidence to face the evening.

For dinner, she would leave off the apron and cap.

"I thought you were wearing that one to the wedding tomorrow."

Beatrice feigned a casual shrug, ignoring Chloe's close regard as she pinned her hair into a careful knot. She would not admit that one of Priscilla's guests had mistaken her for a maid. It was too humiliating.

"I'm going for a quick stroll along the cliffs before tea," she said, instead.

"I'd tag along if I wasn't so tired." Such an admission from this particular woman was exceptional. Despite Beatrice knowing Chloe's secret, the two had not been chummy in the past.

In the nine years since Miss Primm had hired her, Beatrice hadn't been familiar with any of her co-workers. She'd considered it too dangerous. What if she slipped up? It would be too tempting to share her secrets if she had a close friend.

She hadn't even told Primm.

And yet, thinking she might be able to help Chloe, she hesitated before leaving. "I'll seek the captain out if—"

"No!" Chloe's eyes widened. "I'll...I'll speak with him. I just need the right moment..."

"Oh, Chloe." Beatrice shook her head grimacing. "Putting it off won't make it go away."

"I know," Chloe said. "But once it's out there, life as I know it will."

The other woman certainly had the right of it. Chloe was going to have no choice but to marry.

Beatrice had never been the sort of person to intervene in the affairs of others, but as she made her way through the winding foyers and exited the massive manor, she pondered Chloe's circumstances.

As far as Beatrice knew, she was the only person who knew Chloe's secret. She'd suspected for nearly a fortnight.

Often it was those who spoke the least who noticed the most.

And one thing she knew for certain was that Chloe was only procrastinating because she was terrified.

And what lady wouldn't be?

## A FORTNIGHT LATER

"Oh, and Beatrice," Primm rose from her desk to stop Beatrice before she could escape the office. With brown hair tied into a merciless knot at the back of her head, Beatrice's starchy employer wore the traditional olive-brown muslin gown of a true spinster. An apron with large overflowing pockets covered her skirts that swished about practical half-boots.

But although she dressed as though she was in her late fifties, Primm couldn't be much older than Beatrice herself, who'd just turned eight and twenty.

"Yes?" Beatrice hesitated. "Anything else?" She asked helpfully. The headmistress had not been herself recently. She'd been stern but lacked her normal calm demeanor.

And she looked tired.

"Unlock the dorms upstairs, will you? Lord Sexton has offered to take a look into the identity of our *little annoyance* and I'll need you to fill him in. He is scheduled to inspect the premises in"—she glanced at the clock— "ten minutes."

This was how Primm referred to the various acts of

vengeful destruction perpetrated on the grand three-story building over the past year—their *little annoyance.'*

Last fall, someone had taken an axe to the foundation, and over Christmas a goat had broken into the school overnight. And to make matters worse, while they'd all been away at Priscilla's wedding, a fire had been set in the third-floor student dorm room.

Thank heavens the contractor working over at Longbow Castle, Mr. Rowan Stewart, had been passing by and had the wherewithal to extinguish it.

Beatrice doubled her thanks that all the students had been away for the summer.

The school, in fact, was even quieter than usual.

First Victoria had abandoned them to marry Primm's brother, then Priscilla had gone and fallen in love with the Earl of Hardwood, and now Chloe, who'd failed to have that very important conversation with Captain Edgeworth, was on her way to find him in London. Miss Adelaide Royal had gone along as Chloe's companion.

Chloe, of course, wouldn't be returning. If any parents found out that one of their teachers had...Beatrice shook her head.

Beatrice dared not imagined. The school's reputation was shaky enough without yet another scandal to rock it.

Which left Beatrice alone with Primm.

Until that was, Hardwood's sisters, his mother, and their gentleman chaperone had arrived unexpectedly to tour the school.

Forty-eight hours following the teachers' arrival home, Captain Edgeworth—hopefully Chloe's husband by now—had descended on the school with what seemed like half the guests who'd attended the wedding.

Including Lord Sexton.

Who had never apologized for his boorish behavior and instead had persisted in being all around disagreeable.

When she'd caught his gaze during Priscilla's wedding ceremony, he had only scowled, and later at the breakfast, he'd seemed to be mocking her and the other schoolteachers from across the room.

Beatrice had ignored him at the time believing she'd never be put upon to suffer his presence again.

And now he was here, *drat it all!*

Worse than that, Primm would expect her to be cordial.

*To that arrogant, cocksure, pompous excuse for a human being!*

Which was typical behavior, she supposed, for a person who's every whim was met on a daily basis.

But he was not only a lord, he was also a detective…

"Don't you think you ought to meet with him personally?" Beatrice offered hopefully. If he could help track down their *little annoyance,* shouldn't Primm be the person to deal with him?

"Trust me, Miss Walcott, I'd far prefer your task over mine." Primm glanced at the mantel clock and the finely etched lines around her eyes deepened from worry. "Allison Meadowbrook's father is due to arrive to discuss the conditions of this year's donations." Allison, a lovely-looking girl on the cusp of womanhood, was one of their more… difficult students, and her father was one of the school's most generous donors. Or had been in the past, anyhow.

After nearly losing his patronage last winter, Primm was trying desperately to mend that relationship.

"What of Adelaide—Miss Royal?" Beatrice suggested

hopefully. "She gets on well with that sort." Meaning that Adelaide would have no difficulty nodding and smiling.

"Miss Royal has accompanied our dear Miss Fortune to London, remember?" Primm's fine lines transformed into full blown wrinkles. "You are the only one available, and I am counting on you to persuade Lord Sexton to take on our case." Primm touched her fingertips to her temple. "Whoever is causing us all this trouble, needs to be stopped. If our arsonist can be located, the marquess is the one man in England who can do so."

Beatrice knew they were having troubles, but she hadn't yet seen Primm looking so disheartened. Normally, Beatrice was not at all inclined to show affection, but the urge to give Primm a hug tugged at her.

Not that Primm would appreciate it.

So instead, Beatrice set aside her own reluctance about the marquess. "I'll do my best."

"As I'm sure you do all your duties."

The headmistress dipped her quill into some ink and then flicked a meaningful gaze toward the exit.

Beatrice had been dismissed. But as she opened the door, Primm's voice stopped her.

"Beatrice?"

"Yes?" She turned around cautiously.

"If you can, keep the marquess away from my office, will you? I cannot have Mr. Meadowbrook seeing an investigator lurking about. Even without the threat posed by our *little annoyance,* it's going to take everything I can do to convince him to continue sponsoring us."

"I'll do my best." Beatrice nodded. She could see how such a situation might have the potential to end rather poorly for the school. Hopefully, it wouldn't be too difficult to keep the two men from running into one another.

After closing the door behind her, Beatrice smoothed her hands down the front of her gown and drew her shoulders back.

Though she certainly did not envy Miss Primm her task, Beatrice was not much more pleased with her own. Perhaps his lordship would be tardy for the meeting, or better yet, he might not show at all.

Turning to climb the stairs, guilt settled on her shoulders. Because such thoughts weren't at all helpful. They were in direct opposition to Primm's request.

If spending ten minutes in Lord Sexton's company ultimately resulted in the arrest of their vandal, then the school could reopen without the ever-present shadow cast by this unknown threat.

*Nodding and smiling*—it was the least she could do.

She'd pretend the incident at Hardwood Cliffhouse never happened. She was a grown woman and had dealt with far worse individuals—horrible, horrible persons—she shuddered at the memory.

She wasn't some simpering debutante. She could handle one marquess—a marquess who investigated England's worst crimes when he wasn't lazing about at house parties or hunting helpless animals.

A hint of unease that had nothing to do with his arrogance crept over her skin.

Ten minutes. That's all she'd give him.

*Ten minutes.*

Stepping inside the student dorm room a few moments later, Beatrice glanced from one end to the other. The dormitory spanned exactly one half of the length of the school, and aside from a few private student chambers, it housed most of their girls—girls ranging from eight to eight and ten.

But glancing toward the far end, expecting to see the damages from the fire, her heart plummeted. Because it looked nearly as pristine as the rest of the dormitory.

Soot and ash had been washed away, no doubt by Mrs. Driver. Their caretaker's wife would have believed she was being helpful.

Unfortunately, along with the debris left over from the fire, she'd also cleared away the evidence.

Evidence that Lord Sexton would be expecting to use to lead him to the person who'd set the fire. How could the marquess solve a crime with no evidence?

Beatrice exhaled a shuttering sigh.

Lord Sexton was unpleasant under the best of circumstances, from her observations anyhow. Such an important person would be annoyed to have been summoned to a crime scene that had been thoroughly cleaned.

From her reading, Beatrice was well aware that any detective worth his weight would want to examine the aftermath just as the perpetrator had left it.

It wasn't Mrs. Driver's fault. Not when no one had thought to inform her.

With nothing to do but wait, Beatrice decided to conduct her own study of the near pristine crime scene. She tilted her head back, eyeing the places where the fire had scorched the ceiling. Some of the old crown molding had been cut out. It had been hand-carved and was likely half a century old. *Such a shame.*

Beatrice absentmindedly reached out as if to brush her fingers against the place where the fresh, bare plaster met the undamaged portion of the wall, but she managed to stop herself just before she made contact. It might not matter, what with how much evidence had already been destroyed, but still…

"What the devil do you think you're doing?"

At the sound of Lord Sexton's voice, Beatrice jerked back as though she'd been caught setting the fire herself.

Glancing behind her, there was no mistaking the identity of the gentleman now standing in the doorway. He wore an elegant black jacket and his black hair, which ought to appear mussed from the hat he held in front of him, was perfectly smoothed away from his face.

But his most notable feature was his physique. Lord Sexton was slim but not overly so. His capable shoulders were in perfect proportion, and for such a tall man, he was not at all ungainly.

Some might consider him handsome, even.

*Not her!*

It still irked her that he'd never apologized for accosting her. All it would take was a kind smile, a few humble words, and they could move past that initial meeting.

"My Lord," she said. "I was only—" Fisting her hands at her sides, Beatrice made a half-hearted curtsy. It was obvious he was not the sort of man who cared for excuses.

"The scene has already been compromised enough." He strode into the room, all his focus on the empty space near the broken window. "Too many do-gooders think they're helping when they're only sabotaging the investigation." He shook his head.

*Too many so-called experts assume they know everything when they're as human as the next person.*

"My apologies for the condition of the evidence," Beatrice said instead. "In our defense, we were not aware that you would be so... *charitable* as to offer the school your assistance."

"That remains to be seen."

*Then why did you come?* Beatrice huffed in exasperation and he slid his gaze down from the damaged ceiling.

"Do you have something to say?" he demanded.

She shrugged, widening her eyes in feigned innocence. "No, my lord."

He narrowed his eyes. She ought to be intimidated by him, and yet, he could huff and grunt all he wanted, he was only a man.

Albeit a more handsome man than she'd remembered. And that made him even more annoying.

Anxious to get through this meeting with as little bother as possible, she gestured toward the empty place where the fire had been started. "Our groundman's wife, at times, can be a tad too efficient." There was virtually nothing significant remaining, but for the copper pot and its contents, all of which had been stored downstairs in Primm's office. But honestly, did he expect they would leave the burned bed, the drapes and ash and soot untouched, like a shroud, on the off chance he'd deign to offer his services?

"Was anything salvaged?" His voice came out flat even though she noted interest lurking in the back of his black eyes.

"A few items we deemed significant are in Primm's office."

"But how do you know what is and is not significant?" He flicked her a less than complimentary glance and then dragged his gaze around the room with apparent indifference.

The casual mask was misleading, she was certain. This man, she'd wager, wasn't casual about much of anything. He pulsed with an intensity, a buzzing almost.

It made her uncomfortable.

"The arsonist left flint sitting on one of the beds, along with its container." They weren't idiots. "And the pot in which the fire was started."

"I'll dust all of it for fingerprints." He strolled across to the window and withdrew a magnifying glass from his jacket. "*If* I take the case." He proceeded to examine the sill and framing.

Her feelings about this, all in all, were conflicting. Because she wanted him to solve their mystery, she was curious how he'd go about doing it, but she also wanted him gone.

He was a detective for heaven's sake!

Beatrice watched him study the window in a painstaking matter until she could no longer endure the silence.

"What are you doing?" She took one step forward to try to see what he was seeing.

"Detecting," he answered. Did the corner of his lip jerk up just slightly? But it cannot have. That would mean he'd have to have a sense of humor.

"I'm Miss Walcott." Lacking a proper introduction, she'd attempt to insert some manner of propriety.

He went right on working as though she hadn't spoken.

"Beatrice Walcott. I teach composition and literature."

Still nothing.

Clasping her hands behind her back, Beatrice rocked on her heels. "We were never properly introduced at Hardwood Castle last week." Would he apologize for his mistake with this prompt?

He acted as though nothing of significance had occurred —when in fact, he'd all but ruined her afternoon.

"I am well aware." He murmured in a distracted manner, staring intently at what appeared to be nothing more than stained wood.

"Mrs. Driver is very thorough. I doubt she's left a spec of useful evidence." *If any had existed in the first place, you buffoon.*

"That is where you are wrong, Miss Walcott." He dismissed her attempt at civility, directing his attention beyond the happenings at the wedding festivities the week before. Instead, he removed a tiny pair of tweezers along with a small drawstring bag, from that same bottomless pocket inside his jacket.

The sill had been wiped clean, surely he cannot have discovered anything there. Nonetheless, she took a step closer.

"What do you mean?" she asked, more curious than she'd like to admit.

"I'm of the believe that any crime scene can never be perfectly cleaned. The criminal cannot help but leave something behind—something that will lead to his door—a combination of clues that are unique to his person."

"Such as…?"

"A particular kind of grass, or soil, or thread—specs of evidence so small they can only be seen by the most powerful of microscopes." He redirected his attention to the window. "Your Mrs. Driver has, indeed, made the task more difficult than it has to be. With fewer pieces of the puzzle to analyze and put together, the culprit will be more difficult to identify." He exhaled. "But that does not make solving this case impossible."

Beatrice leaned in again, squinting her eyes this time. "How can anything be deduced from essentially nothing?" She watched as he squeezed the handles of the small tweezers, noticing the elegance of his fingers, which were slim but capable looking.

When he held his hand up so light from the window could illuminate the item, his sleeve drew back to reveal a light dusting of black hair on the back of his wrist.

She dragged her attention back to the task at hand. "What do you see?"

"This could very well have fallen off your arsonist's head," he said. "But we cannot know for certain."

"Can you tell the color?"

"Black."

"Like yours."

He sent her another one of his annoyed glances before studying the hair some more. "The texture is coarse." He turned back to the window. "Here is another."

Beatrice began slowly shaking her head. She could see how such insight might be helpful, but it was difficult to imagine gathering enough information to catch the culprit from just a few hairs and discarded trinkets.

"But if you don't have all the pieces to the puzzle, how do you solve it?"

"It's a specific kind of puzzle. It requires one to not only collect evidence, but also eliminate unessential information and then deduce the relationships between what's left. It's possible, for instance, that we can eliminate persons with red or blonde hair, which lowers our pool of suspects significantly. You may wish to take notes, Miss Walcott, and you'll see that as we discover more evidence, our pool of suspects shrinks."

When she didn't move, he stared at her. "Primm said you would assist me."

So it wasn't a suggestion then. He actually wanted her to take notes.

Was she to act as his secretary now?

Doubtful he was going to even take the case, she reached deep into her apron pocket. Removing the small notebook she usually carried, along with a very short and dull pencil, she paused and then spoke out loud as she wrote: *black hair.* And then she added. *Short.* Perhaps, underlying the word with slightly more force than necessary.

"Anything else, my lord?"

If she had spectacles, she would have placed them low on her nose so that the next time he condescended to glance her way, she could glare over them.

Lord Sexton either ignored her sarcastic attitude or failed to notice it at all. Likely, the latter, because he methodically proceeded to analyze the rest of the window and the wall surrounding it. With no more than a chair, the towering marquess managed to reach the ceiling, where he plucked off a piece of the burnt debris from inside the plaster.

Which he sniffed.

"Tar."

"We found tar at the bottom of the container used to start the fire."

He met her gaze and dipped his chin. "Write it down, nonetheless. The accelerant appears to have been tar." Stepping off the chair, he then returned it to its proper desk. "So you see, Miss Walcott. We are now looking for, a presumably dark-haired individual who's been in possession of tar."

Beatrice glanced up and resisted the urge to roll her

eyes. "Why, that's simply brilliant. And that decreases the size of our pool of suspects immensely."

He narrowed his eyes at her. Had she pushed too far?

"Indeed." He brushed his hands together. "Now, let's go have a look at this box of evidence being so carefully preserved in your headmistress's office."

Only… Primm needed her to keep Lord Sexton away from Mr. Meadowbrook.

"Er," she stalled. "Wouldn't you like to inspect the rest of the school first? In case the arsonist left any evidence elsewhere?"

"Has he?"

She couldn't exactly lie to him, could she?

Because she herself, along with Primm, Mr. Stewart, Lord Rosewood and Victoria had inspected it from top to bottom. They'd found nothing out of the ordinary.

"We believe he entered through the front door," she admitted.

"And why is that?"

"Because we discovered one of the publications on the floor there—as though he'd dropped it and been in too much of a rush to pick it up."

"Aside from the one shattered by the fire, were any other windows broken?"

"No."

"Was the building left unlocked?"

Beatrice was already shaking her head. "It was locked up plenty tight. We were, as you know, away at the—"

"Wedding," he filled in for her. "It's possible our arsonist had a key—highly likely, actually."

"But how would he obtain a key?" she asked.

"That's an interesting question, isn't it?" The marquess

held her gaze, and for reasons beyond her comprehension, she felt a warm fluttering low in her belly.

"It is." But when her voice caught in her throat, she cleared it. "It's a very good question, indeed."

The marquess then returned his magnifying glass to inside his jacket, along with the drawstring bag where he'd stored the strands of hair, and the tweezers. And then he gestured toward the door. "I'm finished here. Take me to the other evidence."

No *please would you*... No *if you'd be so kind...*

It truly was a miracle that he hadn't been raised by wild animals. But marquesses didn't need miracles. Nor did they need to worry about little things such as kindness, and manners, or hurting people... Unlike normal people, they did whatever they pleased.

Along with dukes, earls, and viscounts...

He wasn't the first and she doubted he'd be the last.

Dragging her feet as she headed toward the door, a small sigh of frustration escaped her. Because if she was to keep this man from barging in on Primm's meeting with Mr. Meadowbrook, she was going to be the one who needed a miracle.

She sent up a prayer but doubted it would be answered. Not twenty minutes had passed, and it was doubtful that Primm's meeting was over.

If she was going to keep Lord Sexton away from Mr. Meadowbrook she was going to have to come up with something fast. She quickly considered various strategies.

Because she'd learned a long time ago, that when push came to shove, a lady had no one to rely on but herself.

Unfortunately, sometimes, the best course of action could be a little drastic.

# WHO IS THIS MISS WALCOTT?

"Shouldn't you inspect the second floor?" Miss Walcott moved to lead him around the school as though this was a tourist visit.

Ranulf, however, was not the sort of gentlemen to waste time. It was an irreplaceable commodity which he was unwilling to sacrifice without good reason.

"That won't be necessary," He continued descending the steps quickly enough that he managed to get in front of her.

She scurried to catch up from behind and Ranulf frowned. Not thirty seconds ago, she had been moving along at the pace of a snail.

What was this Miss Beatrice Walcott woman up to?

She thought he hadn't remembered her, but of course he had. He'd caught her glaring at him more than once during Hardwood's wedding ceremony, but then when he'd had the opportunity to be introduced, she'd turned away as though wanting nothing to do with him.

By God, she'd practically given him the cut.

Resolved to locate the headmistress's office on his own,

if necessary, he shoved the image of the too-thin, too-gangly spinsterish woman chasing behind him out of his thoughts. He also dismissed the recollection of her sapphire blue eyes, which were too large for her face… and her lashes that were too long, her brows too expressive.

This particular schoolteacher was…

*A little too everything.*

"What of the back staircase?" She was closer than he'd realized. "It's possible we missed something there. Now that I think about it, that tiny stairwell would be the perfect place for an intruder to hide."

It was almost as though she was stalling to keep him from meeting with Miss Primm… which only made Ranulf more determined to locate the headmistress.

"Later perhaps—if necessary." He continued marching down the stairs and, when he reached the first floor ahead of her, intentionally ignored her scrambling behind him.

He glanced to his left and then his right, and surmised where the headmistress's office was likely to be—in the direction of the adjacent residence that looked to have been constructed several decades after the original building had been erected.

Failing to slow him down, Miss Walcott let out a protest. Not a cry, but more of a chirping sound.

It reminded him of the Eclectus Parrot, a common species he'd only ever seen in Papua New Guinea. Upon graduating from Cambridge, many of his cohorts had walked about Scotland; Ranulf had sailed the world.

And his father, recognizing his eldest son's stubbornness, had allowed it.

Ranulf dismissed the memory because the creature coming up behind him was no bird.

"Are you chirping, Miss Walcott?" he asked without glancing back at her.

"I don't know what you're talking about," she answered.

If he was any other man, he might have found her… charming. But in this moment, he remained focused on the business at hand.

Ah… The door at the end of the corridor opened, followed by the unmistakable figure of Miss Primm along with an older but vaguely familiar gentleman. Ranulf went to raise his hand so as to capture their attention, but before he could do so, in a startling turn of events, he was accosted from behind.

By Miss Walcott.

This spinster was indeed, doing her best to delay him.

She gripped both of his arms and—only because he allowed it—dragged him into what, judging by the shelves surrounding him, was the closet where the helpful Mrs. Driver stored her supplies.

Despite the lack of square footage available, Miss Walcott hastily pulled the door closed behind her. When he went to speak, she hushed him.

*She.*

Hushed.

*Him.*

But that was not all.

Forced into such a confined space, the two of them were pressed together in a most intimate—most inappropriate manner.

He'd initially considered her too tall and also too thin, but in this proximity, Ranulf had no choice but to admit that she was neither of those things. In fact, her height seemed just right, and smashed against him in this manner, he quickly acknowledged that although she was thin, she was not without curves.

This was, indeed, an interesting turn of events.

"I thought you'd said everything was in Miss Primm's office." Not quite sure of her intent, he resorted to sarcasm. "Is there by chance, important evidence stored in here?" When she hushed him again, he frowned.

Despite the pleasant sensation of having her form pressed against his, he didn't play games.

"I—I thought this was the teachers' lounge." Miss Walcott's lie could not have been more obvious. In the dim light from a window near the ceiling, Ranulf could just make out a rosy hue ebbing up her neck and into her cheeks.

The sound of footsteps approaching had her tensing up.

Surely, she wasn't attempting to trap him into matrimony? More than one teacher from Miss Primm's had proven these schoolteachers were not above ruining themselves to capture an aristocratic husband. And yet, panic flared in this woman's eyes. Furthermore, she wasn't taking the opportunity to lure him into a more intimate embrace.

Ranulf reached around her waist to grasp the door handle, but Miss Walcott refused to move away so he could pull the door open.

When he went to speak again, she reached up and touched his lips.

"He cannot see you," she whispered.

*He?*

"Who cannot see me?" Ranulf ignored the feel of her breath near his jaw, and he certainly did not give into the urge to open his mouth and bite her fingertips.

Even if she did deserve it.

That and… other carnal urges had no place under these circumstances—even if the blood surging through his veins seemed to have his nether reasons gathering forces to disagree.

He'd been a widower for three years now and the few affairs he'd had had been with widows or women of experience. Never with ladies, and especially not with spinsters.

"Mr. Meadowbrook—he's the owner of Meadow—"

"I know who Meadowbrook is. Why don't you want him to see me?" Ranulf spoke around her fingertips. And then it dawned on him. "He is considering withdrawing his donations."

"Well, yes." He could hear her wince in the whispered answer. "Seeing as several of your investigations have been written up in the Gazette, you are rather notorious. And if he sees you—"

"He'll know there is trouble here at the school."

"Shh…" She increased her pressure on his mouth. What would she do if he trapped those fingers between his teeth?

She shook her head. "We cannot lose his support. And as a professional, you don't wish to break confidentiality, do you?"

When he took on a case, he eventually had to conduct interviews. Following a few of his interrogations, People inevitably realized what he was up to.

But as for this one…

He'd only come today at Lady Hardwood's request—as a favor.

And as he had no intentions of spending a week, possibly longer, looking into one small fire at an all-girls' school. Best he not get anyone's hopes up.

"I haven't said I'd take the case yet." This time, when he

spoke, he got a taste of her soft skin. She tasted like he'd imagine a schoolteacher would taste.

Like chalk, and paper and ink and that indefinable scent one always detected in schools.

But beneath all that, she tasted clean, with a hint of some undefinable flower. And her hair smelled sweet, like a combination of exotic fruit.

She jerked her head, knocking her skull into his chin. "But you must! We've already begun collecting clues."

Anything sweet about this woman was an illusion.

He deliberately removed her hand from his mouth, holding it down at her side. "I've had quite enough of your games, Miss Walcott, if you would be so kind as to step aside, I'll see that evidence in Miss Primm's office now."

# OF COURSE, HE KNEW

"Very well," Beatrice exhaled and then gestured toward the only space they weren't occupying. But when she went to move in one direction, he was there.

And when she tried the other.

He was there.

"If you'll excuse me..." She stared at his cravat while he moved them both in what was surely the most awkward dance of all time. He gripped her upper arms to pivot them, but in those few seconds, she felt him everywhere.

*Literally everywhere.*

He inhaled and she felt his chest grow. He exhaled and his breath teased her forehead. With each move, she felt his tendons tense and then relax. She felt the muscles in his arms, his torso, and his legs. And something else—something foreign and hard... *No!*

She closed her eyes. She should not be feeling that! Heat flooded her cheeks while she pretended not to notice. She could hardly blame him for it when hiding in the closet had been her idea.

Should she apologize?

Only when she was practically sitting on one of those shelfs was there enough room for Lord Sexton to squeeze his large frame through the opening and escape. *Did he know?*

Of course he knew.

*But did he know that she knew?*

Sliding out behind him, she stared at the floor, begging her composure to return.

What had happened in that closet was nothing more than an unfortunate consequence of her clumsy attempt to help Primm.

*For the good of the school.*

"T-t-thank you," she hated the quiver in her voice. "For your discretion." Head down, she followed him into the corridor.

He responded with another glance, this one dripping with blatant annoyance.

She was almost grateful for it, because now she could focus on being annoyed back.

But then he responded. "Is that what that was?" His voice was low and grumbly. "Discretion?"

How dare he? A true gentleman would never give any indication…!

He was the worst—the very worst.

He certainly brought out the worst in her.

With such long legs, and not bothering to adjust his stride to hers, he arrived at Primm's office before her.

But then Beatrice enjoyed the fact that he then had to wait. And she took her time digging the keys out of the deep pocket she'd sewn into her skirts.

Grateful to her composure for returning, she listened for

the click in the latch and then pushed down and pulled the door open.

When she indicated that he should go ahead of her, he didn't move.

"Ladies first." His voice sounded level and his expression remained unreadable.

Unsure as to the protocol one followed under such embarrassing circumstances, Beatrice nodded and then marched across the office to Miss Primm's small storage room and unlocked that door as well. This time when she pushed the door open, she did not enter, but stepped back and gestured for him to examine the copper pot and its contents they had left sitting on the floor.

And of course, he did not thank her.

Oh, but he was one of the upper members of the aristocracy. They weren't required to follow rules. She folded her arms in front of her while he slid on a pair of white gloves and then reached down to extract the cauldron of evidence. She did not offer to help as he lifted it out and set it on the surface of Primm's desk.

"After allowing every amateur sleuth in Warwick Village to touch this, did you invite the local villagers as well?

Beatrice tilted her head back and stared at the ceiling and while summoning her last ounce of patience, imagined what he'd look like with a bucket of cold water poured over his lofty head. She imagined his inky hair hanging around his face and long streams of water soaking the knot of his pristine white cravat.

"Did you have any constructive questions, my lord, or do you intend to waste both of our time with sarcastic ones?"

Lord Sexton's hands halted, his gaze shooting to hers. "Just so long as you answer them, I don't see that it matters."

His arrogance aggravated her all too easily. Because although he did seem to be rather intelligent, she hated that he acted so superior!

And utterly unbothered.

Primm would pretend to be shocked if she knew what Beatrice had done, dragging him into the closet like that, but in the end, she'd approve.

So Beatrice would not regret her actions.

She owed the school her loyalty. She'd accosted the marquess out of duty.

Furthermore, being so close to such a man, feeling her heart race like that... had been a considerable sacrifice on her part.

"No." she answered.

"No?"

"The entire village was not allowed to access the evidence. Only a few other teachers, a repairman, an earl, a viscount, and an army captain." She could be sarcastic too. "And now, a marquess as well," she added.

But he knew this as he'd arrived with half of them.

He cocked a brow. "Touché."

Beatrice wiped her hands on her apron and clasped her hands together at her waist. He turned his attention to the cauldron in which the fire had been started.

"Did you still expect me to take notes?" she asked.

She waited for him to mock her, and was almost disappointed when he merely dipped his chin and without looking away from the cauldron, plucked the tweezers out of his pocket. "Of course."

Silence. Then more silence...

"And what would you like me to take note of?" she finally asked.

"My observations. And yours, if you have any."

Her observations? "But… What good would—?"

He rose, cutting her off with his stare. "Tell me what you know about these partially burned items."

His ability to change subjects was almost dizzying. Perhaps that was part of why he was a famous detective—he knew how to disrupt a person's balance.

"The books were from Miss Fortune and Miss Primm's personal collections," Beatrice grudgingly pointed out. Although she'd felt badly for Primm and Chloe's loss, Beatrice had never been more relieved than when she'd discovered her own possessions safe where she'd left them.

No one could know about her brother's existence. If Jasper's letters had been in that pot of ashes, there would have been questions.

Questions she dared not answer.

"Miss Fortune—she teaches philosophy and dance—or did, anyhow, until, well. I mean…" This was not her secret to tell.

But the marquess waved a hand. "I'm aware."

Two words. Oh, poor, poor Chloe!

"Anyway," Beatrice searched for her train of thought. "She was devastated—as anyone would be. Several editions of her *Monthly Repository*'s had burned. Primm's copy of *Vindication of Rights* was one of her most prized possessions."

He grimaced. "Is this everything?"

"Everything else was beyond saving." A rebellious urge had her adding, "We had no way of knowing such a famous detective might like to have a look at the evidence."

His aura of condescension made it impossible for her to

offer any sort of apology for wasting his time. Sincere or otherwise.

Lord Sexton pursed his lips as he stared into the copper tub filled with ashes and burned books. Safe from his scrutiny, Beatrice took the opportunity to study him.

His stern jawline, imperfect nose, full lips, and pale complexion oughtn't to make for such an attractive package. And his black hair, when studied closely, had a few silver strands near his temples. It was a little too thick which caused it to stick up more than was generally considered fashionable.

The man's head of hair definitely shouldn't cause her fingers to itch to run through it.

She clenched them into a fist. His lips had felt soft and firm beneath her fingertips. What would it feel like to be kissed by him?

And then she caught herself.

Any attraction she had to this man needed squashed.

He was a marquess. He not only associated with other lords, but he regularly investigated crimes. He was the last sort of person she ought to associate with.

Besides, she didn't like him.

She stepped into Primm's storage room and pointed at the small tinderbox sitting on the middle shelf. "The arsonist left that behind as well..." Remembering the gloves Lord Sexton had used on the copper pot, she did not touch the final piece of evidence.

Before she could move away, he'd stepped inside, crouched down and examined it at eye-level.

His scent, wafting off his perfectly combed hair, took her right back to those few minutes in that other closet. A leathery spice, but also orange, clover, and… something more organic than any of those.

Her gaze trailed down those thick strands at the back of his neck to his broad shoulders and back. "A vagrant wouldn't own such an item," she said.

She wouldn't tell him that she had, in fact, studied the engravings herself, because if he chose to examine it, he'd likely discover more of her fingerprints there than anyone else's.

"There must be more than eight different sets of prints on this. I've no doubt one of them is yours. Tell me what you've deduced."

This felt more like a classroom exercise than an actual question, but she answered anyway.

"He was either a gentleman or a thief—which would not come as a surprise to me."

Sexton suddenly rose and all the air left her lungs. Although he wasn't touching her, he was standing inappropriately close. This time, she was the one who was trapped. Was he getting back at her for earlier?

He stepped backward and Beatrice's heartbeat returned to its normal rate. She must have imagined anything deliberate.

And, as luck would have it, Primm chose that particular moment to return to her office.

With Mr. Meadowbrook nowhere in sight, thank heavens! Beatrice met Primm's stare and the two of them seemed to exhale a silent sigh of relief without making a sound.

Unaware of their silent exchange, their marquess/detective strode across Primm's office in slow, easy strides as though he owned it.

"Miss Primm."

"My lord," Primm extended her hand to shake his, a gesture that normally took most men off guard, but not this one. "I see you've begun the investigation. We'll have you to thank this autumn, once our students and staff are no longer at risk."

Lord Sexton sent a tight glance in Beatrice's direction and she barely managed to bite back a grin. Primm had inserted her assumption far too easily.

People normally found it impossible to deny Primm anything.

The marquess, however, either wasn't easily manipulated, or was apathetic toward the welfare of women and children.

Neither of which would come as a surprise.

"No promises, Miss Primm." He sounded rather grim.

"But we have a pool of suspects already," Beatrice spoke up encouragingly. "A dark-haired person, and the length of the sample suggests a male. And he'll have been in possession of tar—oh, and he's either a thief or a member of the nobility."

Primm nodded and Beatrice turned back to Lord Sexton. "Upon examining the evidence we deemed important enough to save, have you any other characteristics to shrink our pool of suspects? Did you find anything *of significance?*"

His mouth pinched into a thin line, making it quite clear that he didn't appreciate her interference.

"This case," he gestured toward the box. "Is not unsolvable."

"Oh, but that's marvelous." Primm's face lit up, but Beatrice didn't trust the tone in his voice.

Primm waved toward the chair facing her desk. "We have a good deal to discuss then. Won't you sit down, my lord?"

Beatrice turned to leave, but the marquess stepped back so she could take the second chair. He didn't sit until Beatrice had lowered herself first.

Only after everyone was comfortable, did he deliver his blow. It was just as Beatrice expected. "I said it is solvable, but I won't be doing the solving." He spoke somberly, his shoulders tensed. He didn't sound as though he'd made his decision lightly.

"As Miss Walcott has already mentioned," he continued. "You have a pool of suspects. At this point, it's a considerably abundant pool. The task of eliminating individuals who lacked opportunity will require time that I do not have."

"Oh, but Miss Walcott can assist—"

"Even with the very capable assistance of your Miss Walcott, I cannot take on your case. My apologies, madam."

Unfortunately, or fortunately, as the case may be, Lord Sexton did not really know Miss Primm.

Therefore, he could not comprehend the cunning to which Primm would take to protect her school.

The corners of Primm's mouth turned down. "I will not deny that I'm disappointed, but I quite understand. "It would be too much, I suppose, to assume that such a talented investigator as yourself could find time to protect the innocent lives of our students."

His ensuing frown was the deepest Beatrice had seen yet.

"I am a very busy man." He gripped the sides of his chair

to rise but, as all gentlemen were taught to do, waited for Primm and Beatrice to rise first.

"Of course you are." Primm leaned forward, hands clasped together on her desk.

Beatrice suspected what Primm was up to and followed the other woman's lead. She kept her hands folded in her lap and purposely avoided Lord Sexton's eyes.

"But you must join us for dinner now that you're here. We are not the sort of ladies to withdraw our hospitality merely because our guest cannot lend his services."

The marquess sent Beatrice a glance that could almost be described as pleading.

*In your dreams, my lord.* She barely kept from smirking. If he thought she would take his side, he had a good deal more thinking to do.

"Lady Hardwood will be expecting me to join them for dinner in the private dining room they've reserved at the inn."

"I'll have Mr. Driver deliver a message." Primm's smile was quite serene.

"I hate to impose."

This time, Primm held up one hand. "Not at all. I refuse to send you back to the inn to suffer inferior offerings when Cook has taken the time to prepare a gourmet meal for you here."

Lord Sexton went to speak but then clamped his mouth shut. As a famous detective, the marquess would not be so applauded if he lacked the ability to read people.

Which meant he'd conceded it would be simpler to relent rather than argue further.

He relaxed his hands on his chair and forced a tight smile.

"Very well, Miss Primm."

"And while you're waiting for dinner to be served, you'll have plenty of time to go through the evidence again, perhaps take notes in regard to this—what did you call it? This pool of suspects." Primm rose, gesturing at her desk. "If you'll excuse us a moment, Miss Walcott and I will look in on Cook to ensure dinner preparations are on schedule."

Beatrice was more than a little surprised that the Marquess did not simply insist on taking his leave. But Primm was… well. She was Primm.

She'd bamboozled this lofty gentleman in the same way she dealt with many of the upper-class girls.

"My notes, my lord." Beatrice placed them on the desk and then rose to follow Primm into the corridor and towards Primm's personal residence.

"I won't be surprised if he escapes the second we're out of sight," Beatrice whispered.

"But that wouldn't be gentlemanly of him."

"True but…" Beatrice sought for the right words. Because, although he'd accompanied the Hardwood ladies to the school out of what could only have been duty, he didn't seem the sort to be manipulated by propriety. "I doubt the marquess cares much for his reputation. He showed a considerable lack of manners at Lady Hardwood's wedding."

"True, he's not a typical sort of lord, what with his involvement with The King's Society. But he's only been a widower for three years. Great loss tends to overshadow societal expectations." Primm opened the door to her small apartment.

"How did his wife die?" Primm wasn't one to gossip, so Beatrice took full advantage when her employer deigned to share information. "Childbirth?" It was the most natural assumption.

Primm dropped her gaze to her hands. "She was kidnapped and then murdered. And despite a major investigation, they never caught the person who did it."

Beatrice was stunned into silence as she followed Primm into the front of the apartment. People were killed every day without so much as a report being filed—that in itself was a travesty. But the death of a marchioness would have demanded a thorough investigation—and once found, the guilty person would surely hang.

Unless his late wife's killer had been a nobleman, that was.

Beatrice had learned the hard way that the authorities were more than willing to ignore evidence when it pointed to one of England's elite.

Beatrice halted, surprised that they'd stopped at one of the linen closets.

"I know this isn't one of your regular tasks," Primm said. "But I need you to air out one of the private rooms. The bed needs made up, of course, and Jenny can provide you with anything else you think he might need." Jenny was Primm's housekeeper and cook, and had been with the headmistress since the opening of the school. "Do whatever you must to ensure Lord Sexton is as comfortable as possible."

"So..." Beatrice rolled her lips together and then said, "There is no gourmet dinner, is there?"

"Not exactly."

But of course not. Cook possessed fine culinary skills, but she mostly excelled at serving large groups of young girls.

"And your plan is to… encourage him to take his lodgings here tonight as well?"

Primm blinked, not at all ashamed. "But of course."

Beatrice pondered the plausibility of such a coup, and then remembered Primm's earlier meeting. "What did Mr. Meadowbrook have to say?" She winced hopefully. "Will he continue sending his usual donations?

"For now," Primm answered. "But he wouldn't promise anything for the coming year."

Well, that was something anyway.

"It buys us time, I suppose," Beatrice said as Primm stacked folded linens onto Beatrice's outstretched arms.

"It also makes finding the identity of our *little annoyance* all the more important."

"So…" Beatrice balanced the growing stack of linens. "A private chamber?"

"I'd put him up on satin and silk if I could," Primm answered.

The headmistress chuckled to herself as she marched off to inform Jenny and Cook of the change in plans for this evening.

Beatrice, meanwhile, very carefully picked her way back inside the school and up the stairs to where she'd make up a bed for Lord Sexton. As she passed the second floor, she contemplated the wisdom of her employer's manipulations. Primm could be rather single-minded.

And devious.

Sometimes Primm's dedication to her school, surprised even Beatrice.

Arriving on the top floor, she passed through the student dormitory, opened the door to their best private room—not much larger than the closet she'd shoved him in earlier—and, scrunching her nose, opened the small window to allow some fresh air to enter.

And then shook her head. Likely, all of this would be in vain.

Lord Sexton may have conceded to stay for dinner, but Beatrice doubted even Primm could change his mind about taking on the investigation.

And as she smoothed the sheet across the mattress, an annoying revelation struck her.

She was changing his blasted linens after all.

# THE BATTLE

Ranulf swiped at an insect, cursing as he strolled around the cobbled walk to the front entrance of Miss Primm's beleaguered school. For an all-girls' school, Ranulf admitted grudgingly to himself, the exterior of Miss Primm's Private Seminary for the Education of Ladies loomed rather impressively.

The three-story building was in the center of a massive park, set on the outskirts of a small village named Warwick Crossings.

It was, in fact, less than a mile from the Gray Swan Inn and Tavern where a hot meal and a private chamber awaited him.

And he'd be sitting down for his meal right about now if not for the... persuasive abilities of Miss Walcott's headmistress.

Instead, he would take dinner prepared at a school. He'd eat his hat if it was even close to what Lady Hardwood and her daughters were being served at the Gray Swan.

Nonetheless, he'd make the most of his present circumstances.

Having spent half an hour reexamining the evidence in Miss Primm's office, Ranulf had come outside. He'd wanted a look at the exterior of the building, and then another of the actual scene. He walked out a few measurements and then continued along.

The case was a challenging one, and seeing as he had agreed to remain for the evening meal, he might as well make a few inroads. Later, he could hand it off to Lord Rosewood—Primm's brother who lived about six miles to the north—or to Hardwood.

The earl would have some interest in the school's troubles, having just married another of Primm's teacher. And if neither of them was interested, he could ask Rowan Stewart.

Ranulf wouldn't be handling the case personally, but that didn't mean others couldn't look into it.

Reaching the front steps, he glanced around and frowned. No fences, no security. They might as well be asking for another attack, which, although it would provide more evidence, wouldn't be great for the school itself.

He rubbed his chin. On the other hand, if the attacks stopped on their own, moving ahead with an investigation might be more trouble than it was worth.

With most of the physical evidence having been swept and scrubbed away, the case was going to require hours and hours of work.

Whoever took it on would be forced to rely mostly on witness accounts and speculation. A speck of guilt pricked him.

Because witness interrogations weren't as simple as they

sounded. The interrogator needed to not only ask the right questions but ask them in the right order. He must know when to keep silent and when to poke at a perceived weakness.

His specialty, so to speak.

But this was not his problem.

He removed the small notebook he carried in his jacket pocket and consulted his schedule. After taking the first holiday he'd had in years so he could attend Hardwood's wedding the week before, Ranulf had left this week clear. And that had been a fortunate decision, what with the mess Edgeworth had gotten himself into. With both Edgeworth and Bloodstone having to dash off to England, they'd turned to Ranulf to escort the ladies home and he'd agreed. Gents did that sort of thing for one another.

Even accounting for the additional travel, he'd have nearly a full month in London before the Society Board members would cast their votes. The old Earl of Southbridge had died in January, leaving the position unfilled—the position Ranulf coveted with every ounce of his being. He wasn't satisfied with being Interim Director; he wanted the seat to be permanent.

And he was closer than he'd ever been. Now was not the time to neglect the members of The King's Society board.

Having picked his way around to the school's front entrance, Ranulf ignored his notebook for the moment, tilted his head back, and studied the brick façade.

Bold letters had been carved into the stone over the double doors of the entrance: *Miss Primm's Private Seminary for the Education of Ladies.*

The institution was empty for what remained of the

summer months—a stroke of luck for Primm and her staff and students.

On the other hand… The timing may very well have been more than luck. The arsonist's timing could have been deliberate. Perhaps the perpetrator had no real desire to harm anyone, but only wanted to cause trouble for the school.

Or, more specifically, the person who ran it—*Miss Primm*. One would think that as such a rational man, he would avoid gossip. And yet between the lines, there was usually a seed of truth. Even as a guest at Hardwood's wedding, he'd overheard a few critical comments.

Which was part of why this investigation could turn out to be a difficult one.

His limps surged with the familiar energy that came with a delicious challenge.

*Dash it all*. Almost any other time and he'd already have officially taken it on.

Furthermore, despite Miss Primm's obvious ploy, these acts of destruction, if allowed to continue, could injure someone—a student, or perhaps one of Primm's teachers. Lives could be at stake. A particular set of blue eyes came to mind and he shoved the image away.

Criminal activity such as this was precisely why he needed to be officially appointed director and to head up the board. The board members were the only ones who could adjust The King's Society's mission statement. Ranulf had grand plans but to effect those changes, he needed to be at the helm.

The King's Society could be of a real service to England. Most British citizens appreciated the centuries-old institution—those who were aware of its existence—but it had become something of a relic. Even the Gazette had stopped printing their announcements, sighting that the breakthroughs were beyond their readers' comprehension.

For decades, The King's Society had limited its focus to scientific hypothesis and tests. If the board approved his plan, it could serve a double purpose—advancing technology but also addressing crimes that went unsolved by local magistrates.

And holding all criminals accountable—not just the convenient ones.

*A national bureau of detectives.*

With a more practical purpose, they'd receive more donations—and be able to provide greater resources to those who worked there—both the scientists and the detectives.

But he was getting ahead of himself.

He needed to win the vote first.

Ranulf squinted up at the damages where heat had shattered a window. Black streaks of smoke had not only colored the exterior stone but damaged a section of the roof.

Not catastrophic, but not insignificant either.

His train of though was broken with the sound of crunching gravel. The rhythm of footsteps was lively, leaving him no doubt as to who was approaching him.

Miss Walcott, whose flowery skin, and sweet-smelling hair had lodged themselves into his senses.

She'd admitted the reason she'd had for dragging him into that closet—to keep a donor from recognizing him. The excuse made perfect sense.

But he'd damn near embarrassed himself.

Furthermore, he didn't trust her.

"Dinner isn't quite ready yet." She didn't meet his gaze, perhaps a little ashamed of their machinations to keep him here. But he would not make an issue of it.

"Anything good is worth waiting for," he said instead. But he deliberately glanced at his pocket watch. "I've never been treated to a gourmet school meal before. I'm quite looking forward to it."

"Oh, yes. As am I," she stammered before stepping forward with her monstrous set of keys. "Primm left the doors unlocked earlier, since we knew you were coming, but otherwise, you'll need the key to enter through the front." She slid the largest key into an ancient looking lock. "Since the fire, we've made it a rule to keep both the front and side doors locked at all times—well, most of the time, anyway."

The apparatus made a loud clicking sound, followed by creaking when she pulled the heavy door open. But when Ranulf gestured for her to precede him into the building, she took a step back instead.

"Do I make you nervous?" he asked. It wasn't something he normally would have asked someone he was only vaguely acquainted with.

And yet following the closet incident, he could almost recite her measurements.

She lifted her lashes, meeting his gaze for the first time since they'd sat in her employer's office. The color of her eyes was truly stunning. Sapphire, like bluebells in spring.

"You are a prominent gentleman," she answered, the corner of her mouth twitching.

There it was again. That smirk. Not quite what one expected from a spinster.

She raised a hand to her mouth. *"You must be used to it by now."* She smothered both the comment and her expression. *"Nervous servants—groveling subjects..."*

"I beg your pardon?"

"Normal people aren't accustomed to mingling with the nobility." she clarified. "Seeing you is the closest most will ever come to having an audience with the king."

Before he could even begin to think of a response, she'd spun around, leaving him to stand there damn near frozen with shock as she marched away.

Was she implying that he wasn't normal?

"Little witch," he hissed but, oddly enough, found himself smiling.

Unwilling to ponder all that might go on in a spinster's mind, Ranulf entered through the tall door and climbed the stairs. Perhaps he'd find something Mrs. Driver had overlooked.

He inhaled and, memories from his own years as a student flooded his mind. Even with the lingering hint of smoke, the aroma of academia hung in the air. This building housed students for nine months out of the year.

Young ladies.

Children—the absolute weakest members of society, dependent upon gentlemen for protection.

A deeper, familiar guilt gnawed at him. But he would not rethink his decision. This situation was entirely different. Susan had been his to protect, but other gentlemen were responsible for the plethora of females who lived at the school.

Lord Rosewood, for one, Mr. Driver, hell, Mr. Stewart even—not to mention some of the villagers, those who benefited economically from the school's very existence.

And yet, as Ranulf arrived at the top landing, he couldn't

keep his thoughts from shifting to a tall, slim blue-eyed young woman who was, even now, flouncing about the grounds unaccompanied.

Vulnerable.

Spinsters were far too independent for their own good. Or foolish. The two words were synonymous where these teachers were concerned.

He ought to have taught Miss Walcott a lesson when she'd dragged him into the closet.

Correction—when he had *allowed* her to drag him into the closet. If he'd not been an honorable gentleman, she might have suffered far more than a little embarrassment today.

These women might think themselves capable of managing the stronger sex. They might even imagine they'd managed him.

Ranulf fought back a smirk.

These women had a good deal to learn.

"I OUGHT to have realized a meal served by the daughter of a marquess would be nothing less than exquisite," Ranulf complimented his host.

The conversation, along with the meal, were proving to be surprisingly pleasant.

And enlightening.

He was not ignorant of the fact that the school's headmistress had twisted his arm into staying, nor that she was digging deep to find something that would convince him to take their case.

She was as hard-headed as a woman could be.

"I must emphasize, madam." He folded his serviette into quarters and placed it to the left of his plate. "I cannot take your case. With Captain Edgeworth and Lord Bloodstone both compelled to travel on to London, I, and I alone, am responsible for the safe return of Hardwood's mother and daughters to Cliffhouse. Along with other… responsibilities, I simply do not have time to pin down your arsonist."

Miss Primm nodded. "I'd be happy to send my coachmen to escort the ladies home," she offered. "As he is an excellent protector. But he has gone on to London as well."

But that would not have been an option. "Even if he had been available, I could not break my promise. I'm sorry, Miss Primm. I simply cannot help you."

The headmistress didn't appear nearly as unhappy as he'd expected.

Miss Walcott turned bright blue eyes on him. "The middle Hardwood sister has arranged to undergo testing tomorrow," she reminded him. "That allows you one day to investigate. You might come up with something. You said the case was solvable…"

Days like this, Ranulf wished he'd never heard the word honor.

Because honor meant putting the needs of others above his own. And in the long run, instituting his plan for The King's Society stood to affect hundreds, possibly thousands of criminals. Remaining at Miss Primm's would affect only one.

So although he felt a tug to stay, he ignored it.

Just as they finished with the dessert, the door to the dining room opened and Miss Primm's cook stepped inside. "Pardon me," she addressed her employer. "A missive, along with some luggage, was just delivered for his lordship—from Mrs. Pratt at the inn."

Primm accepted the note and handed it across the table.

*Lord Sexton,*

*We are terribly sorry for this inconvenience, but your room was damaged this afternoon. Gertrude, a local goat, broke through the tavern, and before we could keep her from going upstairs, she broke into your chamber and has rendered it, for now anyway, uninhabitable.*

*With the school currently on break, I'm quite certain Miss Primm will provide you with acceptable lodgings.*

*My most sincere apologies,*

*Mrs. Pratt of the Gray Swann*

Ranulf glanced up from what he'd just read. "Is this a joke?"

"Is what a joke?"

He handed the note across to Miss Primm and although her expression was all shock and outrage, he doubted very much that she was not somehow behind this nonsense.

"Gertrude is the same goat who damaged the school last winter," Miss Walcott supplied. Was that a hint of mirth dancing on her plump lips?

He tore his attention away from her mouth and forced himself to address the matter at hand.

"A goat, really?"

"She truly is a menace," Miss Walcott answered.

Ranulf narrowed his gaze, demanding further explanation without so much as a single word. Her mouth might, indeed, be plump and enticing. But in that particular moment, the urge to strangle her swan-like neck was more compelling.

"Her owner, Mr. Jonesey, has tried everything to contain her, all to no avail. Mrs. Jonesey suggested making a meal of her, but she's their best milk producer—Gertrude, that is, not Mrs. Jonesey." Miss Walcott winced. "Anyway, when she isn't raising havoc, she really is the sweetest thing."

A sweet goat! Ranulf barely contained a snort.

About as sweet as Beatrice Walcott herself.

Ranulf scowled. What the hell had just happened?

These two spinsters had, in fact, succeeded in managing him. Aside from outright accusing them of lying, he was caught.

But only for one night—and, he supposed, another day.

*Dash it all.*

"Not to worry, my lord," Primm returned to the matter at hand. "You are quite welcome to avail yourself of one of our private student chambers. And how convenient that Mrs. Pratt sent your luggage over."

"Just as well in my mind. It looks to rain. This way you won't have to get wet." Miss Walcott glanced toward the window and then added. "Now that would, indeed, be inconvenient."

There it was. That spinster smirk of hers.

Primm rose from the table. "Will you be so kind as to show his lordship to the chamber you prepared earlier?" She sent a satisfied smile in Miss Walcott's direction. The damned woman was a menace. Both of them! He'd call them out for arranging the unfortunate goat incident himself if he wasn't a gentleman.

"Delighted to," Miss Walcott responded. "If you're

finished eating, my lord?" She pressed her palms down on the table as though to rise.

"I am, and it was delicious," Ranulf admitted grudgingly. "This room isn't, by chance, on the third floor, is it?" The stench from the fire a few days prior was still noticeable.

"Yes. I think you'll be rather comfortable, my lord," Miss Primm answered as Miss Walcott waited for him at the dining room door.

"Let that arsonist try something tonight!" Miss Walcott sounded all too eager. As she led him out of Primm's residence and into the foyer of the school, she rubbed her hands together. "Wouldn't he be surprised to come face to face with a famous detective?"

Ranulf barely refrained from rolling his eyes heavenward at such an exaggerated compliment.

"And don't worry about the smell. Just before dinner, I aired it out and..." Her smile stiffened. "I made the bed up with new linens."

But of course...

His chamber at the inn had not been rendered useless by accident. A goat! He'd wager a thousand pounds the room was untouched by this Gertrude animal, or anyone else for that matter.

"How thoughtful of you," he said. Was that a hint of guilt in her eyes?

It should be.

By Jove, if not for Hardwood's womenfolk, he'd simply take to the road tonight. But he'd made a promise to protect those ladies. A flash of something familiar shot through him, but it was only a flash—like the recollection of a dream.

*If only he could have taken care of Susan.* Ranulf pushed the images away and focused his thoughts on the weeks ahead.

He'd protect Lady Hardwood and his daughters on their journey home with all due diligence. He clenched his hands as memories taunted him. Always from just below his conscious thoughts. Familiar strain began radiating up the back of his neck.

He could look forward to another sleepless night then—one of many.

At least he could spend the time contemplating Miss Primm's arsonist.

Miss Walcott, who'd been marching ahead of him carrying a taper to light their way, turned to glance back. Her silky dark tresses glowed in the candlelight. "Would you like me to bring you up some tea? Or warm milk?"

He sensed sarcasm, but with this woman, he could not be certain.

"I'll be fine, thank you." The prospect of a warm female body lulling him to sleep invaded his thoughts.

Said female would be slimmer than usual, and the woman's face would be staring up at him in ecstasy.

He'd wipe that smirk off of it for good.

By God, he truly was out of sorts if he was contemplating Beatrice Walcott as a bedmate.

Nonetheless, he climbed the steps behind her, chastising himself. It was too late now. He was well and truly caught.

He'd never underestimate the power of a determined spinster again.

And yet they'd only won the battle. Ranulf Winters hadn't lost a war yet.

## GUESTS

With both Miss Fortune and Miss Royal having left for London, Primm had offered Beatrice the spare bedroom in her apartment. But Beatrice had declined.

Others might consider it daunting to spend the night alone in such a large building, but although the additional chamber in Primm's apartment was far more luxurious than the teachers' lodgings, Beatrice enjoyed having her privacy, which was a rare commodity, and would take advantage of it while she could.

And having dispatched the marquess to his chamber for the night, a smile danced on her mouth as she changed out of her shift and into her well-worn nightrail. She and Primm had actually accomplished the rather daunting task of keeping Lord Sexton at the school for another day.

In light of their first meeting, while making up his bed, Beatrice had given into the desire to place just a few tiny drops of her perfume onto his pillow—lemon and lavender. Not that it was strong enough to keep him awake, it wasn't really even perfume, but scented oil. No doubt, it was an improvement since that particular pillow had been stored in the closet for most of the summer.

And yet Beatrice had taken some satisfaction from her uncharacteristic act of rebellion.

Snuffing out her candle, she climbed onto the bed and lay back on her own pillow.

Overhead, the floor creaked, and she conceded that it was comforting knowing there was someone else in the building. With the marquess on the floor above her, she could attribute any sounds to him.

Would he even recognize her scent when he lay down to sleep? Even now she remembered his. With a deep inhale, she imagined the virile scent… leather, clove, orange and… skin.

Her face flushed even as she lay alone on her bed, remembering the moment she'd all but tackled him into the storage closet. She hadn't realized how small the space would be and, although she'd only been doing her job, she had truly been shocked by her own actions.

She'd remember his scent for years to come. The aroma hadn't been overly strong, but it was as though it reached inside of her, tantalizing places she didn't know existed. Such foreign sensations ought to have made her uncomfortable, and yet she'd wanted to linger there.

Until…

Beatrice raised her arm and covered her eyes. She'd never sleep if she dwelt on that…

*Think of something else... Anything!*

She exhaled a long, slow breath.

Her father's scent had consisted of leather and earth. It

had always comforted her. Her heart cracked a little at the memory.

She hadn't thought about that for years. More creaking upstairs was a welcome distraction from her spiraling thoughts.

Because nothing could bring them back.

As his footsteps moved across the ceiling, Beatrice deduced that he had left his private room to go into the large student dormitory. It was just as Primm had hoped; his curiosity was pulling him in.

But then the footsteps quieted altogether. She sat up, thinking he might be coming to her—for tea or perhaps another blanket. But no knock ever came.

No, he was going down to the first floor. Echoes sounded upon echoes and, even as she contemplated how much she could hear in the quiet of the night, she distinctly heard the creaking of the front door opening, and then latching closed.

Was he intent upon escaping them?

She hopped off the bed and dashed across the room to her window where she easily made out his tall figure marching across the lawn. But he did not look as though he was going anywhere. No, he wore only breaches and his long linen shirt, which was untucked. He was barefoot even.

Beatrice stepped to the side so she was only barely able to peer out the window. With her room in total darkness, she knew he couldn't see her, and yet she felt that if she were too obvious, he would feel her eyes upon him.

What was he doing?

But he was walking back and forth, restlessly pacing for several feet in one direction and then back as though deep in thought. When a cloud moved away, allowing moonlight to illuminate the yard, it was obvious the marquess did not look happy. He looked determined, a little tormented, and... sad.

Primm had said he'd lost his wife. No, not lost, she'd been murdered. And he was a detective.

A dark cold feeling swept through her. Murderers looked the same as everyone else. She'd have thought there would be something evil in their eyes—that they would have an aura of danger about them.

But no… They smiled as if they weren't malicious and evil. They ate, they slept, they dressed…

What had happened to Lord Sexton's wife?

Beatrice stood there for several minutes, simply watching the Marquess as he unleashed the hidden energy plaguing him. He adjusted from walking to a slow jog, and then Lord Sexton sprinted around the perimeter of the yard.

Was this something he did regularly, or was he simply uncomfortable to be sleeping in such primitive dwellings? Although the room Beatrice had aired out was somewhat luxurious for an affluent student, it would be considered substandard for a man of his stature.

Her father had often roamed their house late at night. She'd thought he might have heard an intruder or was chasing a ghost.

One night, just after her seventh birthday, she'd climbed out of bed and gone to ask him why. He'd told her it was his favorite time to think.

"About what?" she'd asked.

"About all the things I need to do to make my little girl and her mother happy." She'd been an only child at the time and, upon reflection, more than a little spoiled. Her father had grown serious then, however, and added. "Taking care of the people you love isn't easy, you know. It's a grand responsibility."

For months, following his death, she'd realized he had not been teasing her or making light of the burdens he'd carried. Because with him and her mother gone, she'd had to become the responsible one.

For Jasper's sake, if not her own.

She shivered at the memories of leaving the only home she'd ever known. She'd gladly suffer the troubles at this school to salvage Jasper's future.

As long as both of them were safe.

Down below, the marquess caught her attention once again when he came to a halt and bent over to rest his hands on his knees. When he rose, he ran a hand through his hair, flattening it.

He swiped his arm across his face, and then, in an impatient motion, reached down and drew his shirt over his head, revealing his shoulders and sinewy torso. His pale skin practically glowed in the filtered moonlight, but for the sparse dark hair that spread across his chest, tapering into a vertical line that disappeared into the waist of his breeches.

Beatrice jumped back and then, drawn by an unrelenting force, slowly peeked around the curtain again.

He used his shirt to wipe his front and then tilted his head back to look...

Straight at her.

Only he couldn't be looking at her. She was in total darkness. The notion that he could see her was impossible.

She held her breath.

And then he waved.

Beatrice flew back onto her bed as though shot out of a

cannon. How mortifying for such a man to…! How—! How arrogant—! For him to be capable of seeing into her window, where she wore nothing but her dressing gown.

But then she groaned.

She had been staring at him, and he'd been practically naked. Beatrice squeezed her eyes closed and heat flooded her entire body.

She was so caught up in her mortification that when a knock sounded, she jumped.

"Goodnight, Miss Walcott," a low and gravelly voiced called through the door.

Beatrice squeezed her eyes tighter. And when his footsteps didn't move away from the door, her voice betrayed her by answering. "Good night, my lord." Upon which she promptly buried her face in her pillow.

Unfortunately, even the feathers in her pillow couldn't block out his soft chuckles as they drifted away with his footsteps.

~

DESPITE HAVING ONLY SLEPT INTERMITTENTLY, Beatrice was up and dressed just in time to meet their guests for the day—potential new students and, perhaps someday, future school sponsors.

She'd taken extra care with her appearance, wearing the jonquil gown she'd worn at the house party along with a newly whitened apron.

Primm looked well-put-together as usual, and the two women stepped outside just as the Hardwood carriages arrived—two of them, as there were five daughters, two chaperones, and the girls' mother.

The dowager Lady Hardwood was the first to be assisted onto the pavement, followed by the eldest, Lady Eloisa. Isadora and an older woman whom Beatrice presumed to be one or the chaperones followed them out of the first carriage while Evie, Cora, Maddie, and a younger looking companion exited the second.

The school yard immediately came to life with the sound of giggling girls and squeals of excitement to have arrived at their destination.

Primm welcomed Lady Hardwood while Beatrice merely smiled beside her, keeping her hands behind her back.

Despite the extra work of having visitors, Beatrice welcomed them with genuine warmth. These ladies were the very reason the marquess was here at all. If not for them they'd have little to no chance of capturing their... annoyance.

Primm and Beatrice had decided ahead of time that Primm would administer the teacher's test to Mary Grace, while Beatrice provided the other girls and their mother with a grand tour. Mary Grace was all of seven and ten and, depending on her scores, she could either attend the school for one year or take one of the more elementary teaching posts.

Primm and Beatrice had agreed that neither of them would mention the acts of vandalism. And although it would be something of a miracle if their guests failed to notice the damages from the fire, Primm and Beatrice would do their best to downplay the circumstances surrounding it.

But on occasion, even the best laid plans go awry.

"Is it true someone tried to burn the school down while

you were away?" One of the twins asked. Both of them were five and ten, if Beatrice remembered correctly. Their eldest sister, Eloise, rather than shush her younger sibling, turned accusing eyes on Beatrice.

Lady Eloise had yet to have truly forgiven Priscilla—or any of the school's teachers, in fact. Not because Priscilla had married their oldest brother, but because of the deception she and Chloe had committed on behalf of one of their students earlier that year—Allison Meadowbrook.

Which may not have been wise, but had seemed their best course of action at the time.

To protect the school, of course.

Even so, Beatrice understood. She might feel the same under similar circumstances. But now that Priscilla had married Lord Hardwood, it would be better for all of them if Lady Eloise could forgive, if not forget.

"A vandal," Primm answered. "Most likely a vagrant traveling through. It's rare that we leave the school unoccupied for so long." Effectively closing the subject, she turned to the middle sister. "Lady Mary Grace, have you come prepared for the examinations?"

One glance revealed that Mary Grace, who was usually cheerful and enthusiastic, looked more than prepared. But she also appeared as nervous as a debutante would right before making her bow to the queen.

"Why don't you come along with me. Your mother is more than welcome to join us if she'd like." Primm glanced at the older woman questioningly.

The dowager countess smiled. "I think that would be best."

The younger sisters wished Mary Grace good luck, as did lady Isadora, but Lady Eloise kept silent.

Beatrice hoped the older girl wasn't too difficult to entertain. As a teacher, Beatrice was quite accustomed to dealing with moody young women, but they had all been under the age of eight and ten. Eloise, she believed, was only a few years younger than herself.

"I imagine you girls would like to see the inside of the school first. Have any of you attended school away from home?"

For the next hour, Beatrice answered multiple questions the girls had about life at Miss Primm's as they explored the first, second, and then of course the third floor. Beatrice would have preferred not to enter the student lodgings, but it was one of the areas of the school that the girls were most intrigued about. All of them had lived at home their entire lives and been taught by a governess. The notion of living with other students, away from home, intrigued the girls almost more than the school itself.

But going to the third floor meant Beatrice must face the marquess. Despite his late-night exercises, she'd heard him awake and moving about early. And he'd not come looking to break his fast. Either he was hard at work on the case or avoiding herself and Miss Primm.

But the marquess was not alone, and upon stepping inside, he sent Beatrice an annoyed glance for interrupting his conversation with Mr. Rowan Stewart.

Mr. Stewart was the gentleman who had spied the fire from the road. He'd been riding to a nearby estate that had fallen into disrepair. Longbow Castle, most conveniently, had been purchased by Primm's younger brother—Lord Rosewood—who had married Victoria, the school's former etiquette teacher shortly after Christmas.

Mr. Stewart grimaced and ran a hand over his head of

short black hair. Rather than the natural pallor of most English gentlemen, his complexion was nearly as dark as a cup of tea. He was not quite as tall as Lord Sexton but possessed thick and muscular shoulders, no doubt developed by the labor of his occupation.

He'd designed several remarkable buildings in London, but he was known mostly for being the bastard brother to the Duke of Bedwell.

And the collapse of a grand project he'd undertaken in Mayfair.

"Is there something you need miss Walcott?" Lord Sexton cocked a brow, his tone conveying that she was making a nuisance of herself.

Just when she thought she might think kindly of him, he promptly squashed her softer feelings with his rude behavior.

*Some manners would be appreciated.* But out loud, she said, "These young ladies wish to see the dormitories." Beatrice did not wait for permission, but rather held the door wide for her guests to enter. "Avoid the damaged area, please. Repairs will be made, of course, but until then, best to stay on the undamaged side of the dorms."

She shot a glance in Lord Sexton's direction, using her eyes to silently beg him not to comment on the nature of their *little annoyance.*

His look softened just enough so that she could breathe a sigh of relief.

"By all means." He addressed Hardwood's sisters rather than Beatrice. Of course, as a longtime friend to the Earl of Hardwood, he would be far better acquainted with them than Beatrice was. "Come in, ladies."

All four of them dropped into a curtsy as though it had been choreographed. "Good day, my lord." Lady Eloise spoke for all of them and then strolled along one of the twin-sized beds. "I do hope Mary Grace completes her test in a timely manner so we can return to Hardwood Cliffhouse tomorrow morning. I imagine you feel the same." She addressed the marquess specifically, her tone conveying exactly how she felt about their visit.

Lord Sexton's stare flicked to Beatrice. "I've managed to entertain myself. Such a school as Miss Primm's provides a valuable service to the young ladies who are fortunate enough to attend."

"Indeed." Hardwood's oldest sister didn't argue, but her scowl gave away her true feelings. The girl strolled between a set of twin sized beds, separated by a small wardrobe and desk. "This is how I imagine prison would be—or bedlam." She turned her stare to her younger sisters. "I strongly suggest the two of you rethink your desire to attend such a plebian institution. You'd be crying to come home in less than a week."

But the twins obviously disagreed. "It would be like having sleepovers every night," the more talkative one responded, a mischievous gleam in her eyes. "And it's not as though we'd be alone. We'd have one another."

"And Mary Grace—if she can pass the teaching exam," The youngest chaperone added.

"Oh! Miss Walcott, do you remember our cousin? Her mother has taken ill so she's staying with us for a few months."

Miss Francis—or Miss Fanny, as Beatrice recalled—looked to be about ten years older than the girls. Although mousy-looking in a physical sense, with brown hair, a round face, and spectacles perched on her nose, her smile was infectious.

"It's marvelous such institutions exist for young women," Miss Fanny commented. "And living amongst the other students, it would be difficult to be lonely."

Beatrice liked her immediately.

"Although I doubt all the girls are friendly," Eloise turned to her sisters. "Remember Kate Jones and her group? And all those pranks they played?"

Mary Grace winced.

"It happens." Beatrice conceded. "There is always one or two girls intent on making others miserable. But you'll find people like that throughout your life, and learning how to deal with them earlier is a useful lesson. And you'll not be alone. You can always go to one of your teachers if you're having difficulties." She turned back to Miss fanny. "I'll admit that Identifying these situations and addressing them effectively is one of our greatest challenges as a teacher," Beatrice offered. If the girls chose to attend the school, she wanted their expectations to be realistic.

"You are more than a teacher, then," Miss Fanny said. "You are part older sister—part mother."

"We are." Beatrice smiled to have met a kindred spirit. Inexplicably, she glanced across at the marquess.

His eyes locked with hers and although he wasn't smiling, he didn't appear as irritated as he'd pretended to be earlier.

In fact, he even added to the conversation. "It's much the same for boys. There will always be at least one bully to ruin one's fun."

It had been yet another worry Beatrice had had about Jasper. She'd been happy when he'd attached himself to a few good friends. Although that had given her reason to worry as well…

The temptation to share their secret wasn't always easy to resist.

But the marquess was watching her.

"I hope you weren't one of those bullies," Beatrice gave him a stern look. Sparring with him was becoming her new favorite diversion, and she momentarily forgot that they were not alone.

He raised his brows as though forcing her to guess, but then shook his head. "Never me. I was the peacekeeper."

"Of course, Lord Sexton wasn't a bully! How unkind of you to suggest that he was anything less than the perfect student," Eloise inserted. "Anyway, I've seen enough. And the air is uncomfortably hot up here—the entire building is stuffy. Come on girls, let's find Miss Primm's office. Perhaps Mary Grace is finished with her test and we can return to the inn."

Mr. Stewart stepped forward. "I'm happy to show you there as I need a word with our intrepid headmistress, myself." He did not offer an arm, as most gentlemen would have, but gestured toward the door for the girls to exit. Beatrice wondered if Eloise, as the eldest sister, would have taken it if he had.

"A word, Miss Walcott?" Lord Sexton's softly spoken request halted her while the others filed out of the room. This gentleman's presence affected her unlike anything she could remember. Not in a nervous way, but something else… something that had her skin aching and made her blood run hot.

He was good-looking, she couldn't deny that. And although he was titled, that could not be why either.

Perhaps it was because he'd found such great success outside of the nobility. Regardless, she did her best to wish it away.

But when he stared at her with those black eyes, a fluttery sensation lightened her chest. It was as though molten lava spread through her.

Sensations that threatened to rob her of all intelligence.

Nonetheless, she would remain alone with him—she would hear him out. She glanced at her watch.

Besides, she could take these few minutes to further plead their case.

They desperately needed his expertise. The possibility that the school might be attacked again hung over them like a looming storm, and it was wearing on all of them. It affected not only Primm, but the Drivers, Miss Royal, and the other few servants who dedicated their lives to helping to keep the school running smoothly.

Not to mention herself.

"How can I help you, my lord?" she asked in the sweetest voice she could muster.

# TOO MANY QUESTIONS

The marquess stroked his chin with his fingertips, contemplating her while Beatrice lowered herself onto one of the beds, doing her best not to squirm.

But then he was all business.

"Who has keys to the school?" He'd removed his little notebook and was poised to document her answer. She couldn't help but notice his fingers, which were elegant, well-manicured, but also capable-looking.

If he was taking notes, it meant that anything she said might be of significance.

"Myself," she replied, dragging her gaze away from his hands. "And all of the other teachers—on occasion. The Drivers have a set. Oh, and Coachman John. Cook. And I believe we've even provided Mrs. Pratt with a set for when we host special events."

"What sorts of special events?"

"Parents' Day, Christmas festivals, performances..."

"Hmmm..." Sexton ran a hand through his hair. "So,

essentially every person within a three-mile radius can access the building at will."

"Unfortunately, yes." Beatrice sighed. "Before Gertrude broke in, we never thought it necessary to keep the school locked. This is a school—a girls' school! Who on earth would have reason to harm it—to harm any of us?"

He scratched out a few notes and, standing above her, narrowed his eyes. "When did you join the staff?"

"Er..." Beatrice winced. As a rule, she never discussed her past with anyone. She'd even managed to evade most of Primm's questions.

Or lied.

"About nine years ago. I started in September of eighteen twenty-three," she replied, trying to keep her answer as succinct as possible. She'd had to get Jasper settled first. Luckily, one of his schoolmaster's had known Miss Primm and suggested Beatrice seek employment here.

"And who are your people?"

"My people?" She pretended not to know his meaning.

He exhaled. "Your family."

"Am I a suspect?" she laughed nervously. To answer these sorts of questions could cost her...

A decade was a long time but not long enough for everyone to forget.

His brows shot up. "I was trying to get a sense of whether or not you might be a possible target. Is there anyone you can think of who may want to cause you trouble or harm?"

She stiffened for a moment, but then shook her head. The arsonist had damaged Primm and Chloe's belongings. They'd left her possessions alone.

She could not be a target. She and Jasper had been exceedingly careful to cover their tracks.

In her silence, he watched her. "Are you going to tell me?" His brows furrowed as though slightly perplexed.

Beatrice waved a hand in front of her face. "I'm a nobody. I have no family left, both my parents are dead." That was true, anyhow. She swallowed around the lump that always came with the memory.

"Hmmm..." Again with such an ambiguous sound.

"I'm only a schoolteacher. I'm blissfully insignificant." She shrugged, hoping to appear nonchalant.

"Perhaps..." he grumbled, still staring at her with more than a little suspicion in his gaze. He lowered himself to sit on the bed across from her. "Tell me about the other teachers."

Beatrice was the least talkative of all the staff, but that didn't mean she hadn't been paying attention.

"I'm not a gossip," she said. "But what sort of information are you looking for?"

"Anything. Imagine I'm painting a picture. I need every possible detail you can think of if I'm to get an accurate representation."

She rather liked that analogy. This marquess could be agreeable when he wished to be.

If he were like this all the time, he'd certainly be more tolerable.

"Most of them have married recently," Beatrice said. Over the next half an hour, she went on to tell him much of what she knew about the teachers she'd shared lodgings with, careful not to divulge anything too personal about any of them, but trying to think like a detective.

Because no one was without skeletons. Many of them had come to Primm's to keep those bones locked away.

As he had attended Priscilla and Lord Hardwood's wedding, he no doubt knew that Hardwood's new wife had lied to him about who she was for the first fortnight of their courtship—so Beatrice needn't dive into that.

She supposed she ought to mention the elderly couple who lived on the edge of the school's property. "The Drivers, the school's caretakers, have lived on the grounds for decades—long before Primm purchased it, in fact."

"And Primm purchased the school in eighteen twenty-one?"

"Yes. She was young to take on such an endeavor but she'd inherited a fortune from her mother's mother."

"Hmmm..."

"You think someone is out to hurt Primm," she said.

"Perhaps."

"Primm's father is known for his extreme political views, which are in direct opposition to the school's philosophy—to Primm's ideals," Beatrice offered.

"Which are?"

"Forward thinking—somewhat liberal, especially when it comes to the rights of women." Beatrice frowned. "But do you really think it possible her own father might try to ruin her—put her in danger?" And yet Primm's father was a member of the nobility—a marquess, no less.

Beatrice summoned the image of her own father, a man who would have sacrificed his own life for his family—but hadn't been allowed the chance.

"The Marquess of Starbridge would have been embarrassed, first that she'd jilted her betrothed, a man he selected himself, and then that she'd use money from her mother's side of the family to open the school. There is no telling how the marquess might retaliate." Lord Sexton seemed to be thinking out loud.

"Primm is something of a rebel." Beatrice conceded, feeling more than a little guilty discussing her employer this way. But... she wanted the marquess to find their *little annoyance.* And to do this, he needed as much information as possible, so she added. "From what I understand, she jilted the man her father chose for her to marry—some duke. I don't recall the name." It was one of the reasons Beatrice admired the woman to such a great extent. Not only had she stood up to her father's demands, but she'd jilted an actual duke.

"The Duke of Malum. An unsavory fellow, to my knowledge."

"Does he have black hair? Does he fit in our pool of suspects?" she asked. The name Malum sounded vaguely familiar. And then she remembered. Priscilla had purchased Lord Hardwood's freedom from the man.

"I'll have to look into it, but I can't imagine he'd bother with Primm. His preferences lend themselves to an altogether different sort of woman."

"What do you mean?"

The marquess raised his brows. "Women of a profession considerably less respectable that yours." Oh...*Oh!*

"You mean...?" Blushing, she pinched her mouth shut.

"Precisely." He nodded. And then his lip twitched.

Beatrice quickly turned the conversation back to the topic at hand. "Do you have any other suspects in mind?"

Lord Sexton stared unfocussed at the wall behind her.

"Perhaps Malum, or perhaps someone less obvious," he answered.

"Or any man." She added quickly, turning her head to the side. An uncomfortable silence followed. This case really was an impossible one!

Nearly a full minute passed while Beatrice waited for him to contemplate other possible suspects.

"Were you aware that one of Mr. Stewart's London projects was destroyed by vandals less than two years ago?" he asked. "It nearly killed two people.

"I am aware. The Duchess of Bedwell is a friend of mine. She was a teacher here before her marriage." *For less than a fortnight*—but that wasn't relevant. "She told us about it when we attended her wedding." Beatrice shivered. Poor Collette had been trapped beneath the collapsed structure for nearly an hour. If the Duke of Bedwell hadn't managed to find a way out, the two of them would surely have been killed.

"But that was a good deal more serious than anything we've experienced." Beatrice tried to connect the pieces. "I don't understand how that's related."

Lord Sexton shook his head. "It was Mr. Stewart who repaired the damaged foundation. It was he who discovered the fire. And he says that both those incidences could have been far more damaging if he had not been in the area to put the fire out—or make the necessary repairs to the foundation. Which leaves us to beg the question: is your arsonist a prankster or is he intent on hurting someone?"

She'd known the vandalism was a problem but, before putting it together with the Duke and Duchess of Bedwell's near tragedy, she hadn't truly believed that the danger could escalate.

What if the vandal became more than a *little annoyance*?

"I'm not certain of any connection," he spoke slowly.

"But if it's her father, Mr. Stewart's involvement might only add fuel to the fire."

Beatrice hadn't considered that. But Mr. Stewart was a bastard. The product of his father's affair with a Barbadian woman. Before the duke had married. It wasn't exactly a secret.

The current Duke of Bedwell was the duke's second, younger son. But he was legitimate, and therefore had inherited the title. He'd also married one of Primm's former teachers.

Beatrice nodded. "To Primm's father, a traditionalist such as Starbridge, the nature of Primm's school, along with associating with Mr. Stewart, could be viewed as the ultimate betrayal."

"Your employer walks a fine line."

Beatrice stiffened. "Our girls graduate with skills necessary to succeed in society, but also in life. That's what matters most." She spoke with more vehemence than she'd intended.

He studied her. "A commendable endeavor." And then his eyes twinkled. "I am ninety-nine percent certain I can remove you from my list of suspects." *Was it possible he was teasing her?* She was tempted to look out the window to see if pigs were flying.

"Thank you." Beatrice sat up a little straighter. It was about time!

He'd made her feel comfortable, so she ought to have expected him to throw her off balance again.

"Are you married, Miss Walcott? Is that what you are hiding?"

It was the very last question she expected to come out of his mouth. It was more than laughable, it was ludicrous.

He was unaware of her circumstances, of course, but as a woman living under an assumed name, she would be a fool to marry. The marriage would never be legal. In fact, providing a false name for a marriage certificate in and of itself might be against the law.

The other teachers at the school may have once opposed marriage, but their reasons had been philosophical. Beatrice's very freedom was at stake.

"Oh, no! I've never—" She shook her head with unusual vehemence. "I mean, of course not. I'm one hundred percent, er, spinster."

But how had he guessed that she was hiding something?

"Walcott isn't your real name." He was so damn sure of himself.

"Oh, but it is." And it would be for a very, very long time —perhaps forever.

Dizziness threatened and she pushed away the memories of the weeks following her parents' passing.

She couldn't discuss this with him. He saw too much. She could only be grateful that his suspicions had taken him in the wrong direction.

Beatrice focused on the carefully tied cravat the marquess wore, searching for a way to escape his probing questions.

Lord Sexton had been married once. She could turn the tables on him, even if it meant she was prying into something she had no business prying into.

"You must miss your wife dreadfully."

Rather than rise to the bait, however, he nodded. "Yes."

It was a brief answer, but it was more than she'd thought he'd share. If he missed his dead wife, he must have cared for her—or even loved her.

"But you did not have any children."

"No."

For a man who asked a lot of questions, he certainly was reticent answering hers. Although… she didn't blame him. A person stood to learn a good deal by keeping to oneself rather than filling every silent moment with chatter.

And his short answers showed reluctance in discussing his wife. Had he loved the woman like her father had loved her mother?

"It's unbelievable, really," she added. "That anyone could take another's life." Had the marquess suffered more than usual, given his chosen profession?

Or less?

Her father had been adamant about protecting Beatrice and her brother, but also their mother. Protecting them had been more important to him than anything else. And throughout her childhood, he'd proved that with his deeds along with his words. He would have been enraged at her circumstances if he'd lived to see them.

The marquess stared at her, not giving away a single thought. She wished she could do that—hide the thoughts dancing in her head.

Lord Sexton had failed to protect his wife.

Was it even worse since her murderer had eluded him—a man who spent his life bringing criminals to justice?

When he'd treated Beatrice with such blatant disrespect at Hardwood Cliffhouse, she'd locked onto her first impression of him. But since then, she'd witnessed other aspects of his character. He could be rude, yes, but he was also intelligent, honorable, and she suspected that he possessed a dry sense of humor.

Had she judged him unfairly?

"I'm sorry I pulled you into the closet." The words shot out of her mouth unchecked. "When I saw Primm approaching with Mr. Meadowbrook, I sort of just... panicked. I hope you don't think less of me for it."

He dipped his chin. "You didn't *act* as though you were trying to trap me for your husband." His mouth twitched and something in his eyes sent her heart racing.

Was he remembering how his body had responded to being pressed against hers? She released a shaking breath.

"I would never do that." In fact, she oughtn't be alone with him that very moment. As a spinster, as a woman who'd decided against marriage, it was easy to forget that her reputation was at stake—as was her virtue—or that either mattered.

But her position as a teacher depended very much on her good standing.

With that in mind, she rose suddenly and he did so as well. Standing simultaneously, however, neither bargained for the proximity it would put them in.

Why did this keep happening? It was as though the tension she felt whenever she was around him overpowered all sense of propriety.

And wisdom.

His cravat was a mere six inches from her eyes—as was his chest, and shoulders. Her gaze flicked to the line of his jaw and she inhaled.

Her heart skipped a beat.

"I suppose I could have misread the situation," he taunted. "Sometimes, even I can be wrong."

The backs of her knees pressed against the bed behind her, Beatrice had nowhere to go. His hand landed on her arm and pulled her closer. She should jerk away from him and be careful not to be alone with him again. "Was I wrong, Miss Walcott?"

*You most certainly were.*

And yet her lips refused to move. How could he seem almost kind sometimes, and then be such a beast at others?

"I don't know what to think of you," she said, her voice almost a whisper.

He leaned closer, his mouth by her ear, the familiar scent she'd been craving overwhelming her senses.

"That might be the first truthful thing you've told me." he said.

He released her arm abruptly, reminding her of their first meeting, but instead of running, she kept her gaze locked with his.

He didn't want people to know him.

It was like looking into a mirror.

When people knew you, it gave them a chance to care for you. And when people cared about you, they wanted to know even more.

But it could be lonely sometimes.

The truth of the matter, she realized, was that the Marquess of Sexton, for all his arrogance and insufferable manners, was someone she wanted to know.

Beatrice tore out of the room as though the hounds of hell chased her.

RANULF DIDN'T TRY to stop her.

He had no business associating with the likes of Miss Beatrice Walcott—a teacher, of all things!

He ran a hand through his hair.

She was hiding something. He doubted it had anything to do with this particular case but he'd seen it in her eyes as plain as day. And she'd tried to lead him off the scent of her secrets by summoning a few of his.

No one asked him about Susan. She'd been murdered—a topic not fit for polite conversation. No one asked him if he missed her.

Not being at her side when she needed him was his greatest failure. And yes, it drove him, though he tried not to think about it.

And then Little Miss Blue Eyes brings Susan's death up in casual conversation.

Why hadn't he given her a harsh set down? Or better yet, simply left the room?

Ranulf stared down at his hands. What had gotten into him? Putting his hands on her like that?

Sapphire eyes had gazed up at him, doing her best to shield her secrets even as her body swayed toward his.

He'd taunted her not because she mentioned his dead wife, nor because she was hiding something from him, but because he'd had the ridiculous urge to kiss her. Her running away had been best for both of them.

*Enough.*

Ranulf pinched his mouth together and opened his notebook. He needed to map out a few timelines, interview a few of the locals in the village and then list out all the possible scenarios.

Trouble was, if he was going to do this properly, he needed time—time he didn't have.

Responsibilities pressed in on him from all angles. And no matter how important this case was beginning to appear, he saw no way to fit it into his schedule.

Perhaps next month. But the case would be even colder by then.

And more worrisome. Would following his own agenda result in the injury of an innocent or worse?

Damned Miss Primm, and double damn Miss Beatrice Walcott. Ranulf had never been the sort of man who could turn his back on a case—a case he knew he could solve.

Especially when there was any sort of danger.

The conniving little spinsters might just get their way after all.

# ONE ABSENT MARQUESS

Downstairs, all the way on the first floor, in the familiar comfort of her classroom, Beatrice paced in front of her desk.

She'd thought he was going to kiss her. One moment he'd stared at her with what she could only think to describe as unbridled passion, and then the next, his black eyes had turned as cold and forbidding as the bottom of the sea.

Her heart had raced, but she'd not been afraid.

Opening the supply closet, she withdrew the lemon oil and rag she kept there and automatically began polishing her student's desks. The dust would build up again before the new term began but the activity was precisely what she needed right now.

In fact, her hands didn't stop shaking until she'd polished an entire row.

Unfortunately, although her hands were occupied, she couldn't quiet her mind. And with the troubles at the school, the last thing she ought to be thinking about was allowing that man to kiss her!

If he refused to help them, there must be something she could do. A dozen ideas floated through her thoughts, only to be dismissed for some reason or another.

Because she needed to be careful.

Beatrice rose, placed her hands on her back, and arched. She'd polished every single desk in her classroom. A glance at the clock revealed that she'd been at it for over an hour.

She needed to keep her distance from Lord Sexton.

Because she didn't know who he was, nor did he know her.

And that was exactly what she wanted.

~

WITH SO MANY guests on the premises, Primm had arranged a special evening meal to be served in the student dining hall that night. She'd opened up the room which normally went unused over the summer months for two purposes—partly to allow the twins a chance to experience one aspect of how they would live at the school as students, but also as a celebration.

Mary Grace had passed the teacher's test with flying colors.

Although Primm had already contacted an employment agency to fill Chloe, Priscilla, and Victoria's positions, and the candidates were scheduled to arrive at the school the following week, Primm was going to allow Mary Grace to be in the running for one of the open teaching positions as well.

She lacked teaching experience, of course, but Primm

was of the belief that experience didn't necessarily mean a person excelled at the post they'd been trained for.

The dinner, all in all, lifted everyone's spirits. Even Eloise cracked at least one smile.

Lord Sexton was conspicuously absent. Beatrice tried convincing herself that she was lucky not to have to face him again.

Likely, if she kept herself busy the following morning, she could avoid him altogether.

As the meal wound down, and these refined gentle ladies expressed it was one of the best they'd ever had, Beatrice leaned close to Primm.

"Did Lord Sexton move back to the inn?" Despite everything, her thoughts had returned to him over and over again.

"He went into the village to conduct some interviews. He has promised to pass along his findings before he departs in the morning."

"Ah..." Beatrice did her best to show disinterest.

Primm leaned toward Beatrice. "And why do you ask?"

"No particular reason."

But he'd informed Primm that he was going to be working on the case today—rather than Beatrice.

She wasn't exactly jealous, but it left her feeling... unimportant?

Rejected?

She needed to purge such impossible—impractical thoughts. She would have had nothing to do with him if not for his investigative skills.

Anxious to be done with all of it, she rose and moved about the room collecting plates and cutlery to assist Cook and Mrs. Driver, both of whom had already worked harder than usual that day.

"Normally, the girls scrape their plates into a bin by the door to the kitchen, but as your carriage is waiting outside to deliver all of you back to the inn, you are officially excused tonight." Primm spoke with an unusual twinkle in her eyes.

The day, all in all, had been a success.

This was the reason they taught—to shape young women's lives—to teach them self-sufficiency, among other life skills.

Amidst a barrage of *thank yous* and even a few hugs, the young ladies all eventually filed outside. Primm followed them, but Beatrice remained behind and didn't go up to her chamber until the last dish had been dried and put away.

Who had Lord Sexton interviewed today?

Had he discovered anything of significance?

And the most bothersome question of all… Had he forgotten all about her?

Just as he'd forgotten the day he'd accosted her at Hardwood Cliffhouse?

Carrying a fresh pitcher of water upstairs, Beatrice's arms and back ached a little more than usual. Served her right, worrying over that man all day. Closing the door to her quarters behind her, she then shed her gown and chemise. She took more time than usual at the washbasin, scrubbing her skin, and wished she could do the same with her thoughts of Lord Sexton.

Even after she'd climbed under the thin coverlet and closed her eyes, her thoughts betrayed her by summoning black eyes and strong male features, his jaw peppered with short black whiskers.

Chances were, he wasn't returning to the school that night—not when he could spend his evening with other gentlemen, patronizing Mr. Pratt's tavern.

Her father had been a member of Whites, but he'd mostly visited in the afternoon hours. Some gentlemen, she knew, indulged in spirits well into the early morning hours.

They fought. They caroused. It was in their nature.

Her mother had warned her against men of the *Ton*. If she'd had a come-out, Beatrice had no doubt she'd have never lacked a chaperone.

Footsteps on the stairs cut off her musings of what might or might not have been.

And like the night before, his every stepped echoed. She almost believed she could hear a pin if he dropped one.

She lie perfectly still as the footsteps arrived at the second floor, paused, and then moved along to the third.

Unable to help herself, she sat up, struck a flint, and glanced at her pocket watch. It was nearly one in the morning.

Not wanting to be caught waiting up for him, she blew out the candle on her bedside table and lie back down as quietly as possible.

It was best he was leaving.

# WORTH THE WAIT

Ranulf had found the evening to be an enlightening one, if not tiresome. When he'd first taken a seat in the taproom, the locals had avoided him.

They'd eyed him curiously, of course, with some glances that were suspicious, some envious, but it wasn't until he'd purchased two rounds for the entire room, that anyone deigned to approach him.

They asked questions about a few of his more famous cases, but also about London. A few made complaints to him as though he was the king himself. But eventually, the discussion had turned to the school.

The school which, no one would argue, kept the local economy afloat. It provided more than one job as, whenever possible, necessary supplies were purchased from local merchants.

But aside from that, not all the menfolk approved.

More than one of the farmers referred to Miss Primm as *"that woman"*. It was well-known that she was the daughter of a marquess, and many mentioned their belief that she was ungrateful—to her father and to God. What decent lady walked away from such a birthright in order to fill young girls' heads up with nonsense?

Womenfolk didn't need to learn about books, history, or blasphemous ideas. Made them uppity, and even worse, unhappy with their lot.

As drink flowed, tongues loosened.

And Ranulf listened.

And although Primm lacked unanimous approval, by the end of the evening, He was convinced that the attacks had not been perpetrated by any of the people here. They worked too hard to waste time on such pranks. Even more importantly, they all stood to lose if the school closed.

When the conversation lulled, Ranulf took a slow sip of his ale, which he'd been nursing most of the night, and then stared into the tankard.

"Someone wants to do harm up at Miss Primm's," he pointed out. "And if they keep at it, one of those ladies, or a student, is bound to be injured—or worse."

As adamant as they were in their feelings about the teachings at the school, the men in the room claimed it as their own. "Has to be an outsider," Leroy Mills, the local blacksmith, declared.

Even if he hadn't mentioned his vocation earlier, it would have been obvious by the soot around his face and on his hands. Soot, Ranulf knew, that would never wash off.

Mr. Pratt, who'd joined his guests by now, leaned forward with a thoughtful expression. "There was one bloke, an odd sort of fellow, who took a room here, right about the time the fire was set. He'd come through before, stayed a few days last spring but kept to himself."

Ranulf stilled, and he felt a pricking at the back of his neck.

"Fellows have a right to keep to themselves, but this one nary said a word." Mr. Pratt pushed his spectacles up the bridge of his nose. "At the time, I'd have thought he was running from an irate husband if he was younger. Dressed like a toff, though. Stayed two nights before leaving. Hard to forget someone who pays extra." Pratt looked thoughtful "Signed in as Mr. Smith."

"No first name, I imagine," Ranulf said casually, not wanting to veer Pratt away from this particular subject.

"Do you think he could have set the fire?" One of the other fellows joined the conversation.

"Could have," Pratt answered. "He was gone the next morning. Not sure why I hadn't thought about it before."

"Did he leave anything behind?" Ranulf took another swallow of the bitter drink.

"As a matter of fact he did. And the wife held onto it, of course—a fine sheet of parchment. She said she didn't care that it had one of those aristocratic seals inked at the top. The paper was dear, that was for certain." Pratt stiffened, suddenly looking defensive. "Signs posted upstairs, plain as day. Anything left behind becomes property of the inn."

Ranulf met the innkeeper's gaze. "Can you produce the stationary. If some person is going around the country setting fires, he needs to be caught." Instilling a little fear never hurt. Arson was a hanging offense for good reason. The strike of a flint could not only rob a man of his home and livelihood, but his life.

"I'll fetch it now." Mr. Pratt pushed his chair back and disappeared.

When he returned a few minutes later, he passed it across the table.

Ranulf didn't have to study it for long. He knew the seal. It represented the Marquessate of Starbridge.

He'd remained to finish his drink, but no one admitted to having seen where the stranger had come from, nor what direction he'd gone when he'd left.

It was a short distance to the school, so just as Ranulf made his way earlier, he walked back to Miss Primm's through the dark.

The information was as he already half-suspected, but it was also troubling. Pinning a crime on a nobleman was never easy. It would be nearly impossible to convict a marquess.

He'd interviewed Primm earlier that day and she'd been, for the most part, forthcoming. Trouble was, everyone had secrets.

She had admitted to him, however, that the school was in financial difficulties. Although she was well past the age of independence, her father had illegally withheld her trust—funds from her mother's dowry that had been set aside for any daughters. At the age of one and twenty, she'd claimed money left to her from her grandmother and purchased the school.

The marquess had been withholding the trust for nearly a decade.

Primm had confided that the last time she'd seen her father, just after the new year, she'd threatened legal action.

He'd laughed at her. Of course, he had; what judge would side with a spinster over a marquess?

"Is there anything else?" Ranulf had asked her. "Do you have a spurned lover? A jealous family member?"

She'd paused, but then adamantly denied the existence of either.

"Do you believe your father is capable of sabotaging your efforts with the school?"

At this question, the headmistress frowned. "No!" Her answer had been almost vehement." She'd ended the conversation then, claiming she was running late that day.

Neither of which matched her typical demeanor. In every other instance, she'd been beyond cooperative.

But when Ranulf had spoken with Rosewood, he'd pretty much said the same. Furthermore, he'd pointed out that his father was infirmed and that he doubted the man had the cognizance to undertake the deed.

And yet, in Ranulf's mind, all evidence pointed toward the Marquess of Starbridge.

By the time he arrived on the school grounds, the building was shrouded in darkness. The hour was late and the rain that had been threatening all afternoon had finally begun to fall.

He was grateful Miss Walcott had provided him with keys to enter the school, but he could have used a flint to see what he was doing.

His hands slippery from the rain, he required several tries before the mechanism in the lock clicked. He couldn't help but think back to much smaller hands unlocking the latch in one motion.

Ranulf stepped into the school, locked the door behind him, and then shook the rain out of his hair.

All the while, his thoughts remained on Miss Walcott. *Not-so sweet Beatrice Walcott.*

Or was it his own cynicism that caused him to see her that way?

He climbed the stairs slowly, deliberately ignoring the second-floor landing.

His rebellious thoughts, however, summoned the blue-eyed vixen's image. He'd not allow himself to dwell on those few moments in the closet, when he'd realized that small breasts could be just as arousing as big ones.

The interviews today had been necessary, but they'd also conveniently allowed him to avoid her.

Ranulf had friends, both male and female, but he was able to limit the nature of their conversations. They all knew better than to ask him about Susan.

Susan couldn't have been more different from Miss Walcott. His wife had delighted in the social whirlwind of the season. She'd loved shopping and dancing and being driven through the park in expensive vehicles.

It was how she'd been raised. She'd also been poised, elegant, and volunteered for more than her fair share of charities.

Susan's eyes hadn't been as vibrant, or as wide as Miss Walcott's. Hers had been closer to gray and shaped like almonds to perfectly match the rest of her features. While courting her, Ranulf had told Susan her eyes reminded him of London on a cloudy day.

He chuckled to himself. She hadn't appreciated the compliment.

But Miss Walcott's eyes... Bluebells, a clear summer sky, a classic blue sapphire...

Shouldn't he feel guilty for comparing his dead wife's eyes to those of Miss Walcott's?

Ranulf glance down at his hands, unwittingly remembering how they'd looked caressing his wife's creamy skin. God, that had been ages ago. Her breasts had been plump, her figure voluptuous. Even her belly had pleased him, round and soft.

For the entirety of the first year of their marriage, he and Susan had shared a satisfying life in the carnal sense.

As most *Ton* marriages progressed, however, theirs had followed the typical pattern. Their lovemaking had become less inspired, less spontaneous, and they'd drifted apart, spending their time following very different pursuits.

She'd conceived the first time at the end of their second year as man and wife, but lost the child before the pregnancy was even noticeable.

The subsequent years, the two of them had gradually become polite friends.

But he'd loved Susan. She'd been an excellent partner not only in life but also politically.

He wished he could erase the ending.

Even before they'd pulled back the sheet, he'd smelled the putrid stench of decomposition, of death. He'd nearly choked on his own vomit to see her like that. And although he'd vowed to find her killer, he'd, as of yet, failed to fulfill that promise.

Perhaps in investigating other crimes, he'd catch the villain who'd killed his wife. No one should ever get away with murder.

No one.

He stared at the bed in the small chamber that was adjacent to the student dormitory, surprised to find himself already there.

Like an annoying insect, the throbbing in the back of his head promised another sleepless night. Nonetheless, he would lie down and close his eyes and he would try. If he was lucky, he might catch an hour, maybe two.

Like a man pounding his head against a brick wall, he always tried.

Now, if he could only sleep.

Lying down on the small bed, his feet hanging off the end, he tucked his hands behind his neck and stared up at the ceiling.

Rationally, he ought to be rethinking his strategy leading up to the day of the vote. Over the past eight months, he'd done more socializing than he ever had before, perhaps in his entire life—but could one really call it socializing? It had felt more like finagling—garnering the support of board members, in addition to anyone else with a vested interest, without making any promises he couldn't keep.

And yet there were still a handful of votes he'd not secured—those belonging to the most conservative of board members.

Ranulf's sister, Edith, who was one of his greatest supporters, had suggested more than once that if he had married again, or was even engaged, most of those would cast their votes for him as well.

Even the Duke of Bedwell had suggested he needed to appear more settled.

But marriage? By God! It was the one thing he couldn't do. He'd been through it once and, in the end, it had simply been too damn…

Painful.

*Appear more settled.* What did that even mean? He'd never had a reputation for being a rake, and he'd kept the few affairs he'd entered confidential.

*Appear...*

Engagements could always be broken. He noticed a small crack in the ceiling as his mind worked through the logistics of an impossible idea. Even so, the last thing he'd want to deal with on the heels of taking the new position would be a messy broken engagement.

But, if he and a temporary fiancée had a prior arrangement—agreed beforehand that the betrothal wasn't, in fact, real…

But what woman would accept such terms? He flipped onto his side.

The idea was preposterous!

Wasn't it? Even if it wasn't, he hardly had time to vet ladies who'd go along with such an agreement.

Especially if he was going to attempt to solve the school's case over the next few weeks.

How had he gotten himself into this situation, forced to escort Hardwood's sisters and mother back to the coast, and now contemplating a visit to meet with the Marquess of Starbridge? It would mean Ranulf would arrive back in London with less than a fortnight to complete his hob-knobbing.

Hell, he was already deciding on questions he'd ask the man. He knew himself too well. If there was a chance he could wrap this case up that easily, there was no way he could walk away.

Because lives might very well be at stake.

The throbbing moved up his head, making his limbs jittery and his entire body feel overheated.

Rather than suffer it silently, he jumped off the bed and, reaching down, jerked his shirt off and over his head.

Rain pelted at the windows by now, but this small chamber was feeling more and more like a cell.

He shot out of the room and down the stairs like a man seeking oxygen.

## THUNDER AND LIGHTNING

With so many windows making up the long wall of the teachers' lodgings, the lightning from the storm illuminated every corner of the room Beatrice slept in. She couldn't tell if it was the light or the thunder that woke her up.

Having had such difficulties falling asleep to begin with, Beatrice cursed it, and then slipped out of bed and across the room to the window to marvel at nature's magnificent display.

Thunder and lightning didn't scare her. Fire didn't usually scare her.

People were far more dangerous.

Hugging her pillow, she stood at the window, watching hundred-year-old trees bend at the onslaught of the wind. A few branches lay strewn about the yard. Then her gaze caught sight of something that didn't belong; no person ought to be outside on a night like tonight.

But of course, it was Lord Sexton. Sprinting across the yard and then back again like a madman tormented by demons. But rain at this time of night would be cold. He'd be getting a chill. What could he possibly be thinking? Did he have a death wish?

It didn't matter that she'd rather not have to face him again or that at times he was an arrogant jerk, *someone* ought to ensure the fool didn't make himself ill.

Not stopping to consider the wisdom of being that *someone,* Beatrice scurried down the stairs and toward the school's kitchen to make tea. Luckily, the coals in the stove were still glowing from earlier that night, and after stoking them, she added water to the kettle and moved it to the already hot surface.

Gathering everything she needed to make two cups of tea, she placed them on the table and then hoped she was not being overly presumptuous as she rushed through the corridors to the school's foyer and peered through the window that flanked the entrance.

Outside, the storm still raged…

As did the marquess.

*Foolish, foolish man!*

She glanced down at her pristine cotton nightrail. If she thought it over too long, she'd change her mind.

Taking a deep breath, she pushed the door slightly open.

Before she could even peer outside, however, the wind whipped it out of her hands, slamming it against the wall outside. She let out a cry, startled by nature's violence.

The sound was carried away by the storm but still managed to capture Lord Sexton's attention. His head turned and she felt like he was staring right at her.

Pinned by his gaze, she didn't move to bring the door under control.

"Lord Sexton!" she shouted, but he didn't move. Was he hurt?

She'd heard of people sleepwalking, was that what he was doing?

He bent over, dropping his head and resting his hands on his knees. Not considering the rain or the lightning or the powerful gusts of wind, Beatrice flew out the door toward him.

"My Lord!" she shouted as she got closer.

And then again.

He did not look up until she was only a few yards away, and when he did, he stared at her as though she were a ghost.

She'd always considered herself reasonably fit, but a cramp had formed in her side and her breaths came in gulping gasps.

~

THE WOMAN STANDING before him resembled an ancient goddess. The material of her gown, transparent from the rain and clinging to her like a second skin presented the sort of apparition a man usually only saw in his dreams.

"My lord," she called as she approached in bare feet. "You're soaked." She glanced down and grimaced at her own present state. "We both are. You need to come inside." Her voice sounded weak. "I've put water on for tea."

Midnight had come and gone hours ago. On nights like these, he lost all track of time. If he could tire himself out enough, he could hope for perhaps an hour or two of sleep.

Where had she come from? In between flashes of lightning, the clouds filtered the night with a soft light. He was incapable of stopping his gaze from trailing down Miss Walcott's surprisingly alluring figure.

How had he ever considered her too slim? By God, she was perfect.

The woman had a uniquely enticing appeal. Even the cold rain couldn't cool his blood as he stared at her.

Pert breasts pushed up, the tips tight and perfectly visible through her gown. Her waist nipped in just above delicately flared hips. Even through the material, her legs went on forever. Firm thighs could wrap around a man's waist and those shapely calves and ankles could lock behind him.

His cock jumped to life and he shifted his stance.

At the apex of those thighs, her gown revealed a thatch of dark hair. He suddenly itched to stroke her there, to thread his fingers through the short curling tendrils and locate soft petals of skin.

Her hair was drenched from the cool rain, as was her gown. She'd be wet between her legs, but she'd be warm, slick, and welcoming.

"My lord?" She tilted her head, studying him with concern. Her tone reminded him of who she was.

Of where he was.

"What are you doing out here?" he asked, sounding gruff —annoyed. Miss Walcott had become something of an enigma, one he'd best be wary of.

And he'd best keep his thoughts under control. Giving into this insane attraction was not an option.

Because teachers were a dangerous sort—not debutantes, but not widows either. While dealing with one of them, a man couldn't know what sort of situation he was getting himself into.

"The storm woke me up and then I saw you outside. Why would you come out on a night like this? Why would you come out at all? This isn't normal!"

Ranulf could only chuckle at this.

"But I'm not—isn't that what you said?"

Something in his voice gave her pause. Because she dropped to her knees, presumably so she could see his face better. Her gown gaped open at the neck, and he forced his gaze not to linger there.

"No one is normal, really," she said, the rain falling in droves around them. "Why can't you sleep?"

Such a simple question.

A question with no answer—or with too many to speak.

Water clung to her lashes, and even in the dark, the blue in her eyes shone.

"I'm not sure," he answered.

She paused and then bit her lip. "I hated you, you know. I was not at all happy when Primm asked me to assist you."

He had enemies, he wasn't naïve enough to think differently, but her animosity at the house party had puzzled him.

"But I don't think you're as bad as you want people to think," she continued. "In fact, I think I understand why you were so rude to me the day before the wedding."

Her teeth chattered a little, and she shivered.

Ranulf ought to get her back inside. And warmed up. And back to the privacy of her own bed.

Where he couldn't ogle her.

Regardless, having this conversation now—here—was madness.

As he rose, he took her hand, pulling her to stand as well.

She had followed him outside in the middle of a storm—

in the middle of the night—wearing, for all intents and purposes—nothing.

"I'm leaving tomorrow morning." Ranulf ran one hand down his face.

He couldn't help but notice how her gaze was fixed on his mouth.

"I know." Her voice was little more than a whisper.

And then she reached one hand up and set it on his chest. "Please, come inside."

What did she want from him? Was this some ruse to get him to stay on for the investigation?

Did it even matter?

In a swift motion, he pulled her against him.

The stiff points of her breasts teased his bare chest. Holding one hand behind her neck, he slid his other down her back until he could cup the soft flesh of her buttocks.

"Why should I?" he asked.

Her bottom lip trembled. From desire? From fear? The two of them like this might as well be on fire.

When was the last time he'd been this aroused?

The first year of his marriage? He couldn't remember a single female who'd brought him to life like this.

Another flash of lightning illuminated her delicate face, making her blue eyes look like ice.

He gripped the back of her thigh and lifted it so he could thrust his hips against her center.

"I need..." She tipped her head back and closed her eyes. "I need you to come inside."

She had both hands on his chest, but she hadn't turned pliant in his arms.

And what had she said?

*"I think I understand why you were so rude to me the day before the wedding."*

A more pronounced tremor ran through her and Ranulf exhaled.

She wanted to go inside. She didn't have blood burning through her veins from exercise or anything else.

Hell, she must be freezing.

He dropped her leg from around his hips and placed one arm around her shoulders.

"The water should be ready," she said. "For the tea."

Ah yes, she had mentioned earlier. "Of course." His voice caught.

She walked beside him, head down, her steps almost long enough to keep up with his. He shortened his stride to more closely match hers.

"We can take it in the kitchen, by the stove," she said. "Or you can take it upstairs with you. I have lavender leaves. It's supposed to help a person sleep. I wanted to help you sleep." Another tremor ran through her.

He had totally misread her intentions.

He opened the door for her and, once they were both inside, locked it behind them. He was leaving tomorrow. Thank God. This could have turned into a catastrophe.

"Which way?" He'd gotten control of his voice.

"She gestured toward a small hallway."

Ranulf took her arm to keep her from slipping. Her feet would be wet from the grass. As they neared the kitchen, the sounds of the storm subsided, to be replaced with the quiet rumbling of boiling water.

The stove was hot and the kitchen was warm.

He lifted the kettle and poured water into the tea pot that was already sitting on the table.

Along with two cups.

She really had been concerned about him.

"*Lavender* tea… It sounds interesting." Ranulf kept his voice even. Pretending everything about this was perfectly normal. *No one is normal,* she had said. "Perhaps it'll help both of us get a few hours of sleep."

"Yes, that is what I had hoped." She sighed. "The flavor's a little unusual, I suppose, if you've never had it before. I hope you don't mind." She poured the water over the leaves and then took the chair across from him as they waited for the tea to steep. She wore her hair in two braids, and rivulets of water trailed down both of them. She was still shivering, so he insisted she move to the seat nearest the stove.

"When was I rude to you at the wedding?" he asked once she was settled, watching her expression. As a general rule, he didn't go about insulting young women.

Unless they provoked him, he supposed. But even then, his response was normally to avoid those sorts of games. All that aside, he certainly would have remembered insulting this one.

She glanced up from the tea in disbelief, and then a sad sort of acceptance. "I don't suppose I'm all that memorable." She fussed with her sleeves. "You thought I was a maid." She winced.

Ranulf shook his head. There was a flicker of something familiar, but he couldn't quite hold onto it. "I don't…"

"You ordered me to change the linens on your bed."

"The perfume," he finally realized. "One of the ladies at the party poured her perfume on my pillow. I had actually managed to fall asleep early that morning but woke up with a blinding headache." He remembered… He'd had that sort of thing happen before. Ambitious ladies of the ton, he'd learned, would do almost anything to capture a title for a husband.

It wasn't something Miss Walcott would do. Of that, he was certain. But he remembered stopping a woman out in the hall, in what looked like the typical maid's uniform.

"That was you," he exhaled. "I didn't realize."

"I'm not all that memorable," she said again. "But I had hoped you'd apologize." She shrugged. "It doesn't matter. You are a marquess, after all."

A foreign sensation washed through Ranulf, and in the next second, he'd moved to the chair beside her.

He'd come this far, he might as well put his arm around her shoulders—strictly to comfort her, of course.

"I'm sorry," he said. "I have no excuse." Just a blinding headache and the rage at having his elusive sleep interrupted.

"If your head was bothering you, I suppose you do," she murmured. "Besides the fact that you can be a little difficult at times…" The hint of a smile curved her mouth. "Do you ever sleep?" She was joking now so apparently his behavior outside hadn't left her completely traumatized.

Her lashes appeared thicker than usual, clumped together from the rain. And as she warmed up, the color was starting to return to her cheeks.

But her lips remained almost colorless.

Ranulf touched his fingertip to the bottom one and shook his head. "Usually I get an hour or two—eventually. Occasionally, it eludes me completely."

She didn't push his hand away.

"That would explain why you're so grumpy sometimes."

A most unusual conversation.

"The tea should be strong enough now." This time, as she spoke, he dropped his fingers from her mouth. What would she taste like? The warm scent of lavender wafted from the tea.

"No sugar?" he asked when he failed to spot any on the table.

"I didn't think you took sugar with your tea, but I can get —" She attempted to rise but he held a hand out, stopping her.

"I thought you'd want it." He knew of few ladies who didn't.

She frowned. "I'm not all that fond of sugar."

Perhaps, then, she wouldn't taste as sweet as she looked. Ranulf lifted his cup for a sip. Why was this woman such an enigma to him?

Her gown was beginning to dry and no longer clung to her like a second skin, but his interest in her hadn't vanished as easily as he wished it would.

What would she do if he kissed her? Would she follow him to the third floor and allow him to shove her gown up to her waist? Would she soften beneath him as he covered her on the mattress? He'd unfasten his falls and settle his cock at her entrance.

Replacing his cup on the table, he cursed that his hands weren't steady.

And when he stared up at her again, he saw his own desire mirrored in her eyes. No doubt her imagination wasn't as explicit as his. He could lean forward and kiss her but...

Likely he'd go unsatisfied. She was a teacher, for God's sake!

He exhaled a frustrated hiss. Ranulf did not need this

sort of distraction. Right now, in fact, was the very worst time for a dalliance.

He stood up abruptly, shoving his seat back so quickly that it nearly tipped over.

"Goodnight, Miss Walcott," he said.

But she caught his arm before he could leave. "Promise me you won't go outside again? You'll catch your death..."

Ranulf exhaled a long breath through his nostrils. "Goodnight," he said again. But then he surprised himself by leaning down and capturing her sarcastic little mouth after all.

He'd keep the kiss chaste, short. It required all his self-restraint to break away from her.

She stared up at him with wide eyes and a tentative smile. "In case I don't see you in the morning," she said. "It's been... interesting knowing you."

Ranulf shook his head. "Likewise."

He took his leave before he could change his mind.

# AN INTERESTING GOODBYE

Not having fallen asleep until shortly before dawn, Beatrice allowed herself to lie in longer than usual. She ought to feel guilty for not rising to wish their guests goodbye, but she couldn't face Lord Sexton again.

She had not gone outside for any other reason than to make him come out of the rain. All she'd had in mind was to warm him up with a cup of her favorite tea.

Outside, he'd taken her into his arms—tightly—as though she... belonged to him.

Had they both been mad?

He'd lifted her leg, his hand tantalizingly high on her thigh. That position had left her open, vulnerable. She'd felt his member nudging at her, and it had been much harder and far more insistent than when she'd felt it in the closet.

God help her, she'd done nothing to make him release her.

She'd fought a battle inside—her body doing its utmost to overwhelm her mind.

Thank God her mind had won.

Beatrice might be many things, but she was not wanton. Wantonness led to trouble of the worst kind.

But then in the kitchen, just when she thought they had both regained their sanity, he'd kissed her.

He had barely embraced her—simply placed his lips on hers, kissing her with so much tenderness she'd nearly burst into tears.

She'd felt bereft when he ended it.

And even worse after he left.

Had that been his way of saying goodbye? Or his apology, perhaps, for his behavior at Hardwood Cliffhouse?

If she were to rise and dress, go downstairs to wish the visitors farewell, she'd have to face him again.

All of this would be easier if she could go on disliking him—if he hadn't had an excellent explanation for his behavior at Priscilla's house party, for his foul moods in general.

What must it be like to not be able to sleep? She'd experienced nights when one of the students had been sick—sitting up with one girl or another, thinking there was nothing worse than falling ill away from home.

The days following such nights, she'd usually had to teach her classes anyway. And yes, she might have been less than her cheerful self on those days.

But going night after night without it… she shook her head, conflicted.

A knock sounded at the door. One of the Hardwood sisters, perhaps, coming to say goodbye? Or perhaps Primm, coming to check on her.

Because Beatrice rarely, if ever, slept in like this.

She slipped out of bed and padded across the room.

But it was neither. Instead, it was the man who'd kept her awake long after she'd bid him goodnight.

"Are you going to sleep all day?" Dark circles were etched beneath his eyes as he slouched against the door-frame. But dressed for travel and looking far more awake than he had any right to, he flicked a glance behind her. "May I come in?"

"What—what?" she stammered. "What are you doing here?" She touched her hair, which had tangled around her face by now. She'd changed into a different nightrail before climbing into bed, but she'd not bothered to redo her braids.

She glanced out the door to ensure no one was witnessing their conversation, and then reluctantly allowed him to enter.

"I have a proposition for you," he said.

Beatrice hastily donned her dressing gown, feeling at a considerable disadvantage. Her eyes still felt sticky from sleep.

"Er..." A proposition? She hugged her arms in front of her. This could not be good—not after the way she'd allowed him to hold her outside.

She had obviously given him the wrong idea about her.

"I don't have much time." He wandered over to the window as if coming into her chamber this morning was the most natural thing in the world. "I was going to wait for you to rise but..." He flicked his glance to her unmade bed. "I didn't know when that would be."

*Because of you!*

"I don't normally sleep in..." she said, stopping herself before she apologized.

His eyes flared, but then he turned away from her.

"Lady Hardwood has sent word that they're nearly packed and prepared to depart from the inn." He shrugged. "And as I said, I would have spoken with you downstairs, but, alas, you never appeared."

Beatrice shook her head, trying to catch up. What did he mean, *a proposition?* If he thought she was that sort of woman, he'd have to think again!

"What can I help you with?" Perhaps he wanted her to collect more evidence… but he'd refused to take the case…

"It's more of a trade." He rubbed his chin. "You can help me with something I need, and in turn, I'd be willing to solve the case of your arsonist."

*… Intriguing.*

Beatrice straightened. "You'll take the case?" Primm would be thrilled! They could go forward as a school without having to worry about constant repairs.

Or an increasingly more persistent sense of danger.

"I need you to do something for me."

"Anything," she said without thinking. "Well, not anything," she amended, sending him an admonishing glance.

The same glance she ought to have sent him the moment he'd asked to come into her chamber this morning.

"I need a temporary fiancée."

"A temporary *what*?" She was shaking her head, even more confused than she had been a moment ago. This was the very last thing she'd expected. She ought to know better. Anything that seemed too good to be true most likely was.

"Only for a few weeks."

"But why?"

He glanced down at his pocket watch and grimaced. "I haven't time to explain all of it, but the gist of it is that in order to achieve something incredibly important to me, I need to prove to a handful of prominent people that I'm... settled. Despite my behavior last night"—he cleared his throat— "this is all on the up and up. I'm not suggesting anything... inappropriate."

"This has to do with the upcoming vote and your position with the King's Society, doesn't it?"

He nodded.

"But why only temporary?" Beatrice asked. "Why don't you find some suitable debutante and simply marry her?"

"Because I don't actually wish to take on a wife. Marriage is far more trouble than it's worth." He sighed. "I have brothers and nephews who are more than capable of carrying on my title. Once the vote is over, I'll call the engagement off. It will officially be my fault. You can return to the school before your classes resume." His brows furrowed. "I woke up realizing you are the perfect woman for the task."

Beatrice narrowed her eyes at him. "And why would you think that?"

Was his smile a little forced? "You seem as dedicated to your occupation as I am. I trust you've no inclination to trap me."

She knew why he believed that. It was because she could have, if she'd wanted to—the day she'd pulled him into the closet.

"And the investigation?" How would that fit into all of this?

"It will be my top priority following the vote." His voice rang true.

But, although she actually did trust him, Beatrice could not do it.

She'd watched more than one of the other teachers get themselves caught with no choice but to enter matrimony, and she was not about to become one of them. His proposal, or trade as he regarded it, posed too great of a risk.

And just as concerning, it would mean she'd have to appear in London. It was doubtful anyone would recognize her, and yet… She shook her head. "I'm sorry, my lord—"

"Don't decide yet. Take your time, and I'll stop back here on my way back to London. Please, think it over. Speak with Primm if you'd like, and I'll accept your answer when I return."

His gaze flicked away from her face toward the window again.

He cleared his throat.

"And there will be no repeat of last night. For that, and any other slight, I offer my most sincere apology."

He regretted kissing her. The thought jumped unbidden into Beatrice's mind.

"This proposal… It would be nothing more than a business agreement," she confirmed.

"Yes."

There was nothing romantic in its nature. He had said he didn't wish to marry again. In all likelihood, the loss of his wife had been too great. It must be why he couldn't sleep.

He'd been missing his wife and then she'd come outside. *Of course.*

Everything he was saying seemed almost reasonable.

But it was too risky.

"I'll think it over," she said. "But I've no wish to mislead you. I'm not likely to change my mind."

He nodded slowly. "Nonetheless," he said. "I'll return to hear your final decision."

He turned back to face her, looking grim but determined.

"Until then, be safe." His tone was quite serious. "Be watchful of anything unusual. And don't make a habit of going off alone."

Then, without another word, he disappeared from her chamber.

THE FOLLOWING DAYS seemed dull and quiet in comparison. Beatrice did not go to Primm to discuss Lord Sexton's rather unusual proposal, but it was never far from her mind.

At dinner on the evening of their guests' departure, Primm had informed Beatrice that the Marquess had politely, but firmly, refused the case.

"He's committed to taking over *The King's Society for the Advancement and Ingenuity of England,"* Primm explained. "Unfortunately, for us, the board is voting to appoint a permanent director at the end of August, and Lord Sexton is up for the position. I suppose he feels it's important he be in London beforehand." Primm grimaced. "Although, I'm not sure he stands much of a chance. The position had never been held by a man who wasn't married."

"But he's widowed," Beatrice pointed out.

"True. And yet..." Primm shook her head. "I understand ambition, truly. And I understand his decision. But I am not too proud to admit that I am exceedingly disappointed."

"But whoever set the fire has not returned to cause further damage. Perhaps he scared himself when Mr.

Stewart caught it." Beatrice offered hopefully as she collected a hearty bit of stew onto her spoon.

"It's barely been a week since the fire." Primm dabbed her serviette at her mouth. "I've contacted an employment agency in London asking them to send me three candidates who can begin teaching this autumn."

Beatrice had been expecting this, but her heart still dropped a little. It was never easy getting accustomed to new people. Besides that, she rather enjoyed having the lodgings to herself.

"We need to do our best to downplay the nature of the attacks," Beatrice said. "If we want qualified applicants to be willing to make their careers here." Because…

Reputations mattered.

"My thoughts exactly," Primm agreed. "You did well with Hardwood's girls, by the way. I don't know what I would have done without you here." Primm lifted her fork again. "I swear, if you up and find yourself a husband as well, I'm going to have you tarred and feathered."

"I'm less inclined than even you are." Which said a lot.

Beatrice stabbed a piece of the meat in her stew. The two ladies sat quietly eating, the only sound, the ticking clock on the mantle.

"It's a shame about Lord Sexton, though," Primm finally said, breaking the silence. "I honestly believed he'd come around."

"Yes."

"And I do understand his professional predicament. But his record for solving crime is unmatched. If only there was something we could do to convince him."

Beatrice clamped her mouth shut. There was no telling what Primm would want her to do if she knew about the marquess's proposal—especially if agreeing to such a charade would help the school.

He'd said that this society board wanted to see that he was settled.

They believed he required a wife to keep him grounded in his position. Preposterous! A married man's loyalty must be to his wife and family first.

They'd do better to select an unmarried one…

"He advised me to be watchful." Beatrice felt heat rise in her neck as she remembered that he'd been in her bedchamber at the time.

He'd seemed to care about her wellbeing. Had they become friends then?

"His lordship offered me the same advice. Mr. Stewart has said he'd send one of his workers over to act as a watchman overnight."

Beatrice stifled the disappointment to learn he'd not singled her out. Oh, she imagined herself so mature and accepting of her circumstances but since the Marquess' visit, she'd acted like a foolish, foolish young woman.

Or foolish older woman, she supposed. She'd turn thirty in just a few years!

# STARBRIDGE ABBEY

Upon successfully delivering the Hardwood's womenfolk to the earl's cliffside estate, Ranulf did not travel back in the direction of Miss Primm's besieged institution. No. He rode south to Starbridge Abbey, the home where Miss Primm herself was raised.

Once there, it was possible he could wrap up this case over the course of the next few days. All of his instincts led him to believe the attacks were personally directed to Miss Primm. The fact that one of her prized possessions had been used for the fire, along with the fact that the school belonged to her, led him there. Any damages, whether to her reputation or the building itself would be her responsibility. And since according to all accounts her father had objected so strenuously to her opening the school in the first place, he was the obvious suspect.

But what kind of man would threaten harm to his own daughter?

Ranulf had experienced tragedy when Susan had been

murdered, and it would plague him until his dying day. But up until then, his life had been more comfortable than most.

Although he and his father had disagreed on issues more often than not, his father had never turned against him, nor had he ever failed to support any of Ranulf's siblings.

Not when it counted.

And yes, nurses and governesses had always been a strong presence in their homes, but such was expected of a marquess and marchioness.

However, their parents had not fully turned over the responsibility of raising them. They had been a family.

It was something he'd always hoped for himself, something he'd expected would come naturally.

The sound of a twig snapping in the woods had him stiffening in his saddle. He drew to a halt, but then relaxed when a flock of birds took flight, not because he was afraid, but because he was practical.

As any smart man ought to be while travelling alone.

Had he realized the turn his plans would take, he would not have given the man who served as his valet such an extensive holiday. Although, 'valet' was a rather benign title for Drake, who spent far more time working investigations and handling administrative matters than he did tying cravats and whatnot.

Ranulf had considered bringing Primm's brother along but decided against it. The stationary Pratt's wife found had been marked with Rosewood's father's crest—the crest that would one day be his. Not only would bringing the gentleman compromise the investigation, but the man was working relentlessly alongside Rowan Stewart to bring his newly purchased estate to a more livable condition.

Furthermore, leaving Rosewood behind provided that the women at the school would have some protection.

Despite their spinsterish tendency to be stubborn.

*Beatrice.*

He couldn't help but grin as he pictured her as she'd been the morning he departed. Her hair standing on end and her eyes had been sleepy, but he wondered if she'd ever figured out her nightrail had been inside out.

And the material had been worn thin.

He shifted uncomfortably. He'd done well not to succumb to his baser instincts with that one.

Although he had come close. And yes, he'd kissed her.

He could only vaguely recall the incident she'd referred to—where he'd mistaken her for one of the maids and treated her badly.

It wasn't something he normally did—mistreat servants—and it wasn't something he was proud of.

Miss Walcott certainly hadn't forgotten the incident. Damn his eyes, he'd hurt her. He'd embarrassed her.

Ranulf tugged at the back of his neck.

The trouble with Beatrice was that she was stubborn as hell but also too damned sweet. Her eyes had all but begged him to kiss her and yet she was too refined to take the liberty.

And, he frowned, she was hiding something.

She presented something of a mystery herself, that was it. That had to be the real reason she intrigued him.

But was that why her body had fit so perfectly against his? Was that why he'd gone against his resolve and kissed her in the kitchen?

Nearly a week had passed since he'd bid her goodbye and still, she relentlessly stole her way into his thoughts.

With nothing but time on his hands, and having already pondered the arsonist mystery to death, he might as well consider what Beatrice was hiding. If Beatrice was even her real name…

She'd told him very little about herself. And she'd evaded answering questions about her past as though she'd been doing it for years.

Walcott was neither a common nor uncommon name. Was it contrived on her part?

He'd asked about her people. And how had she answered? Something about being alone in the world and then she'd asked him about Susan.

*Slippery little spinster.*

He considered the woman who'd hired her.

Miss Primm was the daughter of a marquess, one of the village's worst kept secrets, but even if her background wasn't known, her speech gave her away.

Beatrice's speech was not dissimilar to that of the headmistress'.

Other teachers at the school had been born into the nobility, take Hardwood's new wife, for instance. And although illegitimate, Bedwell's wife had been born the daughter of a baron.

Miss Primm made a habit of saving proper English ladies who found themselves in distressing circumstances.

Walcott, Ranulf decided, was likely a fictitious name. But why would a woman such as Beatrice choose to live under an alias?

And why did it even matter to him?

He turned a corner and Starbridge Abbey came into view--a rather ominous looking structure. With haphazard wings extending from the main part of the house and numerous towers of varying heights, the decorative moldings and carvings had mostly crumbled into partial images of what must have once been angels.

Putting the mystery of Beatrice aside, he ramped up his senses.

Ranulf wouldn't have minded going into this impromptu meeting with Drake at his side. Anytime an investigation required asking intrusive questions, he faced the possibility of a violent response.

He wasn't so cocksure of himself not to acknowledge a healthy dose of fear when he sensed pending resistance.

And as he approached the home where Miss Primm had spent her childhood, a snaking awareness slid along his spine—he was being watched. Not unusual for an estate of this size and yet, by the time he'd dismounted and looped his mount's reins to a convenient post, the door hadn't been opened. No manservant stepped outside to greet him, and after climbing the steps of the staircase fanning out from the entrance, he waited at least a full minute before someone responded to his knocking.

"My Lord." A butler stared at him with suspicious eyes. "Lord Starbridge is not receiving guests at this time. I'm afraid you'll have to arrange for an appointment."

Ranulf handed the servant his card, revealing that he wasn't just any guest, but the Marquess of Sexton. "I'd appreciate a word." He cocked an expectant brow and, without waiting for an invitation, stepped around the shorter man into a massive foyer.

The temperature was at least ten degrees cooler than it had been outside—Ranulf vaguely noted that the cold might be an amenity in the summer months, but the marquess and his sons must freeze their bollocks off over the winter.

"Is that you, Sexton?" A familiar voice drifted down from above. Noah Primm was perhaps the most likeable of Starbridge's sons. Lord Noah had changed considerably since Ranulf had last run into him at White's in London. The younger man still had the same thick brown hair and bright eyes, but with a thicker chest and wider shoulders, he no longer had the look of a youth, but that of a man.

"Indeed," Ranulf answered heartily, grateful to have been met with a familiar face.

The young lord smiled, but it was tight—as though he was doing something wrong.

That sense of unease, that the young man wasn't entirely comfortable greeting an unexpected guest in his own home, would be precisely why Rosewood and Miss Primm had decided to dwell elsewhere. It was no secret that the old marquess ruled his family with an iron hand.

Rosewood had not been born the eldest, but when his twin died, he'd inherited his brother's courtesy title and become the heir to the marquessate, a position he'd never wanted.

Two weeks before, while lounging in the billiard room at Hardwood's wedding party, Rosewood, had confided that just after the holidays, he and his younger brothers had banded together to prevent their father from exerting his powers.

According to Rosewood, their father had gone half-mad. They'd insisted he hand over the running of the estate to the next younger brother, Liam. Doing so had been quite unexceptional and if challenged legally, likely wouldn't hold up, but Ranulf wouldn't judge them.

Piers Primm, as the Earl of Rosewood, wanted to make

his own way, and was doing just that with the rebuilding of Longbow Castle.

And Rosewood wasn't the only Primm sibling to turn their back on the Old Marquess. Miss Primm had thwarted him as well.

Was that reason enough for the man to sabotage her?

Lord Noah reached across to shake Ranulf's hand. "What brings you all the way here? Isn't the King's Society Directorship vote set to take place this month?

Ranulf stifled a flinch at the reminder. Outwardly, he only shrugged. "It's on the horizon." But he wouldn't waste time. "I've been looking into some concerning matters at your sister's school."

Lord Noah's expression turned serious. "Is Auggie in some sort of trouble?"

Auggie? But of course. Miss Primm—*Augusta* Primm.

Ranulf glanced behind him to where the butler who'd failed to send him away appeared all too interested in their conversation. "Is there somewhere private we can talk?"

The younger man's eyebrows shot up and he nodded. "Charles," he addressed the manservant. "Bring tea and sandwiches for the Marquess and have one of our finest chambers readied as well. You're staying tonight, I take it?" At Ranulf's nod, the younger man gestured to a room to the right. "We can talk in here."

Ranulf doubted he'd do much sleeping but would accept the offer. He might very well require more than one day to peel back the truth of this family's machinations.

Lord Noah followed Ranulf into the room where a fire blazed in the hearth, closing the door behind him. He waited to speak again until both of them were seated.

"The last I heard, a goat had torn one of her classrooms

apart. I take it you're here about more serious matters."

"You've the right of that." Ranulf pinched his mouth together, watching the other man for any signs of guilt—or that he was hiding something. "Her recent troubles have not been perpetrated by a goat."

Lord Noah's concern and surprise appeared genuine. "Is she all right?" He stiffened. "By God, if anyone's harmed her—"

"She's fine. Your sister's one of the strongest women of my acquaintance." He'd not deny that, but even as he spoke, images of the other teachers came to mind.

To become a teacher, a person required a strength of character non-existent in most ladies of the ton, including his own late wife.

He'd met most of Miss Primm's teachers at Hardwood's wedding, and his impression had been that they not only taught their students, but that they genuinely cared about them. Was it the vocation that attracted selfless individuals, or Miss Primm's school in particular?

Dear, sweet, naïve Beatrice had ventured into a thunderstorm in the middle of the night because *she had been worried about him*. She'd set aside her own comfort to see to his.

It was something Susan never would have done.

He dismissed the disloyal thought and removed his notebook from inside his jacket.

"Do you know of anyone who'd want to sabotage your sister's school?" He'd get straight to the point.

The other man blinked. "How much space do you have in that notebook of yours?"

Just as Ranulf had suspected. "Enough," he said, waiting for the other man to provide him with a more specific answer.

"I'd say my father, first and foremost, but he isn't the same man he was a year ago."

"Is he infirm?"

"He is... isolated. Hasn't left the Abbey for months. As long as he keeps himself locked up in his suites, he doesn't have to face the reality of his failures."

"And those would be?"

Lord Noah grimaced. "The betrayal of his own children—and all the consequences of their disloyalty."

"All of his children, or just your sister and Rosewood?

"He's not happy with Lord Liam, who's essentially taken over the running of the estate."

"How did he do that?"

"Replaced most of the staff who wouldn't go along with the change in... leadership." Lord Noah scratched the side of his face, as though he was holding something back.

"Leadership..." Ranulf repeated the word. "Or do you see Lord Liam's position as something else?"

Another grimace. "He's not all that different than my father."

Ranulf wondered if Rosewood realized this.

"Does he hold ill-will for your sister?"

"Only after he's been to London. He hates having our name bandied about, and when he hears criticism of the school, it inevitably comes up. But aside from that, nothing of concern."

*Interesting...* Ranulf filed that away for later consideration. "But you don't believe your father would have hired someone to sabotage the school?"

Lord Noah shook his head. "He refuses to see anyone. Even his manager answers to Liam now."

"What of his valet?" Ranulf asked.

"He's been with my father for half a century, but his employment is dependent on Liam as well."

"Is your brother at home now?"

"No. He's up north inspecting our Scottish estate." But then Lord Noah tilted his head. "I should have thought of this before, but you might look into that man Auggie jilted at the altar, although as to my understanding, he's gone on to other... endeavors."

"Malum."

"The very one."

This was the second time the duke's name had come up. Ranulf made a note.

"Trouble is, when Auggie failed to honor the betrothal my father arranged, she became something of a pariah around here. The person who's become a threat to the school could be almost anyone. Could be any one of father's old colleagues, other families who'd have paid dearly for their daughter to have such a match, or even a handful of the local villagers. The people around here lost a good deal of blunt when it fell apart. And once you've gone through all of them, you'll want to take a look at some of the parents who disapprove of her teachings. They don't like their daughters associating with the ladies who've graduated from Primm's school."

Lord Noah shook his head. "I doubt even my grandmother would have left her the inheritance if she'd known what Auggie would do with it. Father would certainly have put up a legal challenge if he'd realized her endeavor wasn't the harmless finishing school he initially believed it would be.

Ranulf conceded that some of the subjects taught at Miss

Primm were far more comprehensive than what was taught at most girls' schools.

And not always ladylike.

And yet parents were reluctant to pull their daughters—because Primm's graduating ladies, by far, experienced the greatest success on the marriage mart.

At Ranulf's silence, Lord Noah sat up straight. "But don't get me wrong. I'm not included amongst her critics. In fact, I'm proud as hell of her. What can I do to help?"

Ranulf nodded. Unless he learned otherwise, he believed Primm's younger brother to be sincere. "Introduce me around. I'd like to take a few days to get a sense of who's been where. I don't have much time, but as I've come this far, I might as well take full advantage."

"Absolutely. Are you traveling back to the school from here?"

"Likely." He'd be vague.

"If you are, and if you don't mind, I'll join you. It's been a while since I've seen the old gal and I could use a few weeks away from this tomb."

And, if Ranulf's guess was correct. Lord Noah was worried about his sister. "Additional protection will be appreciated."

Lord Noah's throat moved. "In that case, I'll arrange to depart when you're finished here."

Just then, the door pushed open and the scowling butler brought in a surprisingly appetizing tray.

"But first," the other man said as he rose and crossed the room. "You've had a long day of travel." Opening a cabinet, he withdrew a tall decanter filled with dark amber liquid. "The tea's just for show, Sexton. But this, this will put some hair on your chest."

# YET ANOTHER UNEXPECTED DEVELOPMENT

The school was quiet—for a few days. But before either Primm or Beatrice were able to get too comfortable, both were shocked into silence for all of a minute as they read the London Gazette while breaking their fast one morning.

"Lord Bloodstone didn't look twice at her at the house party," Beatrice pondered. "How can he and Adelaide be... married?"

Primm and Beatrice had considered such an announcement was possible and had been checking the Gazette regularly ever since Chloe had departed for London, but this was not at all what they'd expected. It had been Captain Edgeworth who had been doing the chasing—not Lord Bloodstone!

And Adelaide had only gone along as Chloe's *companion.*

The announcement ought to have named Chloe and Captain Edgeworth as the newly married couple, not Adelaide and Lord Bloodstone!

Primm removed her glasses and leaned down to read the announcement again while Beatrice read it upside down.

"They've exposed her past—the misdeeds of her father. And they refer to her as a virtual nobody." Beatrice groused. "Why must they be so rude?"

But… Beatrice shook her head. This could not be true! The Viscount had not so much as courted Miss Royal.

"It's not an announcement, exactly," Primm leaned back.

"It says the viscount has *shackled* himself to her." Beatrice countered.

"No," Primm pointed to the print. "It merely says they were seen leaving the church together. And the columnist then asks the question, 'why would the esteemed Viscount shackle himself to a virtual nobody?'"

But the most damaging by far, in Beatrice's mind, was that they exposed poor Adelaide's past.

"It must be a mistake," Beatrice noted that the date on the paper was two days prior. "The Viscount will have already demanded a retraction."

But Primm looked less than optimistic. "I doubt they'll print any sort of retraction—admitting they'd published such a blatant mistake wouldn't sell papers."

"That's not very honorable."

Primm cocked a delicate brow. "Honor is their last consideration. Unfortunately, these gossip rags will leap on the latest scandal to feed their readers. Apparently, they recognized our dear Miss Royal from her time in London years ago and saw it as an opportunity to remind their readers of her father's outrageous misdeeds." She exhaled, causing a few stray hairs to fly up to her forehead. "He is quite the character."

Beatrice frowned. Of course, the article was nothing but fiction. "But what does it mean for Adelaide?"

"Trouble, that's what. And Adelaide's trouble is our trouble—the school's trouble." Primm shook her head. "And even if it's a mistake, the damage has been done. People aren't entertained by reading retractions. Once they've bitten into juicy gossip, they're more than willing to swallow it whole."

"Can she not simply return to the school and make no mention of it? We could all act as though nothing happened."

Primm lowered her spectacles to the tip of her nose and pinned her stare on Beatrice. "For such an intelligent lady, Miss Walcott, you have a tendency to be incredibly naïve." But then she exhaled, looking even more tired than usual. "But that's neither here nor there. We don't know all the facts yet. We will wait to learn more. For all we know, our very own Miss Royal has, in fact, captured the heart of England's most sought-after bachelor. Wouldn't that be ironic?"

Beatrice was more than a little horrified for the other teacher. "What if she doesn't like him?"

"She likes him." Primm sent Beatrice a knowing glance. "Although knowing her, the last thing she'd do is act on it."

Beatrice rolled her lips together. "Were you ever... in love?" It was the most personal question she'd ever asked her employer.

Primm scowled. But when she glanced up, her eyes looked unusually bright. "I thought perhaps... But life doesn't always arrange itself for romantic attachment..." And then she folded the paper closed with an air of finality.

"We can only hope Adelaide has more luck than I did. And now, since there is nothing we can do about what is already done, we must go about our day as usual."

But Beatrice remained sitting, shocked not only that Primm had answered her question, but what that answer had been. Primm had been in love once! But with whom?

And when?

As a girl, Beatrice had hoped to marry a man she could love, just as her mother had done. But when she'd left home, she'd left those hopes behind.

What would it be like to make-believe she was engaged to Lord Sexton? Would he behave appropriately, as he'd promised? But in order for such a charade to appear genuine, they'd have to give some indication of affection for one another, wouldn't they?

Would he kiss her again? Beatrice touched her fingertips to her lips, and then just as quickly dropped them. She would not accept his offer.

Her stare landed on the newspaper. Had something happened between Adelaide and the viscount?

Beatrice could only hope, for Adelaide's sake, that the announcement was just a mistake—and that Primm wouldn't sack the poor woman.

Good heavens, half the staff was already being replaced!

"The applicants are expected to arrive any day, are they not?" Beatrice said.

"Yes." Primm rose. "Judging from the resumes sent over by the agency, at least two have a good deal to offer our students. So I want everything to shine. Mr. Stewart has promised to have the window upstairs replaced and Mrs. Driver is already dusting and oiling the wood and floors in the classrooms. When they arrive, I'll meet with each of them one by one while you show the others about the grounds and the school."

Beatrice nodded. Meeting new people wasn't something she was particular fond of but these days, it seemed, she had no choice.

And some of these ladies would become her future colleagues. She'd no longer have the teachers' quarters to herself.

She'd rather enjoyed having her solitude. It had reminded her of before...

Primm stood at the door and then turned round. "And Beatrice—" She winced. "We must keep our *little annoyance* as quiet as possible."

"Of course." Beatrice forced a smile. "Perhaps we've seen the last of him. Wouldn't' that be a relief?"

"From your lips to God's ears," Primm said before leaving.

Beatrice stared down at her empty cup of tea.

She ought to be excited to be moving forward. She ought to be pleased at the prospect of interesting and intelligent women joining the staff.

But ever since Lady Hardwood and her daughters had departed, Beatrice had fallen into an unusual case of the doldrums.

No—she would be honest with herself.

The sense of disappointment had settled in with Lord Sexton's absence.

It made no sense at all. She wanted to see him again. She wanted to listen to him grumble and complain, and yet she would never accept his offer.

Yes, she wanted to help him with his situation. She'd come to sympathize with him even—when he wasn't acting like an arrogant ass, that was. Who wouldn't act thusly while suffering from insomnia?

But posing as his fake fiancé would be too dangerous.

When he'd taken her in his arms outside, she hadn't felt the cold from the wind, nor had she considered the drenching rain.

All she'd felt was his chest pressed against hers.

His chest, and the sinewy strength of his thighs.

And as she'd remained in his arms, powerful sensations had come to life.

Her breasts had tingled, sending a throbbing ache through her belly to settle between her legs. Had she parted her lips?

She'd been kissed a few times—by one of the boys who'd attended one of the local assemblies. Those kisses had been pleasant but barely memorable.

She would remember Lord Sexton's kiss till she took her dying breath.

She might very well be naïve, but he'd been holding himself back. Even sitting here alone, thinking about it, the memory of his touch sent heat shooting to her core.

Beatrice abruptly pushed her chair back and rose from the table.

She had too much work to do to sit around mooning over the marquess.

~

THE FOLLOWING DAYS, Primm and Beatrice went about performing their typical summer in an unspoken sense of heightened anticipation—or doom—depending on any given moment. They were waiting for the new teacher candidates—waiting for Adelaide and the viscount to make an appearance, and also waiting to see if the trouble-maker who'd been tormenting the school would attempt to cause more damages.

But Beatrice, despite her best attempts not to, was also waiting for something else—*someone* else.

Six days had passed. Had he changed his mind? It was also possible he'd been distracted with his other business and simply had forgotten her.

He might have even decided upon another lady to play the part of his pretend fiancé—one of Hardwood's sisters, for instance. Lady Eloise was bold enough to do it.

But a *Lady*, Beatrice knew, could not risk her reputation. A true lady would require the entire prize. She would not walk away from such an opportunity to become a marquess.

Beatrice pinched the bridge of her nose.

She didn't *want* to see the Marquess trapped.

Perhaps that's what was making her anxious. If he'd asked anything else, anything at all…

But a fake betrothal could all too easily turn into a real one. Look at Priscilla! And Chloe! And now possibly Adelaide.

If Beatrice were to agree to his proposal, she'd have to go to London. That alone would be dangerous. No!

The entire idea was absurd!

It was impossible.

And yet… Each time she heard a horse or carriage coming up the drive towards the school, her heart leapt.

Because she wanted to see him again. She missed him in a way she didn't quite understand. He was a marquess, and as a prominent member of the aristocracy, a public person. And although she'd never made her come out, there was always the possibility someone might recognize her.

It was unthinkable.

But when she went to bed that night and listened to the sounds of the rattling windowpanes, she wished he was right upstairs like he had been before.

What was the matter with her?

She missed him.

~

THE POTENTIAL NEW teachers arrived later that week and Beatrice's nerves were wound tighter than a drum. The applicants were exactly as one would expect—or three of them were, anyway. Those three wore starched grey gowns buttoned up to the neck, with black gloves and black hats despite the warm temperatures, and all of them appeared to be somewhere around the age of thirty. The fourth woman didn't fit in at all. Miss Daisy Pepperspring appeared to be a decade younger than the others, wore a mint green gown over her plump figure, and a hat adorned with ivy and daisies.

Beatrice appreciated that despite the disapproving looks Miss Pepperspring received from the other ladies, the younger woman wasn't at all intimidated by them.

And if she was, she certainly didn't show it.

Late in the afternoon, Primm—Lady Rosewood—Beatrice, and all four of the newly hired teachers stood outside discussing various ideas for the school's future along with some of its history.

And, as chance would have it, before Beatrice could take

the ladies on the last part of her scheduled tours, Primm's carriage turned onto the drive. A magnificent horse and rider trotted along beside it.

The serious nature of their conversation forgotten, all sets of eyes settled on the rider.

It was the Viscount Bloodstone, looking even more magnificent than his horse as he sat tall and proud, his blond hair peeking out from beneath his hat, and his violet eyes smiling down at what appeared to be a welcoming committee.

Coachman John jauntily waved as he drew the coach to a halt, and was hardly noticed, but Adelaide seemed to be ducking down inside the carriage.

Although Primm and Beatrice had been anxiously awaiting the couple's arrival, their timing could hardly have been worse.

With an easy dismount, before greeting any of them, Lord Bloodstone reached into the carriage and after a moment, assisted Adelaide down the step and onto the ground.

Beatrice eyed her colleague curiously.

The woman who'd departed for London a few weeks before had had an innocence about her—an easy smile that was more transparent than most.

There was a definite change to her.

"No more vandalism, I hope?" Adelaide addressed Beatrice with a hesitant smile.

Beatrice winced.

They certainly could not discuss this with the new teachers present. "Vandalism?" Beatrice shifted her gaze in a meaningful way toward the other ladies. "There hasn't been any vandalism. Just finally having the window replaced, you know? From the storm?"

Luckily, Adelaide seemed to understand her meaning right away. "Oh, yes. Of course."

But Primm had been waiting several days to speak with the "newlyweds", and so she made a hasty apology to their guests before whisking Miss Royal and Lord Bloodstone away—which left Beatrice with no choice but to carry on with her tour, which she whisked them through as quickly as possible.

Anxious over what was transpiring in Primm's parlor, she no doubt forgot half of what she'd intended to show them.

And with Primm occupied, Beatrice took it upon herself to send the ladies back to the inn where they'd spend one more night before returning to the school tomorrow.

Beatrice couldn't help worrying over the fact that Primm had hired four new teachers... four... when there were only three to replace.

By later that evening, she knew why.

Primm had no choice but to let Adelaide go. And unfortunately, although Adelaide was not at fault for her present circumstances, Primm had not only sacked her, but asked her to leave the area.

The school had barely scraped through all the scandals last year. It would be best all-around if the bride who wasn't really a bride made herself scarce.

Beatrice was the last of the teachers left over from the year before.

Sitting on her bed that night as the moonlight streamed in through the uncovered window, she wondered at her unease. She had never considered her relationships with her former colleagues to be a vital part of her life. In fact, she'd maintained a level of distance between them intentionally.

But this sudden turn of events left her feeling unusually... disappointed.

No, that wasn't the right word for it. She felt... abandoned.

Not only was she going to lose the privacy she'd benefited from for most of the summer, but she was also to lose one of the last of her friends.

Beatrice changed out of her gown and climbed into her bed. It was starting to sink in that Adelaide wasn't coming back.

As much as she'd resisted friendships with the other teachers, she'd come to care for them anyway.

And now they were leaving—the same as her parents had.

Even Mrs. Martle, the housekeeper who'd worked at Rose Height all her life had deserted her and Jasper.

Beatrice realized she didn't like being left behind. It brought back too many bad memories.

She snuffed the candle, lie down, and reminded herself of all the things she had to be grateful of. She had her brother, who was not only safe, but had been admitted to Eton. And he was set to graduate this winter—with top marks if his past grades were an accurate indicator.

And she had security here at the school. Her life had meaning and purpose.

Her students looked up to her.

*And,* she thought sleepily, *she had become friends with Lord Sexton.*

She dreamily touched her lips. *He'd kissed her.* It was no

doubt a one-time event, but it would forever be the singularly most romantic thing that had ever happened to her.

It was the last thought she had before a loud crashing sound devastated the quiet of the night. Glass rained down on her and something heavy landed on her bed.

That security she'd been grateful for shattered right along with her window.

## "I TOLD YOU TO BE CAREFUL"

Lying in total darkness, Beatrice kept her eyes closed, almost afraid to breathe.

She didn't notice the pain of the rock landing on her knee right away, nor did she notice the stinging around her face and neck. She sat up gingerly, but when she swung her feet onto the floor, the stinging on the bottom of one shook her into awareness.

She was covered in broken glass. Her hands were sticky from her own blood, and with shards surrounding her, she was forced to move very carefully.

When she finally managed to strike the flint to the candle, her stomach lurched. So much blood! She stared at her pillow in disbelief, and then down to the foot of the bed where a rock the size of an orange rested innocently, a note tied around it with a string.

If Lord Sexton were here, she would wait to open it for him to examine, but as he'd abandoned them so callously, she'd have to open it herself. But she'd wear a pair of her gloves while doing so.

Could stone capture a fingerprint? Paper certainly could.

Regardless, she could study the handwriting—compare it to every piece of correspondence ever sent to the school.

And to that of former students.

"My God," Primm's voice sounded from far away. Beatrice lifted her gaze to where the headmistress stood in the door clutching a flickering taper. Looking nearly as shocked as Beatrice felt, Primm's eyes widened. "Don't move," she ordered. "There's broken glass everywhere."

But Beatrice was well aware of her surroundings. Because most of that glass covered her.

Another face appeared behind Primm in the doorway, Mr. Driver. "I was just checking the locks when I heard the crash."

"Send for the doctor, will you? No, send for Lord Rosewood and Victoria. Piers will send one of his men for the doctor, but he'll know what to do." Primm's brother was experienced at a little bit of everything. Beatrice vaguely remembered that he'd taught Victoria how to sew up a wound.

Beatrice dropped her gaze to her arms. Hopefully she wouldn't require any sewing up. That would be even more unpleasant than the cuts themselves.

Primm, who had apparently donned half-boots before she'd come running, crossed the room to where Beatrice sat. Each footstep made a crunching sound and Primm cursed. "This has gone too far, by God." Her voice cut through the room cold as ice. "I'll kill whoever is doing this."

Beatrice blinked as she stared at the rock.

The note would be excellent evidence. It would require

proper handling. But when she tried to speak, her mouth refused to move.

Even hearing her most proper employer cursing like a sailor wasn't enough to shake her out of this fog.

"Miss Walcott?" Primm touched the sleeve of Beatrice's nightrail. "Beatrice? Are you all right?" She'd drawn a handkerchief out of her sleeve and was dabbing at Beatrice's face even as she carefully cleared some of the glass away from the bed. "This is all my fault. I've allowed this to go too far." Primm seemed almost to be talking to herself. "I shouldn't have let you sleep in here alone. You could have been killed. As it is, this cut on your shoulder..." Primm's voice caught just as Mrs. Driver appeared.

"Dear heavens! What's happened in here?"

The housekeeper's question went unanswered, but when she went to reach for the rock, Beatrice came out of her stupor.

"Don't touch it," she ordered. "Please."

Both of the other ladies turned to her in surprise.

"It has evidence on it," Beatrice explained. "The more people who handle it, the less we can learn from it."

And when Mrs. Driver began picking up some of the larger pieces of glass, Beatrice stopped her again.

But Primm touched Beatrice's shoulder.

"Broken pieces of glass are not evidence. Besides, Lord Sexton isn't taking our case. As for the note on the rock, we've no choice but to deal with it ourselves. This far from London, there's no one here who can examine it properly."

Primm lifted the rock off the bed and untied the string. The note was crumpled and, once it had been carefully unfolded, the handwriting showed to be elegant and precise.

Mrs. Driver, collecting glass and dropping it into a bin, paused to listen to the message.

*"This is only the beginning,"* Primm read it out loud.

The message was ominous, but not all that telling. What would Lord Sexton think of it?

Beatrice exhaled and then winced at the stinging in her shoulder.

Damage to the school was one thing, attacks on persons quite another. She hadn't really been afraid…

Until now.

"The students cannot return until we're certain they'll be safe here." Primm had never sounded so defeated.

But she was right. What if this rock had hit a student?

"Perhaps I'll write to Lord Sexton. Beg him to send someone else to help us." Primm's stare landed on Beatrice, her expression filled with self-recrimination. "This can't go on. I am so very sorry this happened to you."

But Beatrice wasn't ready to give up. Not when there was one more option.

"We don't need to close—not yet." Beatrice said with a wince. She should have told Primm about the Marquess' proposal days ago. "And it won't be necessary to write to Lord Sexton."

Primm frowned. "Do you know of some other detective who can track down this fiend?"

"Well, no," Beatrice answered. She'd been more than a little embarrassed about the nature of Lord Sexton's offer, and truth be told, partly concerned that Primm would want her to take him up on it.

But now… Primm was right. This had gone too far.

And, Beatrice rationalized to herself. Most of society

was absent from London. She ought to be safe going to a few political events with the marquess. Doubtful anyone would even notice her.

Ignoring her various cuts and the throbbing on her leg where the rock had landed, Beatrice explained, "Lord Sexton is concerned about that upcoming vote you mentioned."

"To head up The King's Society for the Advancement of Ingenuity in England," Primm provided. "An admirable endeavor, which would be even more admirable if they didn't exclude half the brain-power of England."

Beatrice stared at Primm, confused.

"They don't allow women."

"Oh, well…" That went without saying, didn't it?

"Anyhow, he apparently has grand plans that would make their work more relevant—more useful. He did not go into great detail. But he has a problem. You were right. The board members are partial to gentlemen who are… settled."

"I'm not surprised. It doesn't matter that Lord Sexton isn't one of those rakish fellows, or that I've never heard so much of a whisper of him being involved in unseemly behavior." She made a face. "Such practices are marinated in tradition."

"Yes, well, his chances at winning the position, he told me, would be greatly improved if he were betrothed."

Primm touched Beatrice on the head. "I don't know what you're going on about, Beatrice. Are you certain the rock missed your head?"

Beatrice tilted her head to evade Primm's searching hands, but when the pain in her shoulder pinched, she immediately regretted it.

"Lord Sexton needs a betrothed—a temporary fiancé, Primm. He asked if I'd play this game of make-believe with him for a few weeks in exchange for him taking the case."

Primm stilled, finally comprehending what it was that Beatrice was saying.

"You told him *'no,'* of course." Because it had all the makings of a grand scandal.

"Of course," Beatrice said. "But he asked me not to decide just yet. He is coming by the school again—after he delivers the Hardwood ladies and fulfills a few other responsibilities in the area."

"Did he say when he would be returning?"

"No. And to be honest, I thought he'd have come through already." Beatrice scrunched up her nose. "But whoever is out to sabotage the school cannot go on getting away with it."

"Lord Sexton doesn't want to remarry, I take it. That makes someone like you the perfect person to pose as his fiancé. Although, I suppose I could do it…"

For some reason, this didn't sit well with Beatrice. Primm was needed here, at the school. "But you've just hired new teachers. What will they think if you suddenly announce an engagement?"

"I don't expect you to put yourself at risk." Primm's words had Beatrice stiffening.

"At risk?" Was it possible Primm knew of Beatrice's past after all?"

"Your reputation. If the ruse doesn't go as planned, you might be compelled to marry, in the end. Look at Adelaide…"

"But if I took every possible precaution—took a chaperone along—"

"Victoria is the only person I would trust to protect you. The two of you could reside at her townhouse there. And if Coachman John drives, you'll have his protection as well..." But then Primm was shaking her head. "No. Now is not the time to decide something like this. You've just had a most harrowing experience."

"I can do—"

"Where the devil is Piers?" Primm glanced toward the door. "We need to get you out of this mess. You'll spend the remainder of the summer in my residence. And as for the new teachers, they'll have to stay at the inn. Perhaps Mrs. Pratt will discount their rooms..." Primm paused in her planning and lifted her fingertips to stroke the skin along Beatrice's shoulder. "This one is bad. It's going to need sutures."

"But what of Lord Sexton?" Beatrice asked. Truth be told, although she was getting stiff from sitting amongst the hundreds of pieces of broken glass, she was reluctant to attempt climbing out of the bed.

"We'll deal with him later." And then she added, "if that's even necessary."

Sounds of footsteps and masculine voices floated up from downstairs. Help had finally arrived! Primm exhaled. "It's about time."

As though he'd been summoned by their conversation, the first face that appeared in the threshold was the one most prominent in Beatrice's thoughts. "My lord?" Was she imagining him?

Behind Lord Sexton, Lord Rosewood and another gentleman who looked oddly familiar appeared.

But it was the marquess who marched across the room first, his eyes blazing and his scowl, dark and stormy.

And as though Beatrice was some sort of priceless artifact, he carefully scooped her off the bed.

But then he frowned at her and growled. "I told you to be careful!"

# CONCOCTIONS

The marquess's lack of hesitancy spurred the others into action as well.

"I'll locate the suture kit." Victoria announced. Beatrice hadn't realized she'd come along with her husband.

"I have a spare room for her in my apartment," Primm announced and shuffled ahead of Lord Sexton. "Follow me."

"What are you doing here?" Beatrice asked him, sliding her uninjured arm up and around his neck while he carried her. Was he a mirage?

*Had* she wished him here?

"I told you I was coming back, you little fool. I had just arrived at Rosewood's when Primm's man arrived in a panic." A shaft of light from Primm's taper landed on Beatrice and Lord Sexton paused. As his gaze traveled along the by now large amount of blood soaking her sleeve, an unreadable expression transformed his face. "My poor Sweet Bee," his voice sounded hoarse, but as quickly as he'd paused, his stern look returned and he began descending the steps to the first floor.

*Sweet Bee?* Perhaps the rock had hit her head after all.

Being held aloft by a man of his height, the bottom of the stairs seemed a long way away.

And yet, she felt perfectly safe.

"For the record," Beatrice said, "I have been careful. How much more careful can a lady be—lying in her own bed?"

He groaned as though he didn't want to hear it and she resisted the desire to rest her cheek against his chest. Surely, her marquess came across damsels in distress all the time.

He was a detective, after all.

As they entered Primm's residence, Beatrice noticed a cut on her rescuer's chin.

From her. She must have glass in her hair. Pieces of glass clung everywhere. "Be careful," she whispered.

"Don't worry." His voice came out low again. "I'll protect you. Nothing like this will happen again."

Warmth glowed in her chest.

"This way, my lord." Primm led him into the room Victoria had occupied before she'd left the school to marry Lord Rosewood.

"Jenny, spread a sheet on the floor to catch the glass." The woman disappeared but returned a moment later.

"Oh, but it'll get ruined." Beatrice protested. She'd never liked being fussed over.

Aside from Lord Sexton's scowl, everyone ignored her.

And he still held her aloft in his arms. "Check the bottoms of her feet," he ordered Primm.

Primm checked one, removed a few shards, and then did the same to the other. "You can set her down now, my lord," she said.

But Lord Sexton addressed Beatrice. "Can you stand?"

He asked, and only after Beatrice reassured him twice did he lower her feet to the floor.

Primm finished lighting the sconces around the room just as Victoria arrived carrying a small box. Beatrice recognized it as the kit used for the occasional scrape and bruise suffered by various students.

And, perhaps because the headmistress was finally feeling in control of this situation, Primm turned to Lord Sexton. "You're welcome to wait in the parlor," she told him. He didn't move until she added, "where you and I have something to discuss—but later."

Victoria shuffled the marquess out of the room and closed the door firmly behind him. She then turned to Beatrice, tweezers in hand. "I don't know where to start."

"It's going to be tricky getting her out of that nightrail, but she can't sit down with it on. Most of the glass fell on her front, but we can't be sure."

"Suture that gash on her shoulder!" A male voice called out from behind the door. "She's already lost too much blood."

Victoria and Primm's glances slid to one another, both raising their brows.

"Thank you, my lord. We've matters well in hand," Victoria answered even as she opened the medical kit. "I never would have imagined that a single pane of glass could shatter into so many pieces." She spoke as she removed catgut and a needle.

Beatrice avoided looking at either. "This is going to hurt, isn't it?"

"Drink this—all of it. It'll help in more ways than one. I can't help thinking you're still in shock." Primm placed a short tumbler into Beatrice's hand. "I know I would be if I'd been woken up the way you were."

"You must have been terrified." Victoria stepped back. Beatrice wasn't a huge fan of drinking. She'd heard tales of how it could transform a perfectly normal gentlemen into a menace. But, however, Victoria had finished threading her needle. The thought of being a pincushion was enough to induce Beatrice to swallow the contents as quickly as possible.

It burned, but not as much as her injuries, and aside from a mild fit of coughing, she managed to keep it down.

All the while she stood as though frozen in the middle of the room, experiencing the warmth in her throat and chest and belly. Victoria, who'd located a pair of scissors in her kit, snipped the material from Beatrice's neck down to her legs, literally cutting the nightrail off of her.

"Oh, dear God," Victoria gasped as the gown fell open. Beatrice couldn't exactly move to cover herself.

In the drama of her present circumstances, she had forgotten about the scars on her back.

Raised white lines were left over from her uncle's punishment. She rarely looked at them. It required the careful placement of two looking glasses. And if she didn't look at them, she didn't' have to think of them.

But, from Victoria's reaction, not looking at them hadn't caused them to disappear.

"You poor thing—"

"Suture her arm, Victoria," Primm cut her off.

Primm might be a demanding employer, but she'd always respected the privacy of the ladies she'd hired to teach there, unless their pasts affected the school.

Apparently, Primm deemed the school safe regarding

Beatrice's decade-old scars, just as long as no one ever learned who'd put them there.

Flushed from embarrassment, Beatrice didn't say a word while the two ladies helped her to sit on the edge of the bed.

But when Victoria dabbed at Beatrice's shoulder, she jumped nervously.

"Hold still," Victoria said, but Beatrice flinched again.

"I'm trying." Beatrice suddenly felt weak all over. A delayed reaction to her injuries, perhaps, she thought vaguely.

"There's laudanum at the bottom of the kit. I think she's going to need more than a swallow of scotch."

Primm jumped into action and then Beatrice dutifully drank the too-sweet drink. While Victoria pressed a cloth to her shoulder, the room grew warm and soft.

Along with her head.

"There now, that wasn't so bad," Victoria spoke in a soft voice.

"Everything's going to work out just fine. I'll make sure of it." Primm was on her opposite side, assisting her onto the pillows. Had she already been sewn up?

"But the evidence," Beatrice murmured. "And tell Lord Sexton... Tell him..."

"You can speak with him yourself." Primm soothed a cool rag on Beatrice's forehead. "Tomorrow. But for now. Don't think of anything. Just sleep."

"I'll do it," Beatrice said, feeling heavy. "Tell him I'll do it..."

The room turned dark and all thoughts slipped away as Beatrice succumbed to the effects of Victoria and Primm's concoctions.

Beatrice didn't care what they'd given her, for now, she was only grateful for the absence of pain.

And after that, she didn't care much about anything.

RANULF GLANCED up just as Miss Primm appeared.

"She's sleeping," the headmistress announced as she and Rosewood's countess stepped into the parlor. Nearly an hour had passed since he'd left Beatrice with them. "Physically, I think she'll be fine, but such a horrific attack can leave other scars—emotional ones."

Rosewood nodded.

The headmistress looked exhausted and splotches of blood stained both her and the countesses' aprons.

Splotches of Beatrice's blood.

Ranulf rubbed the back of his neck. He shouldn't have left her alone—not with the school being in danger.

He'd wanted to kill someone when he'd seen her blood seeping from that one gaping wound. But he had only himself to blame—until he found the culprit who'd thrown the rock.

She had suffered other cuts—smaller—less dangerous, but they would pain her just the same.

And there was always the possibility that any of them could turn putrid.

"You cleaned the wounds—?" he demanded of Lady Rosewood.

"Every last one, my lord." She stared at him solemnly and then flicked a curious glance toward Miss Primm.

The scenario played itself over and over in his mind.

*Of Beatrice sleeping, believing herself safe in her bed,*

*dreaming and possibly making birdlike sounds as she lie there peacefully. And then the rock shattering the window above her—raining down on her.*

Blood boiled in his veins.

Had the villain known one of the teacher's beds sat below that particular window, or had Beatrice simply been in the wrong place at the wrong time?

Ranulf tugged at the back of his neck again.

He should have taken the damn case and to hell with his position at The King's Society.

And yet deep inside, rational instincts asserted themselves. The King's Society could resolve if he was allowed to expand their purposes.

Magistrates weren't enough—and they had little accountability—if any.

"Noah? I thought that was you." Following all the drama, Primm finally addressed the fact that Lord Noah was standing in her parlor. "What are you doing here?"

"Isn't a younger brother allowed to come to his sister's need?"

She all but scoffed at his response, and then Rosewood spoke up.

"Sexton travelled down to Starbridge Abbey after delivering Lady Hardwood and her daughters to Cliffhouse." The earl shifted a glance toward Sexton, who nodded. "A piece of father's stationary was found in one of the rooms, Auggie, the morning after the fire."

Primm blinked. "But what does that have to do—?" Confusion warred with understanding, so Ranulf explained further.

"As Starbridge Abbey is only a day's ride from Hardwood Cliffhouse, I took it upon myself to make a visit—if anything, so I could eliminate your family members as suspects."

"It wasn't father." Primm pinched her mouth together. And then she reached into her apron and pulled out a crumpled piece of paper. "This was attached to the rock that came through the window over Miss Walcott's bed. Apparently, in your absent, my dear Miss Walcott has designated herself our school detective. She ordered us not to touch it —evidence—she said. But since we were under the impression you weren't returning, I overrode her suggestion." She grimaced. "But rest assured." She slid a glance to one of her brothers and then the other. "This particular message was not written on father's stationary."

Which in and of itself, wasn't enough to absolve the man.

Ranulf had managed a short meeting with the marquess while he'd been at Starbridge Abbey. He'd not learned much, aside from the fact that in referring to his father as half-mad, Rosewood hadn't been exaggerating.

But the marquess had exhibited moments of lucidity. And when Ranulf mentioned the school, Starbridge had become distraught.

Ranulf wasn't fully convinced the old man wasn't behind the attacks.

Lady Rosewood raised her fingertips to her mouth to cover a delicate yawn. Lord Rosewood noticed and put a supportive arm around his wife's waist.

"It's late," he said. "Everything will look clearer come morning. Sexton, you're welcome to put one of our chambers to use if you'd like. Noah?"

Ranulf declined.

"I appreciate the offer, but if Miss Primm is amenable,

I'll take the room I made use of before." Staying at the school, Ranulf could examine the area below Beatrice's window before anyone of Primm's helpful employees took it upon themselves to trample the grounds.

"Of course," Primm nodded. "And sometime tomorrow, you and I will speak privately."

Beatrice must have discussed his proposal to the headmistress. Did that mean he was going to get a good old-fashioned dressing down, or had they considered how all might benefit?

"I'll take a proper chamber, Rosewood." Lord Noah interrupted Ranulf's musing.

Restless with unease, Ranulf made a hasty excuse and exited. He needed to ensure his Dionysia was stabled properly, after a long day's ride, she deserved a decent rubdown.

So far, the shire was the only lady he'd managed to protect with any sort of success.

If Beatrice wasn't safely tucked inside Primm's own residence, Ranulf would have stood guard over her himself. Hell, in a few weeks, the school would be filled with little ladies in need of protection.

He kicked at the dirt, not quite sure when he'd become so passionate about Beatrice, no—*Miss Walcott's*—safety. All he knew was that when he'd heard she'd been injured, he'd felt as though he'd suffered a punch to the gut.

He'd seen red.

Twenty minutes later, and having regained his composure, Ranulf entered the chamber he'd used previously and deposited his belongings on the floor.

But he didn't stay there long. Instead, he went right to work.

With a taper and his magnifying glass, he painstakingly

scoured the grounds outside Beatrice's window, and by the time the sun rose, he'd followed impressions in the grass to the edge of the property, where it appeared as thought two horses had been tethered.

Which meant that they weren't looking for just one villain.

They were looking for two.

# WORDS OF AFFECTION

Beatrice dreamed about him.

He'd come to her and whispered comforting things, the sort of things she never expected to hear from anyone.

Words of affection—*adoration.*

Shifting, she felt a pinching in her shoulder.

Had it all been a dream?

She was half-awake, but weighed down, her eyelids so heavy she didn't want to open them yet.

And her mouth felt fuzzy and dry.

The glass breaking.

The rock with the message.

And…

Lord Sexton *had* come. His carrying her had not been a dream.

Beatrice forced her eyes open and confirmed that she was in Primm's extra room—Victoria's old one.

"You're awake." Primm leaned forward in the chair,

looking as though she'd kept vigil over her through the night. "Try not to move. You don't want to tear the sutures."

But Beatrice couldn't lie here all day.

She moved to sit up but instantly regretted it when a wave of nausea washed over her.

"Did they catch him, whoever did it?" she asked, her voice hoarse and weak.

"Lord Sexton has been combing the grounds for evidence. He thinks it was two people rather than one. But I don't want you to worry about that just now. In fact, I don't want you to worry about anything." Primm pulled back the bandage and assessed the wound on Beatrice's shoulder. "It's a little red, but not terribly so. I know it was only a piece of glass but there's always the risk that it will turn against you. Fortunately, for you, Victoria doused it in all manner of foul-smelling concoctions. I doubt any putridity could survive her horrid remedies." Primm's laugh was only half-hearted and her eyes looked tired.

"I'll be fine," Beatrice said, taken aback by Primm's unusual uncertainty.

"You can't do it." Primm stared down at her hands which she'd clasped in her lap. "You cannot go to London with Lord Sexton. I've made too many poor decisions on behalf of my teachers this year already. I'm not about to allow you to fall into some sort of scandal as well. And if the two of you were discovered, the sort of scandal you'd be embroiled in would be worse than all the others combined."

"He is here, though, is he not?"

"He is." Primm looked a little more like herself as she stared at Beatrice curiously. "He was... distraught at the sight of your injuries."

Beatrice's heart skipped a beat. Sexton was... worried

for her? But no, best to temper such fancies. "Likely, he feels guilty for leaving us to fend for ourselves when he could have sent the culprit to Newgate within a matter of days."

"Guilt can be a powerful motivator..." Primm murmured.

But Beatrice was stuck thinking about that dream, which, it seemed, had caused her to become sentimental—planting foolish romantic ideas in her mind.

"His lordship seemed to believe it was his fault..." Primm said.

He'd carried her down the stairs like a knight in shining armor. She'd felt safe, protected, and had wound her arms around his neck.

He had not complained.

What was it that he'd whispered in her ear?

*"You little fool. What were you thinking?"* Was it her imagination that he'd also whispered... *"My poor Sweet Bee."*

She tried licking her lips but her tongue felt like cotton.

"You need to drink." Primm promptly poured water into a glass. "Dehydration is an unfortunate side-affect of the laudanum."

Good lord, it very well may have all been a dream—a laudanum-laced dream.

Disappointment swooped in. He'd not proposed marriage, for heaven's sake! He'd asked her to pose as his make-believe fiancée.

Primm assisted her to sit up and then handed her the drink.

"Of course," Primm spoke as though thinking aloud. "Our circumstances, our *little annoyance*s are more problematic now than ever. It would be a great relief if we could nab the villain once and for all."

"Villains," Beatrice reminded her. "You said he believes there were two of them."

Primm took the glass back from Beatrice. "But I'd never expect you to risk your reputation for something that wasn't of utmost importance."

"Of course you wouldn't," Beatrice agreed. She had been hoping the attacks were over. That way they wouldn't need Lord Sexton's assistance and the decision would be made for her.

But the attacks most definitely weren't over.

And what if school had been in session and the rock had come through a student's window last night? Or one of the newly hired teachers?

"I can't leave you here alone..." Beatrice provided another reason she oughtn't take the marquess up on his offer. "Not with Priscilla, Chloe, and now even Adelaide leaving the school. There's too much to do to prepare for the new term."

"If we even have one." Primm stared down at her fingernails. "I do have the new hires—and they seem highly capable." But then she glanced up. "So, I wouldn't be without help—if you did decide to accept his proposal—for the school's sake, of course."

Beatrice exhaled a loud sigh. Primm had hired her with no references, without a single recommendation. She'd hired her on nothing more than a five-minute interview.

This time, perhaps Beatrice could help Primm.

It would be a travesty if the school couldn't open up again. The students would have to settle into new schools. The new hires would have to be sent away.

And Beatrice would be out of a job.

"I'll have to take the utmost of precautions," Beatrice said. "To protect my reputation," she added.

"Victoria will make for an excellent chaperone. Who would dare question the integrity of a countess? The two of you can reside in her London townhouse. It would almost be as though you and she were simply on holiday."

Suddenly the notion didn't seem quite so outrageous as before.

"I'd want his word." Primm frowned. "As soon as the board makes their decision, he's bound by honor to solve our case."

"That won't be a problem," Beatrice found herself defending him.

"You don't have to do this. You're an excellent teacher and I quite understand that you'd not wish to risk your reputation for the school…"

Her reputation would only matter if the school closed and she was forced to find a new position.

Primm collected the pitcher of water and made her way toward the door. "Go back to sleep."

But in the wake of Primm's exit, Beatrice had other ideas. And Defying Primm's order, she gingerly crept out of bed and opened one of the bureau drawers.

She'd need to change into something presentable and find the marquess.

She needed to give him her answer before he changed his mind.

Or even worse, left for London without her.

# INDEPENDENT LITTLE WENCH

Ranulf released his hold on the wood while Rowan Stewart finished nailing it into place. With the light from one less window, the room, which had of course been thoroughly cleaned by Mrs. Driver early that morning, seemed eerily abandoned.

It was becoming clear to him that these attacks would persist until Primm either closed the school or they were stopped by the likes of himself.

He rolled his shoulders, contemplating his choices.

Rosewood, Stewart, and Lord Noah could keep watch at the school. Perhaps they could bring in Bloodstone and Hardwood as well.

Ranulf would make a hasty trip to London for the vote but return immediately thereafter. It was the best he could do.

"You've got this in hand?" he asked.

Stewart stepped away from his work and slid him a glance.

"I don't blame you," he said.

Ranulf grunted, recalling the moment he'd arrived in her chamber. She'd been in shock—and covered in blood. He wouldn't be so easy on himself.

"I should have expected the attacks might escalate," he grumbled.

"Not for last night—I mean, that's not your fault either—but for not taking the case. The King's Society needs you at the helm. I've heard of your ideas. You need to win that vote."

The man's words confirmed Ranulf's belief, and…

"I've assigned my men to keep watch here—And Rosewood agrees. Until this is over, Miss Primm's safety." He cleared his throat. "And the safety of the school—take precedence over castle renovations." Stewart scowled. "But we need to stop whoever is doing this."

"I agree."

Ranulf would follow through with is initial plan, but he'd also take the case. It had to be enough.

Only partly satisfied with the compromise, he exited the room and bounded down the staircase. He was going to have to find Primm at some point. She'd be happy to learn that although he would still be leaving soon for London, he wasn't abandoning them indefinitely.

Furthermore, he needed to question her again. She seemed all too confident that the attacker hadn't been from her father's household.

Beatrice would still be abed. He'd have to speak with her later—tell her he'd changed his mind. She needn't risk her reputation to help him. He shook his head. The idea to bring a temporary betrothed back to London with him was ludicrous.

The door that connected Primm's residence to the school flew opened and Beatrice herself appeared.

Shuffling slowly, she wore a nightdress that was a few inches too short for her. The sight of it, however, reminded him of how she'd looked the night before, covered in blood. Her face had been white as a ghost. She'd looked stricken, shocked, and far too vulnerable.

In the light of day, she didn't look that much better. Certainly, she shouldn't be moving about so soon.

"What the devil do you think you're doing?"

His voice caught her unawares and she swayed slightly, grasping the door. Ranulf rushed forward and took her arm.

"Good morning to you, as well," she said.

His chest loosened.

If she was well enough to make jokes, then she couldn't be feeling too poorly.

But still she had no business being out of bed. Although she had a little color in her cheeks, she was still pale. A piece of white linen, stained with blood that had seeped through the material, covered the wound on her shoulder. "You can't go prancing around in nothing but a nightrail. Have you no sense at all, woman?"

But before he could swoop her up again, she clutched onto his arm and managed to steer them toward the staircase. "I can't lie around in bed all day. Not with"—she gestured toward the upper floor—"all of this business going on."

Sounds from above gave away that the building was occupied—hammering, shuffling of furniture.

Annoyed with her stubbornness, Ranulf, nonetheless, couldn't help but admire her tenacity.

It reminded him of himself.

"And I'm dressed like this because all of my appropriate garments are upstairs. I didn't exactly have the opportunity to collect a spare change of clothes last night." She shot him a look of annoyance.

Her sunny disposition was nowhere to be found this morning but her sarcasm had remained intact. She swayed, and Ranulf made a decision.

She needn't walk while he was around.

But when he attempted again to lift her into his arms, she pushed him away and began the climb to the second floor. "I'm fine."

*Independent little wench.*

Rather than argue, however, he walked behind her, prepared and half-expecting her to collapse into his arms with each step.

"Where did you go for so long?" she asked. "Hardwood Cliffhouse is only a few days drive—and that's by carriage. I doubt it took you much more than a day." She glanced back at him. "I've seen your horse."

"Dionysia ." He provided.

She was not wrong.

"So..." She prompted when he didn't answer. "You and Dionysia . Where else did the two of you go?"

Of course she would want to know his business. She'd likely pester him all day if he didn't tell her.

"Starbridge Abbey," he said.

"Primm's father's estate?" She didn't sound all that surprised.

"It seems outlandish to imagine anyone would sabotage their own daughter's dreams, but despite his ill health and Miss Primm's own defense of the man, I'm not prepared to cross him off as a suspect."

"Good," Beatrice's voice held a surprising level of conviction. "He could have sent a servant or hired some criminal to do his dirty work. Or he could be feigning his condition. The nobility can get away with anything."

Ranulf frowned. Should he be concerned at such vehemence? "Do you know something I don't?" he asked.

"No," she said, speaking in her normal dulcet tones. "It's just that...you'd be surprised at what families can do to one another."

There had been more than one instance when he'd suspected her of having secrets. This one most of all.

But were her secrets any of his business?

"I suppose you're not wrong about that, unfortunate though it may be," he conceded. "And the information I have gathered is compelling enough that he remains a suspect for now." He'd leave his questions about Beatrice's past unasked. Already, his involvement had become more complicated than he'd like.

"But that's not why I'm out of bed—not the only reason, anyway." She changed the subject, watching her feet as she carefully lifted herself up each step. "I have something to tell you. I've come to a decision."

She would be referring to the ridiculous bargain he'd proposed. Ranulf cleared his throat. "About that—"

"I've decided to help you with your situation in London." She rushed to speak over him. I'll pose as your fiancée, help you win your vote. I quite understand why the board would wish the person they appoint to be well-established, settled, and responsible." But then she paused and turned to him with narrowed eyes. "Just give me your word that as soon as it's over, you'll find the person bothering us, and regardless of who he is, he'll be prosecuted to the fullest extent of the law."

She was angry and rightfully so.

By God, she also must be terrified. Any other woman would be suffering fits of vapors after the traumatic event the night before. Beatrice was prepared to do what she could to prevent another one.

"Of course."

It was as though he'd come to a crossroads. Or perhaps a better description would be that he was standing on a precipice. His choice involved honor, but also ambition. He'd done his best to live a worthy life, live up to the expectations of a gentleman. But he was also an investigator. He had purpose—a mission to accomplish.

Ranulf had already decided he'd work Miss Primm's case. Not that he still didn't have to make the journey to London for the vote, but following that, he fully intended to make it his top priority.

The noble course of action would be to tell her she needn't do it—that he'd already decided on returning anyway. She was injured. She needed to rest. He could thank her and then allow her to go about her simple life, preparing lesson plans and polishing her students' desks.

But ambition was a powerful motivator.

"You haven't changed your mind?" she inquired. They'd only made it halfway up the stairs but she'd paused to watch him.

"I have not," he answered instead of listening to his conscience.

Satisfied with his answer, she returned to making her slow, steady climb.

And Ranulf followed.

Shackling himself to a fiancée, even a make-believe temporary one, would indeed improve his chances. What had Bedwell told him? They wanted the new director to be a settled gentleman—one who could dedicate the remainder of his career to the Society's endeavors.

And at the age of two and forty, they considered him on the young side. What did they expect, that he'd up and chase wild oats like some free and fancy lordling?

Idiots, all of them. He'd acted with the utmost of propriety since his marriage, nearly twenty years ago.

He wasn't some rakish pup.

And yet, he'd come to the point that he was willing to do damn near anything to secure the position.

The King's Society for the Advancement of Ingenuity in London stood at a pivotal moment. The long-standing institution was either going to succumb to irrelevance and lose a good deal of its funding or become one of the most prominent institutions of its time.

But it could only be the latter with proper leadership. Young blood.

And the best man to accomplish that, was himself. He'd never been a boastful sort of person but he believed in his plan, his vision.

Not because of pride, but because he'd taken the time to put in the necessary work. He'd laid out the possibilities, analyzed the statistics and scouted new donors, donors with deeper pockets than the lords who'd kept them afloat thus far.

Lords who were slowly dying off... *half of whom sat on the board.*

But the mere existence of the organization he envisioned, in and of itself, would prove a deterrent to crime. By putting dozens of detectives to work, corruption and unlawfulness would take a downward turn.

After what had felt like an hour, he and Beatrice arrived at the second-floor landing—where she paused again.

"You don't seem all that pleased. Have you changed your mind?"

"No!" His answer came out more harshly than he intended. "Not at all. In fact, I'm simply thinking through the logistics." And ignoring his own guilt.

"Indeed, we'll need to iron out the details." But when she continued toward the door leading to the teachers' quarters —*her bedchamber*, Ranulf stopped her.

"One moment." He moved her to stand around the corner and out of sight. "Stay here."

She wasn't properly dressed. Furthermore, she lacked a proper chaperone.

He marched into the teacher's chambers. "Miss Walcott requires her chamber," he informed Stewart and the gentlemen who'd joined him.

"Shouldn't she be in bed?" Steward asked.

Although Ranulf didn't disagree, he wouldn't belabor the point.

"She's waiting in the foyer," he answered, ignoring the curious look in Stewart's eyes. "So—" He shrugged. "If the three of you wouldn't mind finding some other chamber for your meeting..."

He gestured toward the door, and the four men cooperated.

"We're finished here, anyway." Rosewood shook his head, and then paused. "Aren't you coming?"

"In a moment," Ranulf didn't feel the need to explain. "She requires protection, wouldn't you agree?"

He and Miss Walcott had important details to discuss.

Rosewood's brows shot up but he refrained from offering an opinion.

The moment they'd disappeared down the stairs, Ranulf returned to escort Beatrice into her chamber.

And once inside, he closed the door behind them.

# A SIMPLE SCHEME

Her gaze trailed to the window, now boarded up, and then to what had been her bed. The mattress had been thrown out, leaving nothing but the wooden platform.

She swayed and Ranulf caught her around the middle from behind.

"It happened, it really happened," she mused almost as though she was alone.

Staring down he could see her pulse racing, like a trapped butterfly beneath the delicate skin where her shoulder curved into her neck.

Ranulf clenched his jaw.

He'd happily take the memory for her if he could. Just as he'd take it from either of his sisters—or his own mother. No lady ought to experience such an attack.

There were three other beds lined along the wall of windows, all looking as though they'd been freshly made up. "Sit." When she didn't move, he all but dragged her away from the sight of last night's incident.

She needed fluids, food, and rest, but if he suggested what she needed, she'd likely do the opposite just to spite him.

But she couldn't spite gravity.

She dropped onto the first of the freshly made-up beds and after a moment, found her second wind. "We'll need to set some rules for this make-believe betrothal—my expectations as well as yours. Primm suggested we draw up a contract," she said.

Intelligent women, these teachers.

"Because I won't m-marry. I… can't." Her feelings on this so strong she nearly stammered. "We need to have a very specific strategy to end it."

Ranulf wasn't worried, but he dipped his chin in acquiescence. "After I win the vote, I'll call it off. That way, your reputation will remain intact and you can return to teaching."

Gentlemen could get away with it. A lady could not.

It was a simple scheme, all in all.

"But if something goes awry," she persisted. "I will be the one to suffer from the fall-out. I won't be able to teach—or work at any other respectable position, for that matter. A woman's reputation is her foundation. If I'm involved in even an insignificant scandal, I'll be ruined. I'll need to distance myself from the school, move to another village and start a new life." Her gaze met his. "So, please. It's vital that we exercise the utmost of caution. Lady Rosewood will be my chaperone and we'll reside at her residence in Mayfair."

Ranulf hadn't expected her to have such emphatic concerns. But addressing them was a simple matter. It wasn't as though she was a fresh-faced debutante, wading through her first year on the marriage mart.

"I'll need your presence at a number of political dinners," he said. "And for good measure, we should be seen together in leisure settings—walking in the park, museums." He grimaced and then added. "Shopping. We'll keep our story simple. I met you at Hardwood's wedding and we decided to make a own match of our own."

She frowned. "A love match?"

"I suppose it would have to be. Unless you've a duke for a father hidden away somewhere?"

She shook her head vehemently, even though he'd only been joking. "No duke."

"So..." he pinched his mouth together. "A love match then."

"Because it would have to be," she added. "But if this vote is as important to you as the investigation is to the school, a little play-acting will be worthwhile. The vote, it *is* important, isn't it?"

It was best she understood the details. In fact, to carry out their charade successfully, they both had details to learn.

About one another.

A little about the past... as though they faced a future together.

This was as good a place to start as any.

Ranulf lowered himself onto the bed beside her and briefly explained his plans. And Beatrice Walcott, even injured, responded with enthusiasm.

"So, this isn't just about the investigation at the school," she deduced. "But we shall be working together for the greater good of England."

While she spoke, he'd kept his gaze on her face—appreciating the way her intelligent eyes lit up, making the blue brighter, like a summer sky. He lowered his stare to her mouth and an odd thrill slid down his spine. She was nothing like other women.

But when he lowered his gaze to the bandage on her neck, another niggle of guilt pricked him. "Has anyone checked your sutures this morning?" he asked.

"No."

She stilled. Her answer had been simple enough so why had the room suddenly filled with tension?

Even as he lifted his hand to the cloth, he knew he ought to send for one of the other women to examine the wound. Furthermore, in her condition, she was going to have difficulty changing into a new nightrail.

God knew he was no physician—nor was he a lady's maid.

And yet he drew the cloth back, slowly, until he'd exposed a dark red line about three inches long, dangerously close to her jugular.

He swallowed hard.

If the glass had cut her a few inches higher, she would have bled to death in less than thirty seconds.

"Do you mind if I take a closer look?" He wanted to ensure the sutures weren't too close to the edges, or too loose, or…

Anything less than perfect.

"No," she whispered. "I mean, I don't mind."

Ranulf removed his magnifying glass from inside his jacket and scowled. Edging closer, bringing the length of their bodies together, he slid one hand around her neck and held the glass a few inches from her wound. Beatrice's delicate skin had been drawn together and closed with precise stitches. Lady Rosewood, it seemed, had quite the knack for this sort of thing.

His own breath shook as he exhaled, and yet he kept his stare focused on her skin.

"I feel like a piece of your evidence," she joked.

But she wasn't evidence. She was a victim.

Ranulf took one last look at her smooth, not quite translucent skin, and then lowered the glass.

He exhaled a shaky breath, nearly overwhelmed by the inexplicable urge to place his lips against the side of her neck. To bury his face in her hair. And to taste her.

Everywhere.

"Is it… all right?" Her voice snapped him out of his inappropriate thoughts and he nodded. This temporary betrothal might be the worst decision of his life.

Somewhere between Hardwood's damned wedding house party and the time he'd spent at the school, a most unlikely attraction had formed between himself and this woman.

At a damned inconvenient time.

He didn't want another wife, and she wasn't at all the sort one could take for a lover. He shook his head.

Because, gentleman that he was, he wanted her. And it was impossible.

A spinster, by God. He adjusted his breeches and did his best to remember what the hell they were talking about.

She blinked at him, her mouth parted to reveal just a hint of raspberry tongue. Ranulf adjusted his breeches a second time.

If women ever comprehended the trials of men, they'd thank their lucky stars that they'd been born female.

Trials of men… ah yes, they'd been planning the details of a charade before he'd had to fight the urge to kiss her.

*Call it off.* A warning whispered in the back of his thoughts.

She had mentioned contracts—rules.

If he were to kiss her, she might get the wrong idea. Kissing her, he concluded vehemently, was a very bad idea.

He inhaled, practically tasting the alcohol her wound had been doused in last night, but also a hint of that same sweet scent he'd noticed on her before.

Something fruity and… lavender. That's what it was. He barely kept himself from savoring it.

*Sweet lavender.*

And she stared back at him with something akin to longing, however, it was quite possible she was still feeling the effects of the laudanum.

He rose and took three steps away from the bed. If he was going to make it through this phony engagement, he needed to check himself. God help him if he gave her the wrong idea.

Any benefits one obtained through marriage were not worth the ultimate trials of entering the institution.

"You'll rest today and tomorrow," he announced. "We'll leave the day after that." She moved to protest but he held up a chastising finger. "While you recover, I can proceed with the investigation here. Two days will still allow me—allow us—time enough in Mayfair before the vote."

"But I can help you!"

"With the investigation? I think not." Ranulf almost laughed. "You'll spend the time resting or the deal is off." He shoved his hands in his pockets.

She stood wearing a nightrail that was so worn he could

almost see right through it. A shadow hinted at the intimate triangle between her thighs, and pert nipples gave away her awareness of him. It took all his self-control to drag his gaze back to her face.

Her scowl lost most of its affect when she swayed, reaching out to him for balance.

"Bed. Now. Before I put you there myself," he moved her backwards in no uncertain terms. It was only after the words came out that he realized how improper they were.

In her chamber.

Alone.

By a bed.

Her eyes had opened wider than he'd ever seen them before, and a soft pink blush blossomed on her cheeks.

This entire encounter was highly improper and yet, his cock sprang to life as she drew back the coverlet.

*She's injured!* He silently reprimanded his less than shameless appendage. Breathing through his nostrils, he closed his eyes.

The investigation. The dozens of interviews he needed to conduct.

His position with The King's Society.

The vote.

He opened his eyes just in time to catch sight of her bottom wiggling as she crawled into the bed.

She had showed him mostly obstinance throughout the course of their acquaintance, why would she obey his orders now?

"I'll have tea and toast sent up promptly." He backed away. "No sugar. And remember. If I find that you've been out of bed, our bargain is off."

Her answer was to blink at him. And then she licked her lips.

"But—"

"Don't test me."

"You're a beast," she frowned.

*Better he was a beast than caught in an unwanted marriage.* But he didn't speak the words aloud.

"Rest." He pointed at her. "Or else." But there was no real bite to his bark and she seemed quite aware. It was almost as though she could see right through him.

"Yes sir," she answered cheekily.

He almost laughed at her audacity.

And as he stepped into the foyer, from the corner of his eye, he caught sight of her sticking her tongue out at him.

*Impertinent minx.*

He'd thought she'd be the best woman to play the part of his make-believe fiancé. But he was beginning to doubt his judgment.

Because Miss Beatrice Walcott, might in fact, be the worst.

Ranulf closed the door behind him and then rubbed his eyes.

If he couldn't get some sleep, he'd be no good to anyone.

# THE ABSENT CHAPERONE

"You're certain you've packed everything you're going to need? A book to read? Your evening gloves? Oh, but this is so very exciting!" Beatrice stifled a groan as Miss Daisy Pepperspring enthused. "I'm traveling with a lady who's going to become a marchioness!"

As it turned out, Victoria was not available to travel to London as chaperone to Beatrice. And although neither the countess nor the earl made any official announcement, Beatrice suspected that the former etiquette teacher might be *enceinte.*

With Primm being required to remain at the school, she'd asked Miss Pepperspring to act as chaperone.

Not only had the young woman agreed without hesitation, but she was also ecstatic at Beatrice's supposed betrothal.

The new teachers had all been told that Beatrice and the marquess were newly betrothed. The less people who knew the truth, the safer their secret was. Trust was something that was earned, and there was no way of knowing that one of these unfamiliar ladies wouldn't risk their position at the school in exchange for the payment they'd receive by selling such a story to the Gazette.

And they had learned, unfortunately, that the Gazette was willing to publish anything.

Another change in plans came when Victoria explained that her townhouse was being renovated. But Lord Sexton, as luck would have it, had the perfect solution.

One of his sisters, Lady Edith Abraham, resided in London year-round. The marquess assured Primm and Beatrice that Edith would keep everything on the up and up. And if she wasn't watching them, one of her three children aged: ten, two and ten, and six and ten would be underfoot.

So despite the changes to their plan, and a last-minute onslaught of nerves, Beatrice climbed into Primm's familiar carriage, feeling determined.

It had been more than a little frustrating having been confined to bed for the past few days. Especially when there had been so much work to do.

Primm must have felt as though she was starting from scratch, having to train an entirely new staff of teachers.

Furthermore, now that the two days of bedrest were over, Beatrice was stuck all over again—albeit this time—in a coach.

It was for the best, she reminded herself for the umpteenth time, as both she and Miss Pepperspring waved after Coachman John flicked the horses into motion.

To soothe the anxiety licking at her, Beatrice reminded herself of the contract that she, Primm, and the marquess had agreed upon.

First and foremost, the marquess had promised that the

school's vandalism case would be his top priority upon the conclusion of the vote.

Secondly, he'd agreed to end the engagement the day after the vote. They would do so with dignity. That timeline allowed Beatrice time enough to return to the school, but not so much time that any unsavory gossip would cause parents to second guess their choice of school for their precious daughters.

The assigned chaperone—Miss Pepperspring—would be present at all times—excluding formal political dinners and/or meetings where there was no risk of Beatrice being compromised in any way.

Primm had, of course, added a few line items that Beatrice would not have thought to include: no kissing, holding of hands only when necessary to lend authenticity to the engagement, Beatrice was to be allowed at least three nights to herself, nights where she was not required to appear in public or anywhere else, and last of all, if at any time she wished to end their agreement, she could do so.

It would void Lord Sexton's desired outcome—an image of responsibility, but that was only fair.

Beatrice wouldn't break her word though. The vote was as important to him as finding the vandal was to the school.

"You must be very excited. Have you been to London before?" Miss Pepperspring broke the silence.

Beatrice had a well-rehearsed answer for this. "Once. Before my parents passed."

In truth, she'd been to London numerous times—where she'd had her own room in her father's Mayfair townhouse, as had Jasper.

As a lord, her father had been required to spend a good

deal of his time in town, and following the season, they'd often drive down to spend a few weeks at Brighton.

The trouble with remembering the good times was that they contrasted so harshly with the bad.

Miss Pepperspring giggled, leaning forward to stare out the window to where Lord Sexton rode alongside. As a tall man, he rode a black Shire—the largest breed in all of England.

*Dionysia* .

Beatrice shivered inside. The marquess wasn't classically handsome, but he was striking.

"He is positively breathtaking," Miss Pepperspring announced, sending Beatrice a teasing glance. "If you don't mind my saying so."

"Not at all." He'd stolen her breath a time or two but she wasn't about to admit that to anyone, because he was also bossy, arrogant, and a know-it-all.

He didn't seem the sort of man who enjoyed flirting. If he had been, it might have been easier to dismiss those moments—moments when the air felt thick and her heart beat so loudly she was sure he could have heard it.

And on those occasions when he'd touched her, staring at her intently, she'd concluded he was as attracted to her as she was to him.

Even if they didn't actually *like* one another.

He'd visited her each day of her forced rest, but he hadn't checked her wound again, and he'd never sat beside her again.

And it was maddening.

Beatrice pinched the bridge of her nose and winced. If she dwelled on the Marquess of Sexton for most of this journey, she was going to be ready for Bedlam by the time they arrived in London.

She forced a smile. "Tell me about yourself, Miss Pepperspring."

The other girl brightened immediately, and with a few leading questions kept Beatrice entertained with stories of her family, schooling, and finally, her elation at having been hired to teach at Miss Primm's.

The idle prattle was enough to keep Beatrice sufficiently distracted for the next three hours of their journey, until the carriage finally drew to a halt and the door opened. A quick glance out the window revealed that they were not at an inn, or in any sort of village. They'd stopped at the edge of a meadow and she could just make out what looked like a distant stream.

The door swung open.

"I thought a picnic might be in order." Lord Sexton looked and sounded exceedingly cordial—not at all like the man she'd come to know.

"A picnic?" she asked.

His eyes twinkled a little. "You know, various foods and drink eaten while sitting on the ground, usually with some sort of blanket provided to keep one from getting grass and seedlings on one's clothing."

He lifted a basket so she could see it through the door. "Primm's Cook very graciously sent this along for us. We're lucky, as the quality of tavern food is never a certainty, unless you'd rather..." He cleared his throat.

And then Beatrice realized. He was already playing the part of her gallant fiancé!

It was just as well. Miss Pepperspring was quite inclined

to conversation and she, perhaps, was one of the most important persons to be convinced.

Beatrice licked her lips, looked into his eyes, and allowed herself to smile at him like the happy bride-to-be they were pretending she was. It came to her more easily than she thought it would. "I'd love a picnic."

Her feelings in that moment were unexpected. Neither of them moved, and she caught her breath, locked in his gaze which almost appeared…

Loving.

But then his smile turned polite as he extended his hand for her to take. "I hope the jostling of the road isn't affecting your wounds."

Beatrice touched her neck, which was healing nicely, and then remembered, they were play-acting. This was make-believe. She was expected to appear enamored with him.

He was far better at this than she was.

"No," she answered after an almost uncomfortable pause before accepting the hand he offered.

And while Coachman John led the horses to water, the small and unlikely threesome consisting of Beatrice, Miss Pepperspring, and the marquess located the perfect spot for their picnic. In the shade, close enough that they could hear the water of the bubbling brook, but far enough away that the ground wasn't damp.

Miss Pepperspring, mindful of Beatrice's sutures, insisted on doing the serving. She set out plates, napkins, and opened the packages of meats, cheese, fruits, nuts, and a few pastries. Once she'd filled their plates, she made up two more. But rather than settle onto the blanket beside them, she pushed up to stand.

"I'll take one of these to Coachman John," she collected the two other plates, winked, and then added. "Picnics can be ever so romantic."

Without waiting for an answer, she left Beatrice and the marquess alone.

Lord Sexton flicked a gaze to where Miss Pepperspring disappeared, before sliding it over to Beatrice. "Interesting chaperone," he commented wryly.

Beatrice was going to have to have a talk with Miss Pepperspring, explaining that her very purpose for coming along was to ensure that Beatrice was never left alone with the marquess.

"I suppose there's no danger here," she answered, aware that, although Miss Pepperspring had not at all discreetly left them alone, she could easily return at any moment.

Which meant they needed to keep up their charade.

"Was your first betrothal an extended one—your real one—I mean?" she clarified. There was so very much she didn't know about him!

"Six months. We became engaged early in the season and our parents planned a July wedding," he answered lazily, looking more relaxed than normal.

"I'm only asking because…" she cleared her throat. "I'm embarrassed to admit that I'm not sure what people will expect."

His stare locked with hers. "Your chaperone is going to be the most difficult of anyone to fool. No doubt, she'll expect that we'll steal a kiss or two. But if we can convince her, we'll have no trouble convincing my colleagues."

"A kiss or two…?" Beatrice swallowed the bite she'd been nervously chewing. "But what about the contract?"

## PRACTICE MAKES PERFECT

In hindsight, Ranulf wasn't sure what particular devil had goaded him into mentioning anything about kissing.

But then he corrected himself. It wasn't a devil at all—more of an angel, actually.

She'd seemed glum the past few days, and most definitely annoyed with him for insisting she keep to her bed.

He'd expected more of the same when he'd opened the door to peer into the carriage.

He had not expected her smile.

Damn near struck him dumb.

And now, with the most cooperative exit made by Miss Pepperspring, he'd suggested the idea without thinking.

Beatrice was mostly recovered from her injury. They were in the full light of day. And… an innocent kiss would indeed, provide a sense of intimacy between the two of them, making their betrothal appear authentic.

Wouldn't hurt to convince Coachman John either.

"Ah. The 'no kissing' rule only applies while in private." He'd slipped a piece of grass between his lips and slid his hand adjacent hand to hers, a few inches closer. "We're supposed to appear betrothed."

She didn't move it, so he shifted again, this time allowing his pinky finger to graze hers.

She sat frozen, staring straight ahead.

"But this is not real," she said.

"A little practice can't hurt."

Ranulf could practically see the wheels turning as she weighed his proposal.

"We did decide that it would have had to be a love match, did we not?" She turned to meet his gaze. With the subtle stroke of his finger, pink suffused her neck and cheek.

His chest loosened. He hadn't realized it had even been tight.

But with that little blush, she looked more like herself than she had since the night that damn rock had come flying through her bedroom window.

Interested. Engaged.

*Aroused.*

She looked as though she cared about the world around her—as though she needn't be afraid.

He stroked her finger again and this time, she responded with a small stroke of her own.

Truth be told, it was important that they appear comfortable with one another. If they were exposed before the vote, his reputation would seem worse than if he'd not pretended to be engaged at all.

And yet, in that moment, he wasn't thinking of the vote.

Good God, he felt like a schoolboy, building up his courage, thinking through the most natural way to kiss her.

But then she upended any idea of choreographing this part of their courtship—no, not a courtship—their make-believe betrothal.

"I thought you wanted to kiss me—a few times before—but then you didn't." She looked up from where their hands touched, frowning. "I'd hate for you to have to do something you'd rather not—"

*Enough!*

Ranulf captured her mouth with his.

When he drew back to adjust the angle, she tried again. "But I thought—Mrmph..."

This was the best method to stop her from uttering nonsense. And this time, she allowed him to coax her mouth open. She tasted of fruit and sunshine and... innocence.

This was not part of their bargain. But for this afternoon, in a place where he didn't have to think about either the vote or the school, for the first time in years...

He simply wanted to enjoy kissing a pretty woman.

When one of her hands reached up to clutch his shoulder, Ranulf pulled her closer and exhaled a low growl.

She hummed back at him, his Sweet Bee, and tightened her arm around him.

Careful to protect her injured shoulder, and without breaking the kiss, Ranulf lowered her backward until she was lying down, half on the blanket, half on the grass.

He couldn't remember the last time he'd experienced such an unadulterated, genuine desire.

Lust, he'd known. He'd even gone so far as to feign romantic want.

But kissing Beatrice... was.

Something he'd not even realized he'd missed.

Were his hands shaking? He kept a good portion of his weight from resting on her, sliding his free hand down her side, learning her curves. She used her palms to cradle his face, her thumbs pushing his hair back. Sweet breath mingled with his and something light blossomed at the sound of her little sighs.

Kissing her here was safe, he rationalized. If the chaperone saw, it would make their endeavor all the more convincing.

And he couldn't allow it to go too far.

Coachman John wasn't more than fifty yards away. They had just enough privacy to indulge in...

This.

Ironic that he'd never considered kissing anything more than a means to fulfill the female's trivial expectation for romance.

But. *Hell and Damnation.* He was going to have to rethink the entire endeavor.

Ranulf nipped at the tip of her tongue.

He couldn't seem to get enough of it.

Enough of *her.*

He explored behind her lips, the corner of her mouth, the delicate line of her jaw.

But since further improprieties were strategically impossible, he did his best to ignore that his cock was rock hard—that he wanted to lift her gown to her hips and engulf himself in her heat.

A high-pitched slightly off-key singing sounded from the short path leading to the spring.

The chaperone was returning.

For now, a kiss was going to have to be enough.

Even if it was only make-believe.

BEATRICE OPENED HER EYES. *Why was he stopping...?*

Confusion swooped in when Lord Sexton rolled off her abruptly, pulling her to a sitting position. She nearly choked on her disappointment until she realized someone was coming. Miss Pepperspring was just stepping out from behind the trees as Lord Sexton moved back to his previous seat.

Beatrice lifted her hand to cover her lips and the marquess, cool and calm as per his usual demeanor, adjusted his jacket.

Of course he was cool and calm. And the fact that what they had been doing must look painfully obvious was precisely what they'd set out to achieve in the first place.

"Coachman John suggests we pack up and get back on the road," Miss Pepperspring smiled knowingly as she gathered Beatrice and Ranulf's plates, along with the two empty one's she'd returned with, and stuffed them back into the basket. "But it was a lovely afternoon for a picnic, was it not?"

"Indeed."

There were times when Beatrice wondered how it was that Lord Sexton could act so cordially with others and hardly ever with herself.

And aside from a curious glance or two, Lord Sexton hardly spoke a word to her while they loaded up the remnants of the picnic.

She knew him well-enough to guess that he wasn't

ashamed, but again, he'd managed to take up a most stubborn presence in her thoughts. He'd kissed her.

And there had been nothing chaste about this one.

Furthermore, Beatrice knew beyond a doubt that he'd enjoyed it. His body had hummed right along with hers. He'd tasted every inch of her mouth, teased and chewed on her lips, and trailed his open mouth around the line of her jaw.

And then kissed her some more.

For the first time since hearing of how Victoria, Priscilla, And Chloe had all essentially sacrificed their careers and livelihoods because they'd allowed themselves to be compromised by men, Beatrice had a sense of understanding why.

Not that she'd allow the same thing to happen to her but…

Kissing involved more than what she'd always considered a kiss to be. She'd imagined two mouths meeting, touching in a perfunctory manner.

But the kiss she'd experienced this afternoon was so much more than that. It was as though one of the kissers was a flint, and the other stone.

She couldn't decide which of them was which.

Nonetheless, kissing like that had ignited other…

Longings.

Even before he'd guided her so that she was lying beneath him, she'd wanted his weight.

He'd rested his large hand on her outer thigh. She'd very nearly spread her legs to encourage more intimate exploration.

Thank heavens Miss Pepperspring had returned when she did.

Beatrice shifted in her seat. Primm had most certainly not meant the *'no kissing'* rule to apply only in private.

Ensconced in the carriage and on the road again, Miss Pepperspring sent Beatrice a knowing smile. Beatrice felt her face grow hot.

The marquess was older than she, and far more experienced. She ought to believe him when he'd told her it was only for practice—and to convince Miss Pepperspring.

She peered out the window, but could barely see his back. Had he forgotten the kiss already—while she analyzed it piece by piece as thoroughly as if she'd had his magnifying glass?

Even if she had full view of his expression, the blasted man was impossible to read!

She sat back and blew a stray hair out of her face. She'd do well to consider his every move to be an act—a deliberate part of their charade.

Well, at least they'd accomplished what they'd set out to do. Her chaperone appeared quite convinced of this betrothal now. Society—what little of them who would be in Mayfair this time of year, would require far less from the two of them for the betrothal to be believable.

She glanced out the window again. She'd had her hands on that back. She'd threaded her fingers through his hair.

No more kissing. She reprimanded herself even as she pressed her knees together. No kissing at all? Or just no private kissing?

The private kissing would be the most dangerous.

All because it offered the possibility of leading to something more.

"I imagine you're anxious for the wedding. Have the two of you discussed a date?" Miss Pepperspring asked.

A date? A wedding?

For a flash of a second, she pictured herself as a wife—something she'd not done in a very, very long time.

But that was the last thing that ought to be on her mind. Two weeks and then she could return to Miss Primm's. Best to focus on the school, her classes, her students.

This wasn't real. They were only presenting an illusion.

# LADY ABRAHAM

After one and a half days of travel, and having shared a room the night before on a most uncomfortable bed at a lively inn, even Miss Pepperspring seemed to have lost some of her enthusiasm for the journey.

In reality, travel wasn't nearly as glamorous as one imagined it to be.

And as Coachman John drove them through the streets of Mayfair, his passengers both breathed a sigh of relief when he finally pulled the carriage to a halt in front of a typical white stucco Townhouse, if not larger than most. The entrance was flanked by two elegant columns, and the symmetrically placed bow windows boasted iron balconies all the way up to the fourth floor.

Upon seeing a perfectly put together woman standing on the steps waiting for them, Beatrice only wished her own dress wasn't so wrinkled as she climbed stiffly out of the carriage.

The woman, who appeared both practical but also lovely, was obviously Lord Sexton's younger sister. With dark hair and eyes, she stood taller even than Beatrice, slim and fit.

It was difficult for Beatrice to believe that the woman could be the mother of the three young ladies who were obviously exceedingly pleased at the arrival of their uncle as they fidgeted excitedly.

He'd ridden ahead on Dionysia when they'd departed from the inn in order to arrive in Mayfair ahead of them. Beatrice took this to mean that he'd not had time to send word to his sister and was going to have to warn her of their arrival.

Beatrice hoped the woman, who appeared as difficult to read as her brother, was not put out by the intrusion. So when a welcoming smile took over the woman's expression, Beatrice breathed a little easier.

"You must be positively exhausted." Lady Abraham took Beatrice by the arm as though Lord Sexton was not present, and then gestured Miss Pepperspring to follow them. "Aren't you perfectly lovely? Ranulf has told me so much about you! But you've suffered a long journey. Just come along with me now. I've had our best guest rooms prepared for both of you."

Beatrice and Miss Pepperspring followed Lady Abraham and her housekeeper up a steep but ornately detailed staircase.

It must be all the stairs that kept Lady Abraham looking so fit. Once they'd arrived on the second landing and turned down a foyer, their host paused and then pushed open one half of a double door.

"This is Miss Walcott's chamber," she said.

Beatrice's breath caught. Even the room in which she'd grown up, on which no expense had been spared, had been much inferior to this one. Set on the back side of the house, the far wall boasted tall windows, one which boasted a faux balcony. She skirted around the canopied bed to look outside and then felt almost giddy to be looking onto an almost fairy-tale-like garden. A glance down revealed that a viny trellis extended up most of the wall.

The affect was delightful.

"Lord Abraham and I had it designed for the girls," Lady Abraham provided, as she strode across to a discreet door. "This chamber adjoins with Miss Pepperspring's. If you wish, the two of you can assist one another with dressing. Nevertheless, I've arranged for a lady's maid."

"Oh, but that won't be necessary." Beatrice turned away from the window. She had once expected she'd be attended to in such a manner, as her mother had, but time had shown her just how superfluous such a luxury was.

And she had long since grown accustomed to taking care of her own needs.

"Oh, but it is," Lord Sexton's sister contradicted her." She spoke like a woman who was rarely challenged. "As my brother's betrothed, people will expect you to appear in the latest fashions. You'll want to feel confident attending political functions, mingling with the ton, or even strolling through the park."

Lord Sexton appeared belatedly, but rather than join the conversation, crossed his arms and leaned against the door frame. How much of the truth had he told his sister? Beatrice met his gaze, but he only shrugged.

She then turned a serene smile back to his sister. "But it is autumn. Isn't all of Mayfair absent this time of year?"

"Oh but this is the little season." Lady Abraham said. "You'd be surprised at who deigns to make an appearance in town, even if it is for just a few weeks. Even this morning, I received an invitation from the Duchess of Dillingham. She is hosting a ball next week and I've already accepted for all of us."

Beatrice's blood cooled as an almost forgotten fear returned.

She'd come to town believing most of society would have retired to their country estates until the next Season came around. She hadn't considered that there would be events in autumn.

She was struck then by the powerful urge to march back down to the carriage and ride far away from here. She clenched her fists. What if they were here? What if somebody recognized her?

But she had made a promise.

Forcing air in and then breathing out, Beatrice reasoned with herself.

While they'd been alive, her parents and most of their friends, without fail, abandoned London at the end of May and didn't return until just before Easter.

What were the chances her aunt and uncle would behave any differently? People didn't change their ways as they grew older. No, they settled into them even more deeply.

With her hands only shaking a little, she exhaled and strolled around the lovely room, noticing the uniformed woman standing in a corner.

The lady's maid.

Lady Abraham rubbed her hands together. "Dora, please show Miss Pepperspring to her chamber while Miss Walcott settles in." And as Lord Sexton had eventually stepped across the threshold, she then turned a warning look to her brother. "You'll meet me in my sitting room won't you, Ranulf? We have a good deal to discuss."

*Ranulf.*

He scowled, and the interaction had Beatrice biting back a smile. Her own brother, although several years younger, could be just as irritable with her.

Not that he'd required any admonishments during the short times they could be together. Once a year, if they were lucky, twice—and only for a day or two.

That familiar pang of missing him struck her as the room emptied out.

Except for Lord Sexton.

In her bedchamber.

Alone.

She might have complained if the door had not been left open, but with the door ajar, the situation maintained a sense of decency.

Just barely.

Beatrice crossed her arms in front of her, feeling curious as to his present mood. Ever since the picnic, the only interactions they'd had between one another had been civil and proper. Miss Pepperspring, in fact, had performed her chaperone duties with all due diligence.

Was that how the next few weeks would play out?

It was precisely as it should be.

And yet… Beatrice found herself staring at his mouth—and…

Wishing the door was closed. She would not resist him if he took her in his arms again.

"You are uncomfortable," he observed and she tilted her head, not quite understanding what he meant. "Mingling with society. I assure you, you'll fit in perfectly. Your accent, your manners, trust me, you have nothing to worry about." The small praise sent butterflies dancing in her chest. "And if my guess is correct, my sister has a modiste standing by to design you an entirely new wardrobe."

"But I can't afford—"

"At my expense of course."

"But that's not proper."

"My sister will take care of that. Aside from politics, of course, spending money is her second favorite hobby." He actually grinned. The expression completely transformed his face. It made him seem, not soft, but... more approachable. Almost... sensitive.

He loved his family.

"Your nieces obviously adore you," she said. She didn't want him to leave yet. How dangerous was it that something deep inside of her craved his presence?

Not the rational part, of course.

"Don't sound so surprised," he laughed. "And I adore them." He did nothing to hide the affection in his voice. But then a wicked light danced in his dark eyes. "I'm only an ogre when I'm around impertinent schoolteachers."

"So why, then, are you an ogre around me?" she teased. "I hold no claim to impertinence."

She was flirting with him! Were... were they flirting with each other?

"On the contrary, when one looks the word up in a dictionary, the definition reads your name, followed by an artist's rendering of your pretty little face."

Pretty?

She couldn't remember the last time anyone had ever called her pretty. Was he pretending to be her fiancé, even now?

But they finally had some privacy. They ought to use it to discuss important matters, such as what all his sister knew, their intentions regarding the contract they had already broken… and perhaps her misgivings about being recognized in public as well. But if she admitted to that, she'd have to provide him with some sort of reason. She didn't want to come across as weak-minded.

And yet, how could she play the part of the blushing betrothed if she was constantly looking over her shoulder?

"I have a confession to make," he turned serious.

Confessions were never good.

"Edith has a dinner party planned for this evening. She's invited a few of the board members."

*"Tonight?"* Beatrice glanced down at herself. She'd brought a few of her nicer gowns, including some of her favorites that she'd taken with her when she'd left home—the ones she'd picked out with her mother several years ago. Although no longer in fashion, they were in good condition—and they were all she had.

Fashionable gowns had hardly been a necessity in her life.

"If you'd rather not, you don't have to attend, but—"

"The sooner we announce our betrothal, the better, I suppose." She strode across the room and quietly closed the door. In a hushed tone, she continued, "Tonight is as good a time as any for them to see that you intend to settle down. But I must admit I'm a little nervous… Does your sister know the truth?"

"I told her I was bringing my betrothed and her companion. When she asked if it was a love match, I told her it was. So she'll be watching us."

"So…" Beatrice's heart raced.

"It's important we be convincing."

Which meant he might send her romantic looks—that he would find excuses to touch her. He wouldn't kiss her again, because even couples who were actually betrothed only ever took such liberties with one another in private.

"I'd wager she's hovering in the foyer as we speak," he whispered.

The hint of his breath sent her back to the interlude in the meadow.

She licked her lips, staring into his eyes. Was he thinking what she was thinking?

"Just outside the door," he said.

Surely he wasn't suggesting…?

"Do you think we should…?"

Just as he'd done in the meadow he didn't waste any time in making the decision for the both of them.

"Practice?" he spoke against her mouth. "Makes perfect."

Beatrice exhaled into his mouth and her insides danced. She should make some show of protest. She should push him away rather than melt against the length of his person.

It was as though she consisted of two parts, one of them prim and proper, the other, starved for intimacy and utterly uninhibited.

She slid both her arms up his shoulders, winding one hand behind his neck and savored the sensation of his solid chest pressed against her breasts. She melted into him, his arm around her waist as he tugged her closer, pressing his thighs against hers.

And low on her belly, his member strained between them.

One of his hands reached down and he lifted her thigh

so she could almost wrap her leg around him. She might have done so if not for the restrictions of her gown.

Standing in this lovely bedchamber like this, so very… together, the most ironic thought struck her.

They were opposites in almost every way and yet they fit. Like two puzzle pieces.

*This isn't real. This isn't' real. This isn't real...*

He tilted his head, drinking from her mouth, one arm around her back like a vice, his other hand cradling her chin.

"And Ranulf…" The voice entered the room before Lady Abraham did and by the time she peered inside, both of Beatrice's feet were firmly on the floor. Lord Sexton smoothed his hands through his hair.

But this time, two small pink spots remained high on his cheeks as he strategically moved to stand behind a conveniently tall-backed chair.

The viscountess frowned, and yet something in her eyes gave away that she was …

Pleased?

She cleared her throat. "I know you wish to spend as much time as possible with Miss Walcott—"

"Please, call me Beatrice." It seemed the proper thing, if this were real—if they were to become family to one another.

Theoretically.

Lady Abraham's expression turned even more pleased. "And you must call me Edith." She turned back to her brother. "But will you come and go over this guest list with me? I don't want to make any mistakes with this seating arrangements."

Dora, the lady's maid, appeared behind the viscountess,

holding what looked to be several gowns over her arm—gowns which were specifically made for formal events judging by the fabrics: silk, taffeta, satin…

"I've arranged a bath to be brought up for you, miss. If you wish to try these on, you can decide which one you prefer, and I'll make the necessary alterations."

Beatrice exhaled. All she wanted to do was fall into Lord Sexton's arms again. And yet…

It had been for show.

The charade was beginning.

And in just a few hours, Beatrice would officially become fiancée to the Marquess of Sexton.

# ONLY A MAKE-BELIEVE PRINCESS

"One day you're a teacher, working for your living at an all-girls' school, and the next, poof, you look like a princess." Daisy practically danced about the room

Beatrice was losing her ability to resist the younger woman's enthusiasm.

Because throughout the afternoon, Dora and a few of Edith's other maids had most certainly treated Beatrice like some sort of royalty. She decided on a lovely silk sapphire gown that cinched at the waist with a gold tie, while waiting servants filled the deep copper bath with hot water—deliciously hot—a luxury not always available at the school.

Beatrice had added a few drops of her lavender oil before climbing in, and once seated, she contemplated that this alone may have made coming to London a worthwhile endeavor.

Dora had then washed Beatrice's hair with shampoo that felt like silk. Afterward, having dried off and wearing nothing but her dressing gown, Beatrice had sat at the vanity while Dora brushed her hair, and then curled and pinned the shining dark strands, very deliberately arranging them like cascading ribbons.

Standing in the gown while Dora made a few last-minute adjustments, Beatrice flicked a grin in the direction of her chaperone.

"Not a princess, Miss Pepperspring, but definitely royalty."

"Oh, please, if you don't mind, call me Daisy. I hate my surname and would change it if I could. It reminds me of running eyes and the uncontrollable urge to sneeze." The girl looked quite relaxed, wearing a comfortable looking morning gown.

Since the dinner was of a political nature, Daisy had the evening off. She'd announced that she was going to finish reading her latest book—fiction, she admitted. And then make use of the softest mattress she'd ever lied down on.

The old Beatrice envied the young woman.

The new Beatrice, the one who liked kissing… the one who'd agreed to this charade even knowing it might all end in scandal, well, she felt a spark of challenge.

And she must be made up of three different parts. Because the third one was looking forward to the evening. It was as though she sensed a serendipitous opportunity to fulfill something deep within her. She yearned to exceed Lord Sexton's expectations, but she was also determined to present herself in such a way that would have made her mother proud.

After stepping into silken slippers that matched her gown perfectly, she plucked at her skirt while Daisy dropped the lacy gold shawl on her shoulders.

One of the other maids knocked and then peered inside

the room. "The guests are arriving. I'm here to show you downstairs."

"That won't be necessary." The maid stiffened as Lord Sexton stepped around her.

He would escort her.

The maid backed out of the room with a curtsey. "My apologies, my lord."

Beatrice clasped her hands at her waist and forced herself to breathe. Seeing her marquess like this, dressed to the nines and appearing every inch a lord, her confidence fled.

She'd become far too comfortable with his casual attire—the detective—the man who'd teased her and goaded her into upending her life in ways she'd never anticipated.

This man—this marquess…quite literally stole her breath.

His hair had been combed back, his sideburns trimmed, and his face recently shaved. A valet had to have performed the artistry of Lord Sexton's cravat, the ends of which had been tucked into his pristine linen shirt.

As for the rest of his attire…

It fit him perfectly and had to have cost the amount Beatrice made over the course of an entire year.

The navy jacket, a brushed velvet, was buttoned low on his torso, allowing a glimpse of the embroidery on his waistcoat. At the ends of his sleeves, intricate lace cascaded over his wrists. And of course, that was not enough. He wore a massive gold ring on the index finger of his right hand, and a smaller but no less impressive one adorned his left pinky.

It was him—the same man who'd kissed her earlier that afternoon. But he was also someone else.

It was only when she lifted her gaze to his that her confidence returned.

How was it that such dark, inscrutable eyes, could lend her comfort?

"You look stunning, Beatrice." He used her given name intentionally. The servants would gossip that his lordship was enamored with this woman—a spinster, a simple teacher— he'd found at Miss Primm's School. "Shall we?" He winged an arm and Beatrice, afraid to speak lest it come out sounding like a croak, merely took it.

She didn't say a word until after the door closed behind them and they were nearly at staircase. "You look terrifying."

He didn't so much as miss a step "Really?" he said. "How positively delightful."

"What do you want me to call you?"

"In public, Sexton will suffice." He gripped her elbow firmly enough that, even if she were to stumble on the steep stairs, she wouldn't fall.

He would catch her.

"And around your family?"

"My dear, my love, darling..." But it was obvious he was joking.

Or was he?

"Ranulf?" She ventured. It was what his sister called him. It suited him.

Not tonight, though. Tonight, he was the marquess—his lordship, etc.

The man who'd teased his nieces, who'd irked his sister —The man who'd kissed her senseless...

Was Ranulf. The name was rough, but also earthy.

And intelligent.

"Ranulf it is." They stepped onto the main floor landing and he sent her a glance that she couldn't quite read. Voices could be heard from behind two doors. Doors so tall that the tops extended well into the upper floors. "Are you ready?"

Beatrice nodded, and together they stepped into the massive drawing room.

An unexpected silence fell, but Ranulf was one hundred percent the marquess. "Ladies and gentlemen, may I present to you my beloved betrothed, Miss Beatrice Walcott?"

~

CHOOSING BEATRICE TO play the part of his betrothed had been an excellent decision. Ranulf stood back while Beatrice greeted one titled colleague after another.

And for an orphaned schoolteacher, her manners and speech could fool anyone into believing that she'd been born into the ton.

"Your Grace," Ranulf introduced her to their highest-ranking guest first. "May I present my betrothed, Miss Beatrice Walcott. Beatrice, the Duke of Dillingham."

Extending her hand to the duke, Beatrice lowered her lashes and dipped into a perfectly executed curtsey.

Upon rising, her demeanor transformed into one that would rival the diamond of any given season. Had she simply learned the nuances of society from the proximity she had with some of her students and their parents?

Ranulf accepted a drink from one of the manservants, and although he remained at her side, he mostly listened.

And watched.

Making excuses to the duke, Ranulf took her arm for

more introductions—a few of which weren't even necessary.

Because, as luck would have it, she was acquainted with a few of the other ladies present. Bedwell's duchess had taught at Miss Primm's for a very short term, and having attended their wedding, Beatrice was familiar with the duchess's sister-in-law, the baroness Chaswick as well.

Their guests that evening were friendly ones—persons who respected and supported Ranulf's vision for the Society.

And although he considered most of them friends, Ranulf found himself keeping an eye on Beatrice while she gracefully mingled.

He'd expected Edith would provide his betrothed with something elegant and fashionable. Was that what had affected his fiancée's transformation?

But no. This was not simple make-over. She glowed with an inner confidence.

Ranulf wasn't sure what to think. Was this her secret? That she'd been born into the aristocracy?

He shook his head. The more he learned about this woman, the more he liked her.

He swallowed his drink, simply watching her. Was it possible she became more beautiful with each passing day?

Truth be told, he'd been intrigued by her back at Hardwood Cliffhouse—when she'd been scowling at him and avoiding an introduction.

How in the hell had he mistaken her for a maid?

Looking at her now, his blunder was even more laughable.

She smiled at something her current companion said.

Not her genuine smile, but the one she donned when trying to be polite.

Lord Shelby, a wealthy viscount—only because of his recent marriage to an affluent American heiress—had been welcomed into the society, not for his character, but for his sharp mind and his now deep pockets.

Ranulf glanced around to confirm Shelby had not brought his wife along. Not uncommon, in fact, couples weren't expected to live in one another's pockets.

And yet…

Ranulf did not appreciate the manner in which the viscount's mouth was almost touching Beatrice's ear—Beatrice—the woman he'd make his wife.

The thought nearly choked him.

But when the blighter's hand dropped low on Beatrice's back, Ranulf shoved his way through the other guests and stepped between them, sending a warning look in the other man's direction.

"We'll be going in for dinner shortly." Ranulf placed Beatrice's hand on his arm. The rules for entering a dining room were one of the most basic requirements of dinner party etiquette, but if Beatrice wasn't assigned someone he could trust, Ranulf was more than willing to break them.

Edith, who had apparently noticed the tension from across the room, inserted herself into their trio. "Ranulf. If you wouldn't mind leading Lady Chaswick in for dinner, I've asked Lord Chaswick to accompany Beatrice."

Chaswick had once been one of London's more notorious bachelors, but that had been a few years ago. Married now and quite besotted with his wife, he could be considered trustworthy.

Ranulf nodded and another lady began chatting with his betrothed.

"What are you doing?" Edith leaned in and whispered. "Beatrice is doing fine. Keep your mind on your goal, brother." She shook her head, muttering. "I never imagined you'd lose your head over a woman."

Ranulf stiffened. Because he had once been *married.*

"What do you mean?"

"You haven't taken your eyes off her all night. Look around you, mingle, use that charm you so rarely exercise to solidify votes."

His sister's admonishment brought him up short.

Beatrice was *not,* in fact, his betrothed. Their affection was feigned, nothing more than a façade. But watching her step so easily into his world, he couldn't shake the niggling thought that having her at his side felt more real, more right, than anything he'd felt in years.

## IT BEGINS

Seated at dinner, Beatrice glanced down Edith's elaborately dressed table. She'd been pleasantly surprised to find that she had a prior acquaintance with a few of tonight's guests—people she'd met while teaching at Miss Primm's.

Even so, she'd had no trouble making conversation upon each new introduction. It was as though all those etiquette classes she'd taken years ago, the long practices and the exercises she'd suffered through as a young girl, had happened only yesterday.

Ranulf sent her an approving stare from where he sat, adjacent to his brother-in-law.

He kept a careful eye on her, in fact, throughout the endless courses and dessert.

And later that night, when the gentlemen rejoined the ladies after finishing their port, he didn't delay in coming to her side.

He touched her elbow and leaned down to whisper, "Is everything all right?"

A resulting shiver was impossible to contain.

"Yes. Were you worried?"

"I thought I would be. But not really. You could school me on a few of my manners."

The compliment ought to have pleased her, but he had only made it because everyone accepted her as his betrothed. And despite knowing this, Beatrice felt an underlying disappointment.

*None.*

*Of.*

*This.*

*Is.*

*Real.*

She knew this.

"Ha," she answered. "As if anyone would dare to question the manners of a marquess." Or anything else.

"Is that not why you are here tonight?" The question was not an admonishment, but perhaps a reminder.

"Of course."

"You must be tired." He touched his hand to her back. "Just another half an hour and you can retire for the evening."

Their first night had been a triumph, but oddly enough, also something of a disappointment.

Beatrice dismissed the notion.

"You are right." And with the power of her words, tiredness washed over her. According to Edith, this was only the first of many such performances. Best not wear herself out on the first one.

"Half an hour," he promised. And he was true to his word. Shortly after, the guests began making their goodbyes.

But it was Beatrice who excused her for the evening. "Ranulf is in Lord Abraham's study strategizing with a few close colleagues."

"Oh." Had she expected he would kiss her goodnight? "Well then. Thank you again, for everything."

But Edith waved her thanks away. "Don't thank me yet. We've a long way to go."

~

THE WEEK THAT FOLLOWED, although a whirlwind, was not altogether unpleasant. And as Primm had made explicit in the contract, Beatrice was allowed three nights to herself.

She had only sacrificed one of them in order to attend a last-minute event. Edith had emphasized that the people who would be there were *very important*. The Duke of Dillingham would be so disappointed if Lord Sexton's lovely betrothed were absent.

The last part, Beatrice knew, was poppycock. Nonetheless, she'd relented.

Because she found herself with more free time than she ever had at the school.

Beatrice had forgotten what it was like not to have to spend her days planning and setting up her classroom and devising strategies for educating some of her more difficult students.

And when she wasn't alone, both she and Daisy found themselves spending a good deal of time with, of all people, the Duchess of Bedwell, *Collette*. In a chance coincidence, a few years before, the duchess had taught at Miss Primm's for less than a fortnight. She'd been sacked for no fault of her own, but then the Duke of Bedwell, brother to one of their former students, had swept her away in a most surprising love-match.

The Duke of Bedwell was one of Ranulf's most ardent supporters. He was also interested in the details of the vandalism at Miss Primm's, seeing as it was his half-brother, Mr. Stewart, who'd made most of the repairs. Whenever they stepped out as two couples, conversation never lagged.

And despite the time of year, Town was not at all dull. In fact, Beatrice felt as though it buzzed—regardless of the hour. As a person who normally appreciated her solitude, Beatrice made an ardent attempt to pace herself, but unlike her experience at Priscilla's wedding earlier that summer, she did not have a constant desire to hide in her chamber.

She was having *fun*—an emotion she'd long since thought existed only in her past. Because teachers must be serious and somber. The ability to have fun wasn't something that would be admired in a spinster.

For a few weeks, anyhow, she left spinsterhood behind.

On days when Ranulf wasn't required to meet with any of his cohorts, he took her either walking or riding atop his splendid curricle to see the sights of London.

When her betrothed had other obligations, Beatrice spent some of her free time with Collette and the duchess' sister-in-law, Lady Chaswick. Sometimes they did nothing more than sit in Lady Chaswick's drawing room, crocheting but mostly chatting. Other days, the two ladies took Beatrice around town, introducing her to the small set of socialites who had chosen London over the country for the autumn months.

Edith joined them on a few occasions, but her daughters and, most extraordinarily, her own political endeavors, often kept her occupied.

At the end of the first week, not one person from her distant past had recognized her. Had her fears been unreasonable? Her concerns over being recognized seemed to diminish with each passing day, and as they slipped away, she wondered that she'd had them at all.

She was careful, however, taking time to look around while out in the open and to always know the names of the ladies they were visiting.

Ranulf asked her about it a few times.

"I don't want to miss anything," she'd answered evasively. "And I want to be prepared."

He never pushed, or challenged her, but he'd narrow his eyes thoughtfully until she'd change the subject to something frivolous.

Apart from going out, days at Abraham House also took on a pattern.

First thing in the morning, Beatrice and Edith took tea together in the morning room. Ranulf, who was residing at his own Townhouse, usually showed up just as they were finishing and looking the perfect amount of disheveled from having gone riding in the park. The exercise made his eyes shine and put a healthy color in his face. Beatrice appreciated the style of his riding hat, the cut of his jacket, and the fit of his riding breeches—giving her a glimpse at another side of him—not the marquess, nor the detective, but the London gentleman about Town.

But her favorite time of the morning came, when, upon interrupting the breaking of their fast, he always made a point to touch Beatrice somehow—on her shoulder, her hand—and then he'd kiss her on the cheek.

They were all gestures meant to keep his sister convinced that theirs was a love match, but knowing he didn't mean them didn't keep Beatrice from savoring each one.

It was all for pretend, of course, and yet that morning, she again anticipated that moment—her heart racing while she conversed with Edith, surreptitiously flicking her gaze toward the door.

"Waiting for your beloved, I see," Edith teased, a happy gleam in her eyes.

Had Beatrice really been so obvious? "I didn't mean—I'm so sorry. I—" Her mouth turned dry at being caught behaving so rudely.

Edith covered Beatrice's hand with hers. "Don't be. I haven't seen my brother this happy in ages." Her eyes were warm and accepting.

Guilt landed on Beatrice like a thick blanket. Had she and Ranulf done too good a job of pretending?

"He'll be even happier if he wins this vote," Beatrice did her best to turn the subject to something else—anything else. "He certainly deserves it."

"He deserves the vote, yes, but he also deserves *love*." The comment had been an unusually familiar one from the viscountess, and it left a lump in Beatrice's throat.

Returning to her chamber to change into another of the new gowns that perpetually arrived from Edith's modiste, Beatrice tried dismissing the heaviness that had set in after the unexpected conversation.

Upon stepping into the luxurious chamber that she was becoming all too comfortable in, she found Dora waiting for her with a smile. "I've steamed the rose linen, if that's acceptable?" The gown hung on the tall wardrobe.

"It's perfect."

*This isn't real*

Soon enough, it would all go away and she'd once again share the small room with the newly hired teachers. She'd clean her own clothing and spend her days chasing after her students.

The staff at Abraham house truly were spoiling their guests. Daisy was going to have to adjust her thinking as well.

"I think a middle parting, for under your bonnet," Dora suggested as she unpinned the simple knot Beatrice wore for breaking her fast.

"That sounds perfectly lovely." Beatrice caught sight of herself in the looking glass.

She'd worry about tomorrow... tomorrow. As for today, she allowed the efficient lady's maid style her hair and then assist her into the fashionable frock.

And after, Beatrice dabbed a few drops of perfume on her wrists and behind her ears.

The decorative bottle had just been delivered—a gift from Ranulf. She sniffed her wrist and smiled. The scent was familiar in that it had lavender tones, but also something sweet.

It reminded her of sparkling nights, beautiful gowns and... romantic walks through a torch-lit garden. Wearing it made her feel... Beautiful.

She stilled, frowning.

Playing the part of Ranulf's fiancée was becoming complicated. More than complicated...

Dangerous?

"The duchess's carriage just drew up." Daisy peered through the door that adjoined their rooms. The plan for today was to visit a few shops on Bond Street, and later indulge in ices at Gunter's. This wouldn't be the first time

Daisy gushed at her luck upon being chosen as Beatrice's chaperone. "Be sure to bring your umbrella," she called, frowning. "I thought we were going to get some sunshine today, but clouds are already gathering."

This is England, her father used to always say. Sunshine never stays, it only makes the occasional visit.

Beatrice shivered. Happiness was the same. And for her, it would soon have to make its departure.

Shaking off her maudlin thoughts, she turned and smoothed her gown.

All of this would be over in less than a week—mulling over inappropriate romantic feelings, over impossible longings, would accomplish nothing. Likely, all these unfamiliar emotions were as fake as their betrothal itself. They were a product of the unique luxury of this experience.

*That is all.*

It would have been helpful if she believed herself.

She slipped into her shoes. "Let's go downstairs, then, shall we?"

~

LATE, the following afternoon, Ranulf kept his gaze on her the entire time she descended the staircase to join him.

Alone.

"But you are alone? Where is Miss Pepperspring today?"

When he did this, Beatrice imagined he could see into her thoughts.

"She caught the sniffles from the rain yesterday. Nothing serious, but your sister and I thought it best she not attempt anything strenuous until she's recovered."

"And riding with me would be strenuous?" he cocked one brow.

Beatrice liked when he was in one of his teasing moods —so often, the demands of his ambitions required he be serious.

"For some of us," Beatrice shot back at him. "You do keep me on my toes."

Taking her wrap from the butler, Ranulf dropped the lacy mint shawl around her shoulders.

"Is it cold today?" She'd kept herself busy writing letters that morning, to Primm, who had written to tell her that there had been no incidents since their departure, and of course, to her brother. As she'd lapsed in her correspondence, Jasper would be wondering what had become of her. His time in school, nearly ten years, had felt like forever, but now that he was close to finishing, her heart squeezed.

He was becoming a young man and at some point, he was going to want to take his rightful place in life. But how were they going to prove his identity?

"A breeze." Ranulf watched her curiously. "Autumn is definitely in the air."

Which meant school would soon be in session.

Ranulf had asked her the night before if she'd like to go driving through the park. With only three days until the vote, both of them had agreed on a quiet afternoon.

Without Daisy, and with no maids available to act as chaperone, Beatrice ought to have cancelled the outing.

Her most gracious betrothed offered his arm and led her outside.

"You're worrying." Ranulf addressed her casually as he assisted her onto the tall vehicle.

"It's nothing," she said. But it was times like this that she wished she could tell him everything. "Have you been sleeping better?" she asked instead. The circles under his eyes were nearly non-existent now.

Swinging himself onto the bench seat beside her, he shot her a knowing glance. He was not so obtuse as to not recognize her change of subject.

"Better." His answer both surprised and pleased her. With Daisy usually listening in, it wasn't often they could speak of such personal matters.

Not until after he'd flicked the reins, turning the matched team onto the road, did he elaborate on his answer.

"The memory is most vivid around our anniversary." He grimaced. "Which was last month."

*When they'd all but trapped him at the school.*

"It's as though my body knows the date even if I try not to acknowledge it."

"You have nightmares?" His widowed state was publicly known, of course, but not once had she heard anyone speak of the circumstances that had widowed him. He most certainly had not.

"If I don't sleep, I don't have them," he said. "It comes in cycles, the sleepless nights."

They drove quietly, the rhythm of the horses' feet hitting the pavement sounding louder than usual, until Beatrice braved the question. "What happened?"

All she knew was what Primm had told her. But what did he go through? Would he be haunted forever?

Ranulf must have loved her very much, to have decided not to marry again.

From earlier conversations, she'd learned that he intended to leave the estate and title to the oldest of his brothers, Lord Frederick, who had two grown sons himself. There was no lack of males to inherit in the family.

*Susan.* Even her name sounded lovely.

"The story isn't a happy one," he said.

"You needn't tell me if you don't want to but… I want to know you better. And if it's a part of you, I'd like to know."

She had no real claim to know the details surrounding his past. He would not be out of line to tell her it was none of her business.

He exhaled.

"We met at the first ball of the Season. I was well aware of my family's expectations—to marry, to set up a nursery. And I was perfectly happy to fulfill my duties." His smile was grim. "Believe it or not, I've never had any aspirations for rakedom."

*Rakedom.*

Beatrice smiled at such a notion. Because the more time she spent in his company, seeing him with his family, amongst colleagues, not to mention his dedication to accomplishing something truly significant for his country, her respect for his character had grown. Aside from a few sarcastic comments, and the occasional snarl while frustrated, Ranulf Winters, the Marquess of Sexton, was generally, a good man—a very good man.

Even if he did have a few grumpy moments.

But he'd since apologized for his treatment of her that day at Hardwood Cliffhouse, and strangely enough, Beatrice found a peculiar sort of satisfaction in bantering with him when he suffered one of his less than delightful moods.

"You married that summer?" she prompted. He'd already told her as much.

He nodded. "And we were content, dare I say happy?" It was as though he was asking her permission.

"Of course," she answered.

"For the first year. We did what was expected. Attended family functions, participated in the season. But not everything worked out as expected." He swallowed hard. "We lost our first child at the end of her third month. Two more unsuccessful pregnancies took their toll on her, and on… us."

Beatrice's brow creased in sympathy. "How could it not have?"

"I felt terrible, putting her through the pain and disappointment, and she'd decided she had failed me."

"But you loved one another," Beatrice pointed out. She could hear it in his voice.

"We did. But after that, it wasn't the same. The romance of that first year was gone. We loved one another, but we were no longer… in love. We were… friends. And that's how I'd describe the remainder of our marriage. If I'd tried harder, If I'd been more attentive, I can't help but wonder…"

This was the ugly part. Beatrice braced herself.

"I should have been there to prevent the attack. So damn senseless. To this day, he's free."

"He?"

"The criminal who killed her—for two pounds. She had a measly two pounds in her reticule. According to her gentleman companion at the time, she screamed. That was when the thief sliced her throat." His voice broke, going rough at the end. "My apologies, Beatrice. This isn't fit conversation…"

"But I asked." She had turned and was gripping his forearm with both of her hands. "I'm so sorry, Ranulf." She could tell him it wasn't his fault. Or that there was nothing he could do. But she, of all people, understood the power of such emotions. How many times had she wondered, *what if*?

Of course he would have nightmares.

"You must miss her dreadfully," she offered instead.

"That's the devil of it, Beatrice." He'd gone back to his growly self again. "I do, but not dreadfully. Every time someone has offered me their condolences, I've felt like a fraud." He brushed a hand across his eyes. "I miss her—I miss the woman she'd been when we first married—and my friend. But I ought to feel more..."

His admission was a rather startling one.

"No one is perfect." It was the most real sentiment she could offer. "You cannot make yourself feel something that isn't there."

Seated beside him, Beatrice physically felt the cloak of self-loathing he'd donned.

How had he been able to trust her with something so private?

Inside, she wished she could tell him her own secret. She trusted him, but chances were, he wouldn't believe her.

Not one person had believed her before. And without a shred of evidence, it was her word against her aunt and uncle's...

"What happens in the dreams?" she asked him, stuffing down the urge to share her burden.

His laugh was short and ironic. "I'm running. Chasing someone without a face. And I've never caught him." He turned the horses into the park. "If I do sleep, I wake up exhausted."

"But you are sleeping better these days?" she confirmed.

"I am." He stiffened his shoulders. "Enough of my problems. Tell me what you've been up to. I hear Bedwell's duchess and Lady Chaswick have been showing you and Miss Pepperspring all the sights. Where did the four of you get off to yesterday?"

A little shaken from his confession, Beatrice put off musing over them until later.

"There were seven of us, mind you, including all our chaperones and whatnot," she answered, quite willing to lighten the conversation. "Nine if you count Collette's dogs."

She felt him relax beside her as she regaled him with the various visits they'd made and then the unfortunate storm she and Daisy had gotten caught in halfway between Lady Chaswick's townhouse and his sister's.

"But you are well?"

"I'm fine," she insisted. His affection might be feigned, but she never doubted that he'd protect her.

"And you are enjoying yourself."

"I did not think I would," she confessed. "But yes, I am. Although…" Beatrice cut herself off before she admitted to more than she ought.

"Although…"

"You are too easy to talk to."

Rather than press her, he pulled the horses to a stop. "Shall we walk?" The groom who'd been riding behind them was already rushing around to attend to the matched pair.

"Yes," she exhaled. It would mean he wouldn't have to focus on driving. After assisting her onto the ground, she took his arm, feeling like it was the most natural thing in the world.

Feeling like he was hers.

"Have you seen the folly in the woods?" he asked.

"I have and it's one of my favorite spots." She answered without thinking. Her mother had taken her there.

*Before.*

"I think your feelings are perfectly normal." She spoke quickly before he could ask when she'd been there. "And you are not a fraud. You are a widow, and you've suffered for her. In your own way."

He had told her something very personal. Entering the thickly wooded path, she felt close to him.

Too close, perhaps. Because the extent of her trust made her feel jumpy, anxious. She'd spent close to a decade trusting no one.

"Tell me about your childhood." He understandably changed the subject again. "Where did you grow up?"

"Near a small village called Briarville." It was the name she'd given Miss Primm and anyone else who'd ever asked—a village as make-believe as this betrothal.

He frowned. "I've never heard of it. Where is it?"

"North-west of Plymouth. It's a *very small* village," she emphasized. "If you blink while driving through, you'll miss it."

And then she swallowed her guilt.

He'd told her one of his deepest secrets, and for her and Jasper's safety, she couldn't even tell him her real name.

# SECRETS

She was lying.

She'd evaded him before but as he persisted, it was becoming more and more difficult for her to avoid his questions.

He had been patient. By God, he'd damn near been crying on her shoulder earlier. What the devil was she hiding?

By now, thick forest surrounded them, leaves, and trees as thick as the wall she'd built around her past. Early on in their acquaintance, he'd realized she was hiding something from him. It hadn't bothered him then.

But it did now.

Why?

He was tempted to avoid the answer to his own question, but it was too late for that. It mattered because he was getting ideas—ideas that involved knowing this woman—knowing both the insignificant details but also the significant ones.

Like who the hell she was—who her people were.

Not that her answers could change his feelings…

Dear God, he had feelings of all things!

But he needed to know her simply because…

He wanted to.

"You must have family somewhere," he would be stubborn today.

She picked her way over a root and then answered softly, so softly that the wind whipped her words away.

"What?" he leaned down.

"I have a brother," she breathed. By God, one would have thought she'd just confessed to murder.

"Younger? Older?" He spoke in a casual tone.

She cleared her throat. "Younger." Thunder punctuated her answer, quickly followed by a flash of lightning. He cursed himself for not noticing the clouds moving in and grasped her hand.

"Let's get to the folly before we get soaked." He walked faster at first, and when a few drops of rain landed on them, they both broke into a run.

They were only partially soaked, but quite out of breath, by the time they ducked into the shelter of the folly.

"I haven't been here in years," he admitted. Thick vines had curled up the columns, run the length of the roof, and then dangled halfway to the floor.

Beatrice walked toward one of the railings, folded her arms on it and stared out at what had turned into a violent storm. The overhanging eaves and direction of the wind was all that kept her from being doused.

Beatrice was taller than most women, and she was not frail.

And yet in that moment, she'd never looked more vulnerable.

She'd told him she had a younger brother but denied the existence of any parents. Where was this brother?

But pushing didn't work with this woman. He crossed to where she stood and curled his arms around her from behind.

"Do you think we'll have to swim back to the townhouse?" He nudged the side of her neck with his chin.

She chuckled softly, turning her head. "I hope not, as I never learned to swim."

"Surely not!" Ranulf exaggerated his shock.

"The students at the school are all required to learn. Primm tried taking me out, but when I persisted in sinking to the bottom of the pond, she decided I was a lost cause, of which, I was happy to agree."

"So, in the case we're surrounded by a lake, I'll have to locate a rowboat to get you to safety."

This time her laugh came out more genuine. "I'm not keen on those, but I suppose with you at the helm, I'm willing to risk it."

"Because you trust me," Ranulf said the words unceremoniously, knowing they held far more meaning than the present discussion would imply.

She spun around in his arms and took his hands. In her eyes he saw… torment.

"I do trust you, Ranulf," she squeezed his hands. "And I want—I want to tell you everything. But I can't. I…"

She closed her eyes.

"I can't." She began to shiver—not from the cold.

"What *can* you tell me?" He resisted the desire to tuck her head under his chin and comfort her because his instincts stood on high alert. "Are you in danger?" She'd never given him reason to believe that she was, aside from the situation at the school, and yet since they'd been in London, she'd been evasive.

And on more than one occasion, he'd caught her searching their surroundings, looking over her shoulder with a fearful look in her eyes.

She shook her head. "It isn't me. Well, it isn't only me." And then her eyes turned apologetic, pleading, and adoring at the same time. "I want to, but I can't. This was all a mistake. I'm so sorry, Ranulf. I'm so very sorry. I don't want to ruin everything for you." She shook her head, her eyes nearly as wild as the storm.

And when she tried to put distance between them, Ranulf kept hold of her hands. "You said you trusted me," he reminded her. "Is there anything at all that you can tell me?"

Something in his voice seemed to calm her and he watched as her breaths became more even. And waiting, he moved his thumbs over the backs of her hands, drawing small circles.

She stared up at him as though she'd been hypnotized. "I don't know," she said.

"How old is your brother?" he asked.

"Eight and ten."

"Is he safe?" he asked.

She nodded. "He's nearly finished his schooling." The very tentative smile she sent him was a proud one. If he were to guess correctly, the brother and sister were one another's only family.

He understood the notion of protection all too well. Was she only protecting the brother, or was she protecting both of them?

Ranulf made mental notes of things he could look into, and then moved his hands up her arms.

"But that's all I can tell you. I shouldn't have even..." she was shaking her head again, that panicked expression returning to her eyes again.

So he did the only thing he knew that would make her feel better,

He tilted her chin back and kissed the panic away.

# SWEET BEE

The rain outside the folly fell hard, in fact, the thrumming was even louder than the thunder.

But it wasn't as loud as the roaring in Beatrice's thoughts. Had she told him too much?

*This is not real...* She did her best to convince herself even as she returned his kiss with abandon. His taste, which quieted her fears, brought her needs to life.

"My Sweet Bee." She barely heard his voice over the storm. His endearment sounded sincere—more than sincere.

Their betrothal might be make-believe but this was not. Emotions, needs, urges as powerful as these could not be feigned.

Could they?

She would have imagined herself exercising at least some restraint under such circumstances, knowing her relationship would soon come to an abrupt end because everything good had an ending.

Even her time at Miss Primm's looked as though it

might soon be over.

When it came down to what a person wanted and what they needed, choice didn't always come into play.

Today, Beatrice not only wanted Ranulf, but she needed him. And he was right here, holding her against the length of his body, kissing her furiously.

He pressed her back into one of the columns without breaking their kiss.

The position left her with no escape. It also increased the friction between their mouths, their thighs, their hips.

"You're terribly sweet." He slid one hand up between them, covering her breast. "For a woman who doesn't like sugar." He laughed softly against her skin.

In the past, Beatrice had considered breasts to be something of a nuisance.

But hers were suddenly the most sensitive part of her body.

Ranulf rubbed his hand over one, cupping it in his palm and giving it the perfect squeeze. So good.

How could he make her feel so good?

He moved his other hand from her neck, and lowered it to tug on her bodice. The cut of this particular fashion offered little resistance.

Nor did she.

And the cool wind swirling over her newly exposed skin only fanned the fire of her need.

"I shouldn't," he groaned.

"Oh, but you should." Beatrice skimmed her hands up the back of his neck and drew his face back down.

Because she wanted more of him. She wanted his mouth on her.

He bent his knees and replaced his hand with his mouth.

His hands gripped the sides of her ribs while he suckled her like a man starved.

"Perfection, you're perfection." His voice rumbled around her breast, vibrating straight to her core.

He lifted her and she instinctively tightened her legs around his waist. She'd experienced the sensation of his member, straining against her before, but never like this.

Poised at her core—hot and throbbing, and so deliciously hard.

The thunder outside cracked, and groaned, but it was nothing compared to the storm raging between the two of them.

She'd been forced to sacrifice a good deal in life, deny herself regularly, of silly things, but also significant experiences. And she'd done so without wavering—for Jasper.

Because her brother was all she'd had left.

And yet…

She'd never wanted anything as badly as she wanted this —as badly as she wanted Ranulf.

It was too… predestined. She would not deny herself this experience. She *could* not deny herself this experience.

In their haste, his falls required both of them to unfasten, and the moment they slipped open, she reached in and grabbed his hot, hard, velvety length.

He covered her hand with his, and placed himself at her entrance.

"Are you sure? My Sweet Beatrice," he breathed her name, sliding himself along her seam.

"Yes, please." His touching her so intimately was slowly driving her mad. She was wet from her own desire, but she didn't care. She had no inhibitions. She had no doubts.

"Inside. I want you inside." She wiggled her hips in

encouragement.

And then he was there, stretching her and filling her.

"You're so tight," he halted. Beatrice glanced down and realized he was only halfway seated.

It hurt a little, but in an oddly, foreign and satisfying way. She lifted her gaze to his eyes, which were darkly possessive.

"Take more," she said.

His gaze locked with hers, Ranulf shifted his hips and slid deeper inside.

Beatrice moaned.

Joining with him was like newfound treasure. It shifted her entire perspective of the world.

She gripped his hips, drawing him in deeper.

Ranulf groaned.

She would have given her life for him in that moment.

He withdrew but before she could complain, thrust inside again. Harder this time. And again. Beatrice clung to him, taking and giving. Making love was its own dance, a celebration of man and woman possessed by a singly unique rhythm.

Sharp anticipation hijacked her entire being. She expected...

She reached.

And even as she embraced the unknown, Ranulf's movements hastened and Beatrice wondered at the joy of being conquered.

And she wasn't sure if the lightening came from the sky or behind her own eyes, but her insides lit up as if struck, and all her sensations tumbled together in the most painfully glorious joy.

"Beatrice," Ranulf huffed. "I'm—." But then he took her

with two last short, but violent thrusts. His body stiffened and she felt an almost ethereal heat inside.

His seed.

In this moment, they were not two separate people, but one complex and magnificent being.

Neither spoke, the sounds of their breathing crowding out the rain outside. Had natures storm subsided as well?

It was the return of sensation in her back, against the wall, that reminded her of where they were. He'd pinned her against a column, holding her weight with his hands and his legs.

She'd been engulfed in this most remarkable act and he'd been holding her weight up.

"How is it that you didn't drop me?" she asked, and he made a sound that was half chuckle, half groan.

"Can you stand?" he shifted his feet, keeping one hand on the wall, the other on her thigh.

He was still inside of her.

"I think so." If her legs hadn't turned completely to jelly.

He moved slowly, sliding out from between her thighs at the same time he lowered her to stand. And with the sensations of the climax ebbing away, her brain began to function again.

Not that it had not been functioning, while…

But other parts of it came back to life.

How had they gotten to this point? She smoothed her skirt down with shaking hands, aware that he was putting himself back together as well.

"I'm afraid Miss Primm's contract is shot to hell by now." Language she wouldn't normally use but she wasn't feeling her normal self. "This," she exhaled. "Was not part of our agreement."

# I LIKE YOU TOO

Their make-believe betrothal had suddenly become all too real, but Ranulf kept quiet. In being wholly honest with himself, he'd wanted her since the day he'd walked into that damn crime scene. She'd scowled at him, defended the school and her colleagues, and somehow weaseled herself between the cracks of his cynicism.

But Beatrice, who was twitching and pacing, trying to make sense of what they'd just done—and apparently not coming up with any good reasons—hadn't even told him her real name yet.

It would eventually be Winters, with the title of marchioness, but he'd have to hold off on that declaration.

"Are you all right?" he asked. A crumbling building in the park wasn't the most romantic place to consummate a relationship, but considering his past experience, it had damn well been the best.

"All right?" She looked at him as though he was speaking a foreign language.

He stepped closer and gathered her pliant form into his arms. “It was your first, was it not? Some women experience pain…” he explained.

“I’m all right. But what does this mean?” she asked, tilting her head back as she did so. “It’s all still make-believe, isn’t it? We aren’t like regular people. No one has to know…”

“No one has to know.” That was the understatement of the century. He touched his fingertips to her chin. “But are you sure? It felt real to me.”

“It was… I know.” But she looked pained.

“You’ve conquered me, Beatrice.” He wasn’t sure what else to say. He’d been firmly convinced he’d never marry again, and now… He wasn’t sure he could live without the little minx.

“I like you too,” she said. “But nothing’s changed.”

Of that, she couldn’t be more wrong. Because even as she was trying to ignore his declaration of affection, she’d melted against him again, and her mouth had gone all soft, her eyes tender.

It didn’t make sense. Why would she resist this?

And then he knew.

Her determination not to marry had something to do with her secret.

A ray of sunlight slanted onto the floor. How long had they been in here? An hour? More?

He’d acted irresponsibly in every aspect of this afternoon’s outing. He’d made love to her—against a stone column, and when he’d gone to withdraw, realized it was impossible without dropping her.

He’d had her away, alone, for far too long. And to make

matters worse, God only knew where his groom had taken the horses and his vehicle.

But she'd told him she *liked him.*

And he was going to discover what she was hiding. Whatever it was, he'd fix it for her. He might have failed Susan, but he was being given a second chance.

He would discover whatever was plaguing Beatrice and make it go away. The challenge was too delicious to resist.

And the prize…

Priceless.

He'd never been more determined as he offered his arm and led her away from the gazebo.

This trip to London was proving better than he ever could have imagined. He'd win the vote, first, and then…

He'd win the girl.

"WHAT DID you say the name of that village was?" Mr. Stork, Ranulf's assistant at the society, scowled as he held a pencil poised above his small notebook.

"Briarville, supposedly northwest of Plymouth." Ranulf glanced up from the file in his hands. With only a few more nights before the vote, Ranulf didn't have time for this—he should be lobbying his case.

And yet, by this point, he was ninety-nine percent sure every single board member had already made up their mind.

A stubborn marquess on the board who had earned himself the nickname, "The Turtle," and a few of his cronies, were the only hold outs. If Ranulf hadn't changed their opinions by now, he doubted another dinner party would make any difference.

And despite their staunch positions, Ranulf was feeling rather confident.

He felt less so, however, where his make-believe fiancée was concerned. It was as though she'd lived with her secret for so long, it had become a part of her—like a disease. And like any malicious ailment, it was eating her up from the inside.

It was his job to find out what it was.

The more he pondered her evasiveness, the more unsettled it made him. He was missing something—something that might be right in front of him.

And so he would send Stork out to make inquiries. He'd trust the case to this man the same as he'd trust him with his own life.

He would follow up on the evidence he had which, admittedly, wasn't much. And he'd see what else he could find in the meantime.

"Walcott, I presume, is an alias?" his aid asked.

"I'm certain of it. We're looking for a brother and sister, both of whom would have gone missing around 1822. The sister would have been close to twenty, the brother... about ten years her junior," he guessed.

People who went into hiding, went by aliases, but those were often some versions of their real name. Stork knew to take that into account during the information gathering process, using a number of variations and rearrangements of each part of the name in his search. Beatrice Clementine Walcott, for instance, offered numerous possibilities. But cross that with the names of young women who'd gone missing from somewhere around Plymouth with a brother ten years her junior, and it limited their search considerably.

Beatrice had admitted her brother was graduating soon. With only a teacher's salary to draw on, she'd likely sent him to one of the cheaper schools.

And yet... She'd seemed inordinately proud. "Check the more prestigious schools first. Send Smithy up to Oxford and you can stop in at Eton. If you both come up empty, check the cheaper schools—everything between Warwick Crossings and Land's End."

By the time Stork took his leave, Ranulf, although pleased to have initiated the investigation, didn't experience the satisfaction he usually did.

Because this was about *Beatrice*. She'd been unusually quiet on the drive back to Abraham House, and although he'd wanted to discuss their circumstances, he'd decided to give her time. Time to realize that whatever this was between the two of them was real.

Time to decide she could trust him with her secrets.

Glancing at his fob watch, he frowned. That had been eight hours ago.

Was eight hours enough?

It was too late to go to her. Edith would box his ears rather than allow him to see his betrothed at such an inappropriate time.

Sleep would likely elude him tonight—not for the usual reasons but because he felt he was close to something important. Not only with the case, but in his life.

With Beatrice?

And good God, the vote! He still had time to try to get a few hours of sleep in—if he could manage to fall asleep at all, that is. He had no choice if he wanted to keep himself sharp.

So, after arriving back at his town house and sending his clothing off with his valet, he snuffed out the tapers and climbed onto his massive bed.

But rather than lie awake restlessly, his limbs felt heavy and relaxed. In no time at all, he fell asleep.

Which he would have been much happier about if he didn't once again find himself chasing an all too familiar villain. But he wasn't chasing the man who'd killed Susan, he was chasing someone else.

Someone who'd harmed Beatrice.

And this time, he caught the man—he was faceless, but finally in custody.

And then, for the first time in what felt like years. Ranulf experienced something he'd yearned for far too long.

Several hours of dreamless sleep.

## NOTHING HAS CHANGED

It was Beatrice who lay awake instead, torn between the necessity of keeping her past a secret and telling Ranulf everything. She trusted him because he was a good man. But in being a good and honorable man, a man who valued justice and the law, she'd be putting him in a position where he'd have no choice but to ruin everything.

She rolled over for the umpteenth time and punched her pillow.

The trouble was, she did trust him. She trusted him enough to believe in her.

The closer they became, the more she liked him, and the more she liked him, the closer she came to putting both herself and Jasper in danger.

Danger she'd spent the last ten years avoiding.

"*You've conquered me.*" His words echoed from her head to her heart and back.

She'd tried to make light of it. After the most earthshattering experience of her life, she'd told him that she *liked* him.

And then insisted nothing had changed.

His expression lent her to believe he disagreed, but he hadn't argued. Had she wanted him to argue? It would have given her an excuse to be angry with him—to march off alone and possibly even make arrangements to leave London sooner.

But she'd made a promise.

And the vote was nearly upon them

And…

She *more than* liked him. In fact, she wanted to spend as much time as possible with him before all of this was over.

Regardless of what he wanted, she was caught in her own trap.

She'd been living under an assumed name, but she was also the very worst kind of person he could associate with. An outlaw.

She knew she was innocent, her brother knew she was innocent, but unfortunately, the only other two people in the world who knew she was innocent would do anything they could to prove the opposite.

She hadn't a shred of evidence to prove otherwise.

So all of this… the rides through the park, their bantering, his morning brushes of affection and being one half of a couple.

Not to mention the kissing, and the…

Making love.

All of it would come to an end.

Beatrice covered her ears with both hands. She'd told him about Jasper! No details, not even his name, but she needed to be more careful in the future.

In the early hours of morning, feeling guilty but resolved, she finally fell into a restless sleep.

Even so, those few hours fell far short of a good night's rest. So when Dora brought in her tea shortly after dawn and drew open the heavy drapes, Beatrice snapped at the unsuspecting lady's maid. "Go away. And close the curtains before you do." She threw an arm over her eyes to keep out the bright light of morning.

"I-I'm sorry," Dora stuttered helplessly, obviously caught off guard. "What shall I tell her ladyship?"

Because Edith would, of course, be expecting her to join her in the breaking of their fast.

"Tell her I didn't sleep well, and that I'm sorry," Beatrice grumbled. She felt truly horrendous, her entire body weighed down by exhaustion, her head seemingly stuffed with wool. But as Beatrice pushed herself to sit up, and while Dora drew the curtains closed again, the memory of that unfortunate afternoon at Hardwood Cliffhouse came to mind—and how being on the wrong end of Ranulf's frustrations had made her feel.

"I'm sorry, Dora," she called out before Dora could close the door behind her. "I slept rather poorly last night, but I shouldn't have taken it out on you. Forgive me?"

The normally cheerful maid peered back in, a sympathetic smile on her mouth. "There's nothing to forgive, miss. Everyone has a bad day now and again, even future marchionesses."

She closed the door and Beatrice lay down on her back, staring up at the ornately detailed ceiling above her bed.

What if she did tell him?

An unrecognizable tangle of feelings engulfed her. She'd told him nothing had changed, but she was wrong.

Something had shifted between them.

When Ranulf thrust himself inside of her, he'd looked fierce. She thought of how he kissed her cheek each morning—how he had shielded her from the crush of crowds whenever they were out in public.

He would never do anything to hurt her. In fact…

He just might be able to help her.

~

HAVING MISSED her breakfast with Edith, Beatrice also missed seeing Ranulf that morning. And absent his usual morning greeting, she could only blame herself for the resulting disappointment.

For this empty feeling.

He was right. What they'd done yesterday had changed everything. Beatrice only wished she understood what that change meant.

But was it only the break in routine that unsettled her? She trusted Ranulf, but she didn't trust her own luck.

Perhaps she should speak with him when she saw him later tonight. They had not one, but two events he'd promised to attend that evening.

Beatrice had known of the busy night and forgone making plans for that afternoon. She'd planned a quiet day for herself.

Quiet that she desperately needed.

And although Beatrice wrestled with the choices she faced, she found some measure of contentment strolling through Edith's magnificent gardens. She drew strength from spending time alone, from thinking, and from appreciating that she could find peace in her own company.

When Dora arrived to dress her for the evening, Beatrice had made her decision.

She was going to tell him everything.

But only after the vote—when the make-believe betrothal was set to end.

He'd told her *she conquered him.* She thought she knew what he'd meant when he said it.

She could only hope that, when she laid her heart bare and gave him the power to destroy her, she would find that she was right.

# THE TURTLE

Ranulf didn't know what to expect when he arrived to collect Beatrice that evening. She'd not been at breakfast that morning, but neither had she sent him a note informing him that she wished to call off their agreement and return to Miss Primm's.

So when he stood in the foyer of his sister and her husband's home, he suffered something most unusual.

Nervousness.

Which made him jump when her voice carried down the stairs.

"Good evening, my lord." She stood on the landing above him looking like a queen. Her smile immediately chased the tension away—replacing it with an odd combination of affection, pride, and…

Yes, lust.

Even if her gown didn't hint at the slim curves hidden beneath it, he knew…

He knew what she tasted like, how her breasts didn't quite fill his hands, and that she fit perfectly against him.

He knew what it felt like to be inside of her, and damned if he didn't ache for more.

"Good evening, Beatrice." He intentionally didn't call her Miss Walcott. Stork had been busy and Ranulf had received intriguing information via messenger. It might lead him to a dead end, but then again...

Ranulf took her hand as she arrived before him. She didn't blush when she held his gaze as he'd half expected, nor did she glance away.

Everything had changed, and he could hardly wait to make it official.

But this particular challenge, perhaps more than any other he'd ever faced, was going to require a light hand.

And, most unfortunately, a good deal of patience.

He'd feel more confident if he thought he had more time, but he'd do what he could with what he had.

"Dinner at Bedwell Manor," she said. "And then the fundraiser at the museum."

"You look more than up to the task." Ranulf tucked her hand in the crook of his arm. Before he could say another word, Edith appeared at the stop of the steps with Charles, the Viscount of Abraham, at her side.

"Getting down to the wire, old man," Charles commented as he escorted his wife down to join them. "You've brought your carriage?"

Ranulf nodded.

They'd agreed ahead of time to travel in Ranulf's coach, which was larger and more impressive than his brother-in-law's. Whether one liked it or not, these were the things that mattered in society. And if they mattered in society, they most certainly mattered to the board members.

Charles and Edith went ahead, and Ranulf followed, Beatrice at his side.

They'd come to London with the intent that the vote would signify the end of their relationship. Afterward, they would drop the façade and he would escort her back to the school, where he'd solve Miss Primm's case. This second part of the agreement was a promise he intended to keep. The first part on the other hand… Well.

The purpose of the charade had been to convince others he'd found his new marchioness. Trouble was, he'd damn well convinced himself.

He'd wager that she, too, was convinced.

Which meant the vote signified the ending of the charade, not the end of the two of them. It would signify the beginning of something else.

Something bigger. And when they moved forward, there would be no more make-believe.

He hoped anyway. Because where women were concerned, a man could never be one-hundred percent confident.

~

HAVING DECIDED she would tell him, Beatrice felt as if a weight had been lifted from her mind—for the most part. A persistent prickling at the back of her neck refused to believe that revealing her secret was the right thing to do. She'd grown up in a happy home, considerably better off than most of the other children she'd known.

And she'd taken that for granted.

Was she a fool to take Ranulf's loyalty for granted? He'd not yet told her he loved her, and he'd mentioned nothing about making this betrothal a real one. When he'd declared that everything changed, had he only been referring to their physical relationship?

Was he considering making her his mistress?

Because he'd have no real reason to protect her if that was the case.

The coach pulled to a halt for the first event of the night, and Beatrice did her best to gather her composure.

With Ranulf at her side, she climbed the steps determined to make the most of their last evening of make-believe.

Ranulf, Beatrice, Edith, and her husband stepped into the grand foyer at Bedwell Manor, and Collette strode out of the drawing room to greet them. "The two of you look beautiful, as usual, this evening." She addressed both Edith and Beatrice.

Lord Abraham clutched his fist over his chest with a pained expression. "I'm devastated that you'd not include Sexton and me in your compliment," he joked.

"Ignore my brother-in-law, your grace." Smiling, Ranulf shook hands with the duke.

"Tomorrow at this time, you'll not only be a member on the board, you'll be at the head of it." Bedwell had good reason to be optimistic, but Beatrice noticed Ranulf's almost imperceptible grimace.

He was confident, but she knew he'd subdue it until after the vote.

With new arrivals sounding the knocker on the front door, Collette and the duke gestured for the four of them to enter the drawing room, which was warm and welcoming while still managing to maintain an understated elegance.

The newly married duchess had had the manor refurnished shortly after their wedding. She'd confided to Beatrice that the dowager, Bedford's mother, who had essentially been banished to the country—with good reason—had decorated the entire townhouse in cold marble, both floors and statues. What wasn't hard and gleaming had been a sterile white.

White walls, white fabrics, white…

Everything.

"One couldn't breathe for fear of breaking something," she'd told Beatrice the first time she and Daisy had visited.

Now though, with the changes the new duchess had made, the home was the perfect venue for the last of the political dinners.

Lord and Lady Chaswick, who had arrived before them and were already settled in the drawing room, rose to greet them. Turning to Beatrice in particular, the baroness lowered her voice. "Are you nervous?" she asked, her thumb tapping each of her fingers one by one, rhythmically. The habit had initially distracted Beatrice, but she barely noticed it at all by now.

Beatrice nodded. She had the utmost confidence that Ranulf would win the vote, and yet an undercurrent of nerves plagued her.

Conversation throughout dinner was lively, tingling with an expectant anticipation. Collette had limited it to only seven courses.

They didn't hurry, but lingered over dessert long enough that they didn't arrive at the Royal Academy fundraiser until a full hour later than the time indicated on the invitation. But that was all part of the plan. It allowed enough of a delay for their group to make a fashionably impressive entrance.

With such anticipation for the vote tomorrow, Ranulf drew the most attention of all of them. Beatrice, however, as Lord Sexton's betrothed, nearly attracted as much.

The first time she'd experienced the phenomenon in public, despite all her earlier training, she'd had to fight to maintain her composure. And although she was comfortable enough greeting people one by one, she would be happy to leave this particular aspect of their betrothal behind.

As luck would have it, by taking the time to study the various paintings, she had an excellent reason to excuse herself from at least a few of the conversations.

The groups that consisted of men, when they weren't commenting on one of the paintings, conversed mostly about politics, horses, and gambling, while the ladies discussed everything else… And *everyone* else.

Except for Edith, of course, who rarely allowed the subject to drift far from political concerns in London. Having become well-acquainted with Ranulf's sister by now, Beatrice understood why she'd chosen to dwell in London when every other lady retired to their country homes.

The featured artist was a gentleman she'd read about, and she had been delighted to have a chance to see his work, which was both controversial and applauded.

Moving about the room silently, she didn't need to feign interest as she stared at one of the larger paintings. Taking up an entire wall, the passionate image had been cordoned off with a velvet rope. Indeed, it was best studied from a distance.

*The Combat: Woman Pleading for the Vanquished,* depicted a woman pleading with one soldier to save the life of another. William Etty was known for the nudity he persisted in including in most of his work, so that wasn't what shocked her.

It was the raw emotion—the darkness of man.

A lump formed in her throat as she stared at it. The work represented war, but it also represented life—and hopelessness.

"Do you think she saved him?" Ranulf had come up behind her. Although he generally didn't allow too much distance to form between them at such events, moments alone with him were rare.

Beatrice shook her head. "I'd like to think so, but look at the soldier's face. He's intent on murder. Likely neither of them made it out alive."

Ranulf touched the side of her face with gentle fingertips. "Have you always been a pessimist?" His breath whispered near her ear.

She turned to him, confused by the question. "Not always."

His gaze flicked to her mouth, and then back to her eyes. "Everything will work out. Trust me?"

It was as though he could read her mind. As though he knew the decision she'd wrestled with all day.

How could she not trust this man?

Something sharp and hot pierced her heart. Surely, she'd not fallen in love with him.

"I'll try," she said. "I'm going to try." She didn't want to make promises she might not be able to keep.

But then Edith arrived to interrupt. "Ranulf, Lord Rothberg wishes to have a word with you." Rothberg was one of the last remaining holdouts, along with a few of the other holdovers from the previous generation. Ranulf essentially had no choice but to meet with the man.

"Work your magic," Beatrice whispered in Ranulf's ear.

But he didn't leave immediately. Instead he bent down to whisper words meant only for her. "When I'm through with him, I'd like to make magic with you, my love. After I've returned you to Abraham House, meet me in the garden, behind the fountain?"

Awareness warmed her skin and she shivered. Beatrice met his eyes and nodded. Because she *ached* for his touch again.

She ached for more than his touch.

And then he was swept away, leaving her heart racing almost as rapidly as her thoughts.

*My love?* This wasn't the first time. And he'd whispered it so she alone could hear.

She shivered.

Would he do more than kiss her again? Would she appear overly eager if she brought a blanket along?

The thought of her doing something so brazen was outrageous. Beatrice bit her lip to keep herself from chuckling at her own thoughts.

She might be wicked, but she wasn't about to be so obvious.

Edith, instead of accompanying her brother to speak with the stubborn old earl, had apparently decided to remain with Beatrice, gazing upon the large painting. Luckily, it seemed the woman hadn't noticed her near slip in composure.

Edith's brow furrowed. "Etty is a master, for certain, but one can't help but wonder if he isn't a little mad. Can you imagine, painting nudes, and then signing your name to them?"

Although an enlightened thinker, Edith was also a mother, so her opinion wasn't a surprising one.

"He is a genius," Beatrice said simply.

Edith turned her back to the painting, her gaze searching the room, already having dismissed the artwork. "He's so close," she remarked abruptly as her eyes finally fell upon her brother. "If Ranulf can secure Rothberg's support, he needn't worry about any opposition the marquess has brought together. I do wish he'd remained in the country though."

"Who? The Turtle?" Beatrice asked.

"Yes."

"I thought he was voting by proxy?"

Initially, Ranulf hadn't been overly concerned about this particular vote—one of the older members, a stubborn marquess whose full title Beatrice had never actually heard. Most of their circle referred to the man as "The Turtle."

"He arrived in town last week. It's rare for him and the marchioness to come to London on the off-season, but apparently he wants to vote in person."

Beatrice resisted the urge to twist around as the inkling of fear she'd been carrying around, for no practical reason, seemed to grow heavier. "Are they here?"

"They're standing with their backs to the painting of the nude woman climbing into bed." Beatrice followed Edith's gaze as it flicked across the room to the mentioned couple. "Lord and Lady Worthington."

Her blood ran cold, and Beatrice quickly turned away. This was what she had felt, the weight of her aunt and uncle's presence. Aunt Ursula and Uncle Titus—of course,

"The Turtle." Beatrice should have paid closer attention. A *marquess*, nicknamed after a cold-blooded vertebrate. She'd taken the nickname to mean only that he moved slowly in his politics, but there was even a physical resemblance.

They had held her parents' titles for ten years now—the Marquess and Marchioness of Worthington.

"Are you all right? You've just gone pale as a sheet. Beatrice?" Edith reached out and touched her arm. "Do you need something to drink?"

Beatrice blinked. The very last thing she could do was turn around. The last time she'd seen them, a decade ago, she'd been a grown woman. She'd changed, no doubt, but not so much that they'd fail to recognize her.

"I—" She stared at Edith. Ranulf's chances would be ruined if she was recognized. "I need to go back to Abraham House." She ducked her head and touched her hand to her head. "I feel ill." She could hardly explain the real reason she needed to escape.

"I'll find Ranulf."

"No." Beatrice stopped the other woman. If Ranulf came to her, he'd bring everyone's attention.

They'd see her. Would she be arrested?

"He mustn't be distracted this evening," Beatrice continued, perhaps a touch belatedly. "I'll have Ranulf's coachman deliver me home, and you can tell him later, when he's allowed a free moment."

"I'll come with you then." But Beatrice needed to be alone—she needed to make a plan. Even that second, she resisted the urge to cover her face and sprint from the room with every fiber in her being.

"I don't want to ruin your evening. And he might need

you," Beatrice pointed out. "I'll be fine; Daisy and Dora can take care of me."

She felt her aunt and uncle's evil presence behind her and couldn't wait a moment more. "I'll send the coach back, of course," she spoke as her feet began moving her closer to the door.

And yet, just before she slipped out, something compelled her to glance over her shoulder.

Neither sighted her, thank God. Her uncle looked older, his shoulders were stooped and he had more gray hair. *The Turtle*. How had she not realized?

Her aunt had hardly changed. She wore her hair high on her head, adorned with jewels and feathers, and rings glittered on her fingers as she emphasized some point with her typical dramatic gesticulations.

But the rings she wore were not Beatrice's mothers. Beatrice had seen to that.

Terrified, knowing that she risked being exposed if she remained even one second longer, she fled outside. A uniformed servant offered to locate Ranulf's coach, but Beatrice declined. She'd find him herself, fearful that her aunt or uncle might decide on an early exit and stumble upon her waiting outside.

She lifted her skirts and ran along the line of parked carriages, whose drivers sat waiting for their prominent—and some not-so prominent—passengers.

Even after she was safe in the carriage, she feared being discovered.

All this time, she'd imagined herself safe. But here they were, her own personal nightmares walking freely and openly amongst the ton in a way that she never could.

Attempting to, even under a false name, had been the height of foolishness.

Seated on the forward-facing bench in the luxurious vehicle, Beatrice raised her feet to the seat and hugged her knees to her chest.

## FITTING THE PIECES TOGETHER

"What do you mean, she left?" Ranulf had been searching for Beatrice for a quarter of an hour and, with each minute he'd been unable to locate her, he'd grown more and more worried.

"She said she wasn't feeling herself," Edith replied. "It seemed to come on suddenly, whatever it was. She seemed fine while we were talking, but then she just turned white as a sheet—perhaps something she ate…? But I'd never mention it to the Duchess. Anyway, your most understanding fiancée insisted you not be interrupted. No doubt, by now, she is safe at home, sleeping like a baby." Edith's words weren't quite enough to reassure him.

Beatrice hadn't seemed ill when he'd left her. In fact, she'd seemed even more alert and vibrant than usual. And she'd agreed to meet with him in the garden. He'd been looking forward to getting her alone tonight, and she hadn't even tried to hide her own anticipation.

He'd intended to reveal his feelings before the chaos that would come after the vote. Knowing his Sweet Bee, she'd insist on returning to the school the second the vote was finalized.

"You're certain she was ill?" he asked as his carriage rolled through the streets of Mayfair. Another thought occurred to him then. "Might it have been nerves?"

Edith's eyes rolled upward with a frown, contemplating. "I suppose it might have been. We'd been discussing some of the more... *difficult* board members you've had to deal with lately. Lord knows, The Turtle and his vile, backbiting wife are unpleasant enough as far as conversational material goes.

"But," she contended. "I have no way to know for certain. But the poor dear looked as though she was going to lose her dinner and, either way, the best thing she can do right now is get some rest." Edith made a most unladylike expression. "And don't get any ideas of looking in on her tonight. With the vote tomorrow, the last thing you need is one of my servants witnessing you leaving her chamber like a thief in the night."

Edith was right about that. Ranulf dipped his chin in a slow nod. And yet as he watched his sister and her husband enter their townhouse, the urge to follow them was powerful. It grew more urgent with each step they took toward the door, where their butler held it wide.

Beatrice was steps away. But if she was ill, he didn't want to wake her.

Ranulf leaned out the door of the carriage. "Send for me if she is still feeling unwell." He ran a hand through his hair. "Damnit, Edith, just send for me if she isn't sleeping peacefully."

"I promise." Edith shook her head. "Now, go get some sleep, brother. It would be best for you not to appear before the board looking as though you spent the night carousing."

Edith knew of his tendency to go running through the darkness when he couldn't sleep. If he did so that evening, it wouldn't be because of his past.

It would be because of his future.

Regardless, he leaned his elbows on his knees, bouncing his feet anxiously as his coachman drew the vehicle back into the empty streets. The hour had grown late.

What were the chances Beatrice would be waiting for him in the garden? Not great, if she'd indeed been ill. But Edith had said Beatrice had seemed perfectly fine until the conversation had moved to—

He jerked his spine upright. *Titus Wiltshire*—Lord Worthington—his estate was near Plymouth. The title wasn't one without controversy, even if it was an old one.

He pounded on the ceiling and his driver opened the small window between his box and the interior. "We're not going home yet, Peters," Ranulf said. "Take me to my offices."

"As you wish, my lord." His driver, accustomed to Ranulf's often unusual working hours, showed no surprise whatsoever.

This wasn't the first time he'd gone to the society's offices late at night, but it might be the most important.

Half an hour later, Ranulf slammed a fist onto his desk, making Stork jump. His assistant had most fortuitously been working late that night, and he'd been able to locate the files Ranulf required.

They'd been relatively easy to find because other information he'd uncovered had led them to that particular case already.

Ten years before, the Seventh Marquess of Worthington had grown tragically ill and died. His wife had followed shortly thereafter. It hadn't been the deaths that had been suspicious, however, but the events that had followed. Charges had been brought against the deceased's daughter, of kidnapping and theft.

The sister and her younger brother—the rightful heir—had disappeared two weeks following their mother's death. Lady Clementine Wiltshire had been eight and ten, and the rightful heir, ten years younger. The late Marchioness's jewelry had disappeared along with them.

The facts in the scenario matched up all too precisely with what he knew of Beatrice. And where investigations were concerned, Ranulf had long believed that there was no such thing as coincidence.

"The boy you told me about at Eton, Mr. Jasper Walcott, bring him to London at once. Tell him his sister needs him."

Stork eyed Ranulf in understanding but then cocked a brow. "You want him at the vote?"

"Bring him here first, but yes. And it's important to keep him out of sight." Ranulf normally collected scads more evidence before he'd attempt such a stunt as the one he had in mind, but with The Turtle in town, this might be the only opportunity he'd get to clear her.

Because it had to be done in public, and it had to be done just so.

Meanwhile, he needed to talk to Beatrice. More than anything, he needed her to trust him. He tugged at the back of his neck.

Because there was more to it than that.

More than anything, he just needed her. And to have her, he needed to save her first.

# IF ONLY

When Beatrice had first realized her aunt and uncle were in town, her instinct had been to run. Without Coachman John, however, she'd been willing to do anything to get away—if she couldn't procure a ticket on one of the mail coaches, she'd been willing even to escape on foot.

The image of herself marching along the road, carrying a small valise, vulnerable to the natural elements as well as the not-so-natural ones, brought her up short.

She hadn't only herself to think about. She had Daisy to consider, and Jasper's tuition to pay off.

Furthermore, she needed to fulfill her promise for the school's sake.

But most of all, the thought of betraying Ranulf, of not telling him goodbye—or worse, never seeing him again—was unbearable.

She would not attend the vote, of course, but she could speak with him after…

A party was scheduled. How long would it go on? She

could keep up her ruse that she was ill, hide in her chamber all day…

And then speak with him the day after, when his position with The King's Society was secured.

Deep inside, at the very core of her person, she trusted him.

He'd help her get away—he'd keep her secret.

She opened the window and inhaled the fragrant scent floating up from Edith's garden below. If everything had turned out differently tonight, she would be down there now.

With him.

Beatrice would not have brought a blanket along, but they would have managed somehow. Her soft chortle sounded heavy with irony.

He had suggested the assignation only a few hours ago, and yet it felt like a lifetime. What a different person she was now than she'd been when he'd whispered in her ear at the gallery. She'd been happy. Excited.

Hopeful.

And he'd seemed equally eager to have her alone. She'd felt it with every glance from him, with every touch. The pulsing energy between them—the attraction—overpowered everything else.

They would have found a private spot, under a tree, where the grass was cool and dry, where they could be alone. They would have discussed the evening. He would have shared his concerns and she would have reassured him. And then he would want to know her impressions.

But there would be more.

There would have been kissing, and closeness. He'd

stroke her leg, sliding his hand up to her thigh, and she'd feel his length grow against her belly.

Or would she take it in hand? Would she act even more boldly than she had before?

She would not be pacing the length of her chamber, contemplating her choices, aching, and feeling urges that wouldn't be met.

She would have been with the man who'd become her lover.

He had called her *my love.* It still seemed impossible. And yet wasn't he her love as well? If only her aunt and uncle had not decided to come to London…

*If only…* Two words that were far too familiar to her.

But it didn't matter. She'd known this time would come to an end, she simply hadn't expected it to happen so abruptly.

Beatrice turned her back to the window. She'd leave it open, allow the fragrant air to cool the room. And although sleep was going to be impossible, she climbed back onto the lovely bed.

She would have slid her hand between her legs, had she not heard thumping and rustling at the window she'd left open.

Beatrice froze.

A vase fell over, but luckily it landed on the rug instead of shattering against the hard wood floor. And then the curtain was very nearly torn off its hooks.

"Beatrice."

*Ranulf?*

He grunted, and she saw an arm and then a leg dangling inside—two familiar limbs which were very dear to her. "Give me a hand, will you? Before I kill myself."

Beatrice flew off the bed so quickly, she nearly toppled onto the floor before dashing over to assist him.

Leaves clung to his hair, and a thin crimson line slashed down one side of his face. He had climbed the trellis to get to her!

She doubted she'd ever been more astonished in her entire life. "What are you doing here? You could have killed yourself, you fool! You stupid, precious fool!" Her voice broke as she berated him even as he threw the rest of his weight into her room, landing on the floor with a thud.

"That looked easier than it actually was," he declared, almost more to himself than to her. "Anyhow!" He lifted his eyes to stare at her. Even in the moonlight, she noticed an excitement she hadn't seen on him before. "I thought I'd drop in and see how you were feeling."

Beatrice blinked. And then blinked again.

She then dropped to her knees, placed her hands on the sides of his face, and gave him what was likely the clumsiest kiss in all of history.

Because, for the last three hours, she'd faced the prospect of never seeing him again. And that… she conceded with all her heart, would be a travesty.

"Mrmph…" She parted her lips when he took control of the kiss. "Ranulf," she gasped when he turned his head, taking a breath. "You're here."

"So." He kissed her again with a chuckle. "You're feeling better then?"

He was here, on her floor, kissing her! Nothing had changed, and yet this had to mean something…

Didn't it?

But there was so much to talk about. She had so much to tell him. Doing her best to gather her composure, she tugged her gown back down to cover her legs and pushed against his shoulders.

"I wasn't sick," she admitted. "But I had to leave."

"Hold that thought. It's too damn dark in here, I can't even see you properly," he asserted, seemingly full of an unusual energy as he burst off the floor. "Where the devil's a flint?" He strode around the room, searching with only the moon for illumination.

"Hush." If he made too much noise, his sister would hear them, and everything would become even more complicated. "Right there." Beatrice pointed to the flint she'd used earlier and, within a few seconds, he'd ignited one of the candles.

With the flickering light now, she noticed that the vines outside had not only scratched his dear face but also torn his shirt to reveal the skin beneath it. A hint of dark hair showed on his chest, and it contrasted with his pale skin, looking inordinately masculine.

She'd never seen a more beautiful sight in her life.

"Why did you leave the exhibit, Beatrice?" He finally broke the pregnant silence between the two of them.

This was her moment. It was now or, perhaps, never.

"You might as well take a seat. I have a story to tell you. It's something I've not told anyone—not even Primm."

Only after he had seated himself in the tall-backed chair did she lower herself on the bed to face him.

She opened her mouth to speak, but then closed it again and shook her head. "I'm not sure where to start," she said.

"Tell me where you grew up," he suggested helpfully. "Because despite scouring the most detailed map of all of England, I've yet to come across a village near Plymouth with the name of Briarville."

"Yes," she nodded. "I mean, you are correct about that. Although I spent most of my childhood in that area, I actually grew up closer to Garden Cove—on my father's estate." She inhaled a shaky breath. "Rose Heights."

"Worthington's seat."

Her eyes flashed up at him. She should not have been surprised that he knew that. He was a learned man. And yet…

"My father was the Lord Magnus Wiltshire, Seventh Marquess of Worthington. The current one is an imposter. The title belongs to my brother." But she was getting ahead of herself. She'd wanted to explain what happened to him in a tempered, methodical, and calm manner. She'd learned before that panic erodes one's credibility.

"How did your father die?" His question cleared her thoughts for her.

"My father was hardly ever ill. And if he did catch the occasional cold, he'd take to the fields insisting that fresh air would cure him. He was a strong man—a good and loyal man. I loved my father. Jasper and I didn't realize how lucky we were, to grow up in such a loving, *normal* home."

"Jasper—you mean Lord Cedric?"

"Yes."

"What happened to change it?"

"My uncle and aunt came to live with us. My mother had never gotten on well with Aunt Ursula, but mother felt sorry for her. My uncle, who'd never been good with finances, was forced to sell off their estate. After they arrived… well, Rose Heights never felt the same. My aunt didn't like children, and I caught my uncle kicking our dog." Her chest tightened at the memory. "But our troubles didn't really begin until the rats came."

"Rats?" Ranulf's brows raised.

"Dozens of them—they appeared after we'd had some flooding. And my aunt was terrified of them. Insisted they carried disease and that they'd be the death of all of us.

"But shortly after their number began decreasing, my father started getting sick... not just a little sick, but horribly sick. He couldn't keep his food down, his skin turned a darker shade than usual, and he'd begun wrapping his hands. My mother said he didn't want to frighten us with the sores." Beatrice swallowed hard.

"And then mother became ill as well. Everyone thought it was the rats." She narrowed her eyes, her gaze unfocussed as she remembered. "Except me. Father hadn't been bitten—in fact, none of us had ever come into contact with any of them. And they mostly kept to an abandoned cellar. It didn't make sense."

"What did make sense to you, Beatrice?"

Beatrice paused.

She remembered being a young woman of only eight and ten, trying to explain her suspicions to anyone who she thought might be able to help her. She remembered being shut down and turned away every time. From the back of her mind, that part of her was begging for her to stop now.

But as she took a deep breath and looked up into Ranulf's eyes, almost glowing with the reflected light of the flickering candle, she saw something she'd never seen in any of theirs. Absolute sincerity, openness, and his full attention.

That meant something. It had to. And either way, he deserved to know.

"Jasper said he'd seen Aunt Ursula put the rat poison in my mother's tea," she breathed. When he didn't interrupt her immediately with the denial she'd still somehow half-expected, Beatrice continued with growing confidence. "It was a white powder—almost identical to sugar. And she kept the powder on a shelf in the larder, in a container that was very similar to the one in which Mrs. Martle kept the sugar. By this time, both our parents were bedridden. One day, Mrs. Martle caught Aunt Ursula mistaking it for sugar, so she moved it to one of the lower cupboards and labelled it distinctly. A few days later, the label had been removed and the container was back on the kitchen counter. She said that my aunt had insisted she couldn't go searching through the cupboards every time she saw a rat.

"Mrs. Martle left shortly after that. She simply disappeared." Mrs. Martle had been the last person Beatrice had trusted.

"And then the worst happened. Three days after Mrs. Martle left, F-father died." Despite her best efforts, Beatrice's voice cracked and her throat ached with the familiar swell of grief. But she pushed it back down; she had to make him understand.

"And then your mother died."

"Two weeks later," Beatrice held his gaze again, his gentle contribution helping her to regather her thoughts. "I couldn't help but wonder about the white powder and the rats. My aunt and uncle insisted on a year of mourning, but they seemed pleased enough to take over our home. With each passing day, I grew to... hate them more and more. And I didn't bother hiding my feelings.

"Their coming resulted in the death of our parents. I knew the two had to be connected. And I wasn't quiet about it. My aunt accused me of being ridiculous—and spoiled. She accused me of blaming them for having to delay my season. But that had nothing to do with it…" Beatrice shook her head, remembering the confusion. That was when she'd first experienced her ever-present fear.

The jar of poison had disappeared, but Beatrice had been incapable of letting go of her suspicions.

"I didn't pursue the issue seriously until Jasper woke up retching one morning." The symptom had been all too familiar, and her brother was the only true family she had left. "I realized he took sugar on his oats in the morning. He liked his sweets."

"You did some detective work," Ranulf observed.

"I did! And I took some of the powder to the lady who owned the local apothecary. She confirmed it was poison—arsenic—she'd said. But my uncle had become Worthington. She sent me home and told me she was sorry about my parents, but that I needed to let go of my pain and face the future." She was met with the same advice from the local midwife, as well as a chemist who came through with a traveling carnival.

"No one believed me. And every time I tried…" Beatrice winced. "My aunt and uncle were outraged. Suffice it to say, they were not happy with me." It had been the first day of her life that she'd ever been whipped.

Ranulf's gaze hardened.

"So you took your brother, and the two of you escaped."

"Once I was allowed out of the attic." She nodded. "My uncle was legal guardian to both of us. But Jasper's condition had grown worse while I was confined for my punishment. I couldn't afford to wait any longer. Jasper's life depended on getting away."

She held Ranulf's gaze without wavering. "I am a criminal, Ranulf. Not only did I kidnap my brother, but I took all of my mother's jewelry." She folded her hands in her lap. "Our luck changed after that. We met with one of the masters at Eton, who was all too happy to accept a bribe to secure a spot there for Jasper under his new name. It was he who suggested I meet with Miss Primm."

"And all went well until you nearly came face to face with your aunt and uncle last night."

"Yes." She rose from the bed and removed her lap desk from a drawer. Dropping to her knees before him, she opened the container and extracted two of her most important treasures. "I managed to keep these as well. This one is my family. It was painted while we were in Brighton, the summer before..." She handed it up to him.

He reached out and touched the side of her face. "You don't look much different now than you did when you were just a girl." But he became serious then, removing his magnifying glass from his pocket to study the miniature with sober deliberation. After a moment, she handed over the other.

"This is my brother. Legally, he is Lord Cedric Jasper Wiltshire. Before father died, he held the courtesy title of Viscount Farthington." Her heart raced to speak his name out loud. She swallowed hard, and then took a deep breath. "He has been living under the name Jasper Walcott."

"And you?" he asked.

"Clementine Beatrice Wiltshire—Lady Clementine. My parents called me Clem." The name she'd given up long ago caught in her throat.

"He looks a little like your uncle."

"Yes—my father's younger brother." She sighed. "I was terrified someone would recognize him. And if something were to happen to me, there would be no one to pay his tuition—no one to look after him. Even if he managed to stay hidden, his life and his future would be in tatters. So, you must understand why I have to leave. You are on the brink of tackling crime in all of England, and even though I only did what I had to do to save my brother, I am... I am an outlaw. Last I heard, there were rumors that I had something to do with my parent's death. If it gets out, it'll ruin you."

"It would be even worse for you."

She was all too aware of that. She could be hung—or worse, forced to live the rest of her life in prison. And then Jasper would have no one.

"I'd never let anything happen to you." His voice caught.

But his expression gave nothing away. Did he believe her, or did he simply take her for a woman who'd imagined something ridiculously fantastic in order to cope with the loss of both of her parents?

All the emotion of her story settled in her throat. She didn't realize she was crying until Ranulf tucked the miniature into his pocket and touched her face again. When his fingertip grazed her cheek, he caught a teardrop.

"My Sweet Bee." He leaned forward and kissed her cheek. "Carrying this alone for so long."

He lifted her off the floor to cradle her on his lap, stroking her hair.

"I had to save him." Beatrice buried her face in his shoulder, shaking now. "You believe me, don't you?"

"Every word." He held her close. "You should have told me before. I could have helped you sooner."

She lifted her head, frowning. "But there's nothing you can do, Ranulf. The fact remains that I did take Jasper away. We snuck out of the house in the dark of night, and I stole valuable jewelry—I have no evidence to prove my innocence. Jasper and I have talked circles around our options. All we can do is wait for my aunt and uncle to pass. Then…"

He cut her off with a kiss, long and slow and... "I'm going to take care of this." He spoke against her mouth. "I've my own confession to make."

"You?" The wonder of his kiss warred with her despair over everything else. But what could he have to confess?

"I suspected you were hiding something." He drew back and moved his thumb to her chin, staring at her mouth. "Under normal circumstances, I wouldn't have bothered looking into it. Everyone has some sort of secret; the vast majority of them are meaningless. But you…" He kissed her softly. "Are far from meaningless to me. So I…"

"Did some investigating?" Beatrice tilted her head, allowing his mouth to trail down her throat. She was partly flattered by the last part of his admission, but also discouraged that she'd been so transparent. Had anyone else suspected she was not who she said she was?

Had Primm?

"I did," Ranulf answered.

"Was my secret so easy to discover?" With him touching her, sitting on his lap like this, she was beginning to struggle to maintain this conversation.

"Not at first. But now that I know everything, I can help you."

"And you'll help Jasper…?" He shifted out from beneath her, lowering himself to the floor and easing her onto the chair. He moved his hand from her shoulders to slide down her arms.

"I'll help your brother."

"But there is no evidence, Ranulf." He kissed the sensitive skin on the inside of her wrist, and it was more than a kiss… "I have nothing… Even you can't help me." His hands moved to her thighs, and then down her legs.

"What did I tell you about evidence? That first day at the school?" He paused and pinned his gaze on hers.

She gazed into his dark, almost black, eyes. How had she ever believed those eyes were cold? Beatrice had to search her brain to come up with the answer. What had he told her about evidence…?

"That no crime scene was ever completely void of it," she remembered. "That if you had enough pieces of the puzzle you could eventually put it together."

"I have the pieces." Certainty transformed his face. "Will you trust me to reveal the picture?"

"I don't want to go to Newgate." Every time someone new visited the school, her chest had grown tight at the possibility that she'd been exposed. That she'd be locked up forever and Jasper would be left alone.

"I won't let that happen." His confidence confused her. And yet…

"I trust you," she said, that fear inexplicably fluttering away. "Just tell me what to do."

"Later," his hands slid up her legs and under her nigh-trail. "But first I'm going to take care of you."

He lifted her knees onto his shoulders, his face poised at a place that ought to make her feel exceedingly embarrassed. "Trust me?"

"Always."

# I'VE HEARD OF THIS...

Sitting there, listening to Beatrice calmly explain how her aunt and uncle had killed her parents and then gone on to dismantle the innocence of her childhood, Ranulf's plan to expose The Turtle for who he really was grew crystal clear.

He'd be taking a risk. Plan A was to expose the imposter after winning the vote. And Plan B was to expose the imposter after losing it.

Either way, he'd need finesse.

And a little luck.

Ranulf hated to imagine all that she'd gone through—how strong she'd had to be to leave her home—to take the risks she'd taken.

All along, he'd sensed that Beatrice was special, independent and fierce in a way he hadn't quite understood. It wasn't something she exhibited outwardly, but something that glowed from inside of her.

That strength had intrigued him initially, even as she'd drawn him in with her intelligence, her wit.

Not to mention her eyes which had enchanted him, as clear as the sky on a summer day, and a mouth ripe for tasting… along with other attributes that appealed to his more primitive nature.

Hell, if he hadn't come along, her plan likely would have played out to the conclusion she'd decided on.

But this was better. She'd lived in fear for too long.

Ranulf was going to make Titus Wiltshire and his manipulative wife pay for what they'd done.

*Tomorrow.*

Because tonight. Tonight, belonged to the two of them. And he was going to help this incredible woman forget the worries she'd been carrying for years.

*His Sweet Beatrice.*

With his blood singing, he settled in comfortably before her. He'd been thinking about this for too long and his hand damn near trembled as he pushed her nightrail up to her hips, exposing the small triangle of silky curls nestled between her thighs. She squirmed even as her lips parted in anticipation.

"I'm going to make you mine—every inch of your skin—in every possible way." He'd never felt this possessive of anything—of anyone. The need to know her inside and out wasn't a question of if, but when.

"How does one go about doing that?" The corners of her mouth tilted up. A promising blush had tinted her cheeks a delicate pink, and her eyes stared at him trustingly.

And yet her words were a challenge if he'd ever heard one.

"How, you ask?"

Keeping his gaze locked with hers, he leaned forward,

tilting his head just enough to drag his open mouth along her thigh, from her knee toward her center.

"Like this," he said.

He'd memorize her texture and taste—silken skin with an aroma of lavender soap and feminine desire.

When they'd made love in the park, he'd not taken the time for nuance. He'd simply wanted her. And when she'd responded with equal enthusiasm, she unleashed him.

He inhaled, heady from anticipation. He ignored the throbbing in his cock. Later…

Ranulf smoothed his hands up higher, widening her and glad for the light from the candle. A jumble of flowery compliments danced in his mind, but he'd compliment later —when his mouth wasn't otherwise occupied.

"I've heard of this act," she said.

Ranulf glanced up when he sensed her hesitation.

"Are you sure?" She asked the question before he could. But she was not hesitant about *her* desire to be tasted, but for his—*to taste.*

He licked his lips. "Does it rain in London?" he asked. "Do the British drink tea?"

Her response was gentle laughter. "If you say so…"

He dipped his head and kissed her.

"Oooh!"

The small nub of flesh was swollen and he rolled his tongue around it.

Her hands tightened on his shoulders followed by another whispery gasp. "What… Don't stop... Ohhh!"

He ought to have teased her a little, stroked the delicate folds of skin around her opening, but she was already slick, practically soaked.

Impatient with his own desire, Ranulf placed one finger

at her opening, circling her entrance even as he flicked his tongue, tasting her everywhere.

She trembled.

Not just her legs, but her core, her hands. He felt her trembling in his chest and throughout him, even as her knees clutched the sides of his head. Encouraged, he added a second finger, this time thrusting both inside—deeper, exploring and searching to learn where she was most sensitive.

If anyone had asked him a month ago if he could be this besotted, he'd have told them to go hang. But his Sweet Bee, she truly had conquered him. He'd not exaggerated when he told her that.

And being conquered by this woman was…

A gift.

Her fingers threaded through his hair even as her inner channel throbbed. She pulsed around him—ignited—a desire so hot the flame would be blue, the same color as her eyes, which had mesmerized him for days now, dancing with secrets.

Secrets she'd finally shared.

Ranulf exhaled a hot breath along her center.

She was close, and *curses on his cock,* its engorged state forced him to pause, adjusting his breaches which had grown unbearably tight.

"Ranulf." She let out a tiny moan of protest, moving to urge him along. Little cries of need showed him that she hovered on the brink—that brink of exquisite sensations that teased one, right before thundering pleasure roared in. He dragged his jaw over sensitive flesh, the scruff of his whiskers catching in her intimate curls.

"Yes!" This cry tore from her very depths.

And it was loud--very loud.

*Too loud.*

Ranulf covered her mouth with his free hand. The very last thing they wanted was for his sister to interrupt them.

He lifted his gaze, and nearly laughed at the expression on her face. Because she realized what she'd done.

"Don't look so horrified, we're not finished yet," he half whispered, and not wanting her to become distracted by the possibility of his sister pounding on her chamber door, he resumed his erotic assault.

And as he increased the pace of his ministrations, bringing all her sensual nerves to life, Ranulf deduced it had been wise to cover her mouth.

Curling his wrist, he reached deep inside, and then took a more shallow stroke. And as he sucked her clitoris into his mouth, she stiffened, biting down on his hand as she achieved her climax.

Ranulf didn't care if she drew blood. Seeing her like this exceeded the wonders of the world. It exceeded any expectations he'd had for his future.

Because it was more than sex. Blast and damn, was this love?

While Ranulf grappled with the startling possibility, Beatrice slumped and her inner muscles tapered to a less frantic pulse. Ranulf wanted nothing more than to rise up, unfasten his falls, and fill her with his own throbbing organ.

Instead, he pushed up onto his knees again, and pressed a tender kiss to her mouth. Because now, she looked... peaceful. For a few moments, he'd succeeded in chasing away her fears. She opened her eyes, and stared at him looking exceedingly satisfied.

After he tomorrow, those fears would be gone forever.

A slow smile spread across her mouth. "I liked that," she said, her eyes hooded, satiated and sleepy.

The night was more than half over and Ranulf needed to check back in the office. He needed to formulate the questions he'd ask in his interrogation, take into account every possible scenario, ensure he was never caught off guard.

If he was to succeed in clearing her name tomorrow, he needed to be at the very top of his game.

Sliding one hand under her thighs, and winding the other around her back, Ranulf rose, carrying her to the bed. The way she looked at him challenged his resolve. Her flushed skin and parted lips nearly broke it.

But as badly as he wanted to climb in beside her, to make love to her properly, on silk sheets and a soft mattress, he couldn't indulge himself tonight.

If he had his way, they'd have hundreds—thousands of such nights together. But in order for that to happen, he needed to clear her name—and help her brother reclaim his title.

"Tomorrow," he forced the word past his throat as he rose, still looking down at her.

She shifted, her expression changing as she remembered there was work yet to do. "Yes."

"Don't arrive at the Society Assembly room with Edith. I'll inform her of the change in plan and send a separate coach for you. The vote begins at precisely ten in the morning. At two minutes of, enter through the east door and take a seat in the back. Wear a cloak or one of those droopy looking hats ladies wear that cover their faces."

"A bonnet?" Her lips twitched.

"Wear a cloak or *a bonnet*," he amended without skipping

a beat. "Don't speak with anyone. Blend in as much as possible." He needed to be clear.

"But how can I help? What can I do?"

Ranulf touched her arm, hearing the strain returning to her voice. "You'll know what to do when the time comes."

"But how?" She was sitting up, her lethargy all but forgotten.

And yet her gaze dropped to the front of his breaches. Ranulf licked his lips, savoring her taste. The longer he stayed, the harder it was going to get—literally, and physically.

"You'll know." His voice came out gruff sounding.

"Be careful." Her voice trembled, and he realized how difficult it was for her to trust him. She'd kept this secret for a decade.

One last kiss, and he crossed back to the window.

"Ranulf?" Her voice stopped him just as he lifted one leg to climb out of the bed.

He looked over at her and cocked a brow. If she asked him to stay, he was going to have one hell of an internal battle with himself.

But she was biting back a smile. "Are you sure you don't want to use the back door?" she asked. "I'd hate for your plans to fall through because you'd injured yourself climbing down the trellis outside my window."

For half a second, he seriously considered her suggestion.

But, hell, he'd come this far. "Until tomorrow, Sweet Bee." He saluted her and dipped out the window.

# TRUST

The following morning, Beatrice awoke before Dora had the chance to bring in her tea. Remembering Ranulf's means of departure, she burst out of the bed and crossed to the window.

If not for the damaged trellis and the vase lying on the rug, Beatrice might almost have wondered if she'd summoned his late-night visit in a dream. Then again, if it had been a dream, how could she explain the fact that her inner thighs were red and tender.

His whiskers…

Ah, yes, last night had been all too real.

Before he'd appeared at her window, she'd been preparing herself for the end of their make-believe betrothal—for possibly having to leave Primm's, having to find new employment.

Her outlook had not been hopeful.

Then Ranulf had come along and changed everything.

But now she must face today.

She was nervous—*of course,* she was nervous. But

although her old instincts urged her to pack her small valise and take the first mail coach out of London, an unfamiliar resolve had taken over.

No, it was not unfamiliar. It was similar to the feeling she'd had when she and Jasper had stolen away from Rose Heights all those years ago.

Courage.

And Trust—in herself.

She would show courage today in trusting Ranulf.

Despite exhibiting all the confidence in the world, there was no way he could know for certain that his plan would succeed. And yet, Beatrice knew, he would do everything possible to ensure that it did.

She trusted him. As her lover, but also, as an investigator.

He'd come to her last night with a plan to solve her troubles, and then he'd made her forget them.

Beatrice replaced the vase on its table and then used the washbasin to clean up. Just as she finished, Dora entered, carrying a bright jonquil linen draped over one arm. It had been specifically purchased for Beatrice to wear on the day of the vote.

But at the sight of it, Beatrice winced.

She would not be wearing the colorful dress today, nor would she don the spectacular hat, adorned with bright silk flowers, which had been made to compliment it.

"I've changed my mind," Beatrice announced. "I want to wear the navy."

The maid's smile fell. "But…?" She looked as though she might go to war with Beatrice over this.

"I don't want to invite bad luck," Beatrice insisted. "And by wearing such a celebratory gown before knowing the outcome, I'd be doing just that. So I'll wear the navy, along with my grey cloak."

If anything, the maid looked even more horrified by Beatrice's explanation. "Are you... jesting with me?"

Beatrice levelled a somber gaze in Dora's direction. There was no room for compromise in this. "I've never been more serious in my life."

It took a few seconds, but she would not argue further. Dora nodded with a jerk and then swept out of the room. "I'll have to steam them."

Alone again, Beatrice inhaled a deep breath. She was going to do this. She was going to attend the vote and watch for some unknown signal from Ranulf.

And then do what?

Dear God, what if she missed it. What if she did the wrong thing?

Why hadn't he been more specific?

Her knees turned weak and she lowered herself onto the nearest chair.

He'd assured her he had a plan. Why hadn't she insisted he provide her with all of the details?

*Because,* a voice whispered in her head, *you were in a haze of satisfaction after he'd done wicked, wicked things to you.*

Was she insane to believe everything could work out to her and Jasper's advantage?

She stared down at her shaking hands. She was about to make the worst decision of her life or the very best one.

Either way, everything was about to change. She straightened her back and lifted her chin. Come what may, she was done living a lie.

One way or another, the truth would win out.

It had to.

RANULF HAD IMAGINED that when this day finally came, his entire being would be focused on the outcome of the vote. As it was, it was going to be close.

He'd done everything he could to persuade the board members—it was time for them to make their choice. Would they remain in the past or take this step to embrace the future?

The door he'd been watching pushed open. A gray cloak covered her face, and her gown managed to hide her figure, but he knew her by the way she moved, the tilt of her head.

Just looking at her, his chest loosened, and his mind cleared.

The seating area was made up of observers, consisting of a sizable assembly of serious-minded individuals. He'd not expected so many to be curious about something most of the ton would dismiss as boring.

Edith sat up front, along with Charles. Ranulf hadn't expected to see the faces beside them, however. Looking quite somber, his brothers, Frederick, Alexander, and Ambrose provided that four of the six Winters siblings were in attendance.

He'd never had cause to doubt the support of his family.

The pounding of the gavel brought the chatter to a small murmur, and then silence.

All eyes turned toward Lord Hamish, one of the older members who, due to the nature of this particular gathering, would preside. For being such an anticipated event, it began the same as any other meeting would.

"I call this meeting to order. Will the secretary please do roll call?"

As the secretary took attendance, the tension in the room grew thicker.

Or was Ranulf the only one who felt it? He'd waited so long for this moment.

"Today is the thirty-first day of August, the year of our lord, eighteen and thirty-two," the secretary spoke evenly. "This is the meeting of the Board Members of *The King's Society for the Advancement of Ingenuity in England*."

Beatrice lifted her gaze and, for what felt like less than a second, locked it with Ranulf's. Neither acknowledged the other, and yet it was exactly what he needed.

Normal procedure took up the next half an hour until Hamish finally acknowledged their observers, reading them the rules. "There is to be no applause or chants or expressions of either approval or disapproval.

"At the last meeting, the board approved the nomination of Interim Director, Lord Ranulf Winters, to hold the position indefinitely—with the final vote scheduled for today. Before we collect member ballots, are there any further questions or arguments?"

Ranulf held his breath. It was possible the nominating board could introduce a second nominee. Or any of the members could challenge his own nomination.

But general consensus coming in was that all of this had been discussed *ad nauseum* at the prior meeting. What hadn't been discussed there had been resolved informally.

The large chamber remained silent but for some shuffling and the clearing of a few throats, so the speaker continued. "Very well, members. As this is to be a private voting process, I ask you to check either *'yay'* or *'nay'* on Lord Sexton's nomination and fold your vote in half." The process was rather efficient, really, and within a minute, the members waited quietly while the secretary collected votes in a locked box.

Hamish then called a short recess to count the votes. Not a single person left their seats. Five minutes later, their murmurs quieted with the speaker's return.

Lord Hamish slammed his gavel on the podium three times.

"Having counted all the votes..." He paused for what surely must be dramatic effect. "The vote proves incontrovertible support by the board that The Society moves forward with Lord Sexton at the helm." The speaker shifted his glasses lower on the bridge of his nose and stared down at his notes. "We have sixteen for the marquess and five in opposition."

He then turned to Ranulf and dipped his chin. Despite his instructions earlier, applause broke out amongst most of the spectators.

There was no mistaking the joy on Edith's face, and when Ranulf glanced toward the back corner, Beatrice's eyes sparkled with a cautious satisfaction.

But also determination.

Ranulf glanced over his shoulder to where the board sat on two separate levels, maintaining their somber demeanors despite the excitement in the gallery. Due to the dignity of their position, they, of course, withheld applause.

Ranulf knew precisely who had cast the five opposing votes.

"My Lord, Director," the speaker called, and then gestured toward the podium. "Congratulations on behalf of the board, in addition to every other member of The Society. We look forward to making great strides under your leadership."

This was a moment Ranulf had worked toward for years. He ought to be celebrating.

And yet, this meeting was only half over.

Ranulf rose.

They would expect a speech from him now, of gratitude, acknowledging the value of The Society, and expanding on his vision moving forward.

And they would get a speech, but not the one they expected. As long as his plan succeeded, they'd be treated to a demonstration of the value that would be added in the future.

A most unexpected demonstration.

He tapped his pocket, reassured when he felt the hard squares of Beatrice's miniatures beneath the fabric. He then stepped up to the podium and stared out at the audience. He did not clear his throat as this was not the time to show uncertainty.

"Good morning." He spoke firmly. "And my thanks to those of you who have taken the time to be involved in this great institution which was purposed over two centuries ago with the objective of enhancing every aspect of our Kingdom. Through science. Through research, experiments, and practical debate." He narrowed his eyes. "It's no secret that one of my primary goals moving forward is to repurpose a portion of the society's resources to focus on one aspect of English lives that plagues all of our citizens —crime.

"Although our magistrates are putting forth their best efforts to capture criminal elements within their jurisdiction, in many cases, they lack the resources necessary to investigate the most puzzling offences, and on occasion, they lack the authority to pursue suspects of status. Lacking accountability, in certain cases, criminal activity such as horse-theft, corruption and even murder perpetrated by the underbelly of England's elite goes unchecked. I'm not talking about victimless crimes here, I'm speaking of activity that undermines our entire system. Because it is upon honor, which we, as England's leaders, have built our foundation. As director, I have the full legal backing of the crown." Ranulf lifted his chin.

"Rather than expound on the extent of this issue or try to convince anyone of the necessity of my proposed mission, I will demonstrate the necessity by addressing a particular troubling case involving our nobility—one that has gone unsolved for a decade."

Those present murmured in surprise upon this announcement. Ranulf took the moment to open the case file and gather his thoughts as he stared down at the podium.

# JUSTICE

Ranulf took a deliberate step back and shifted his body so that he deliberately faced the half of the board that held the Marquess of Worthington's seat.

He could not think of the man as the Marquess. Titus Wiltshire had stolen Beatrice's parents from her. He'd stolen her family.

A good deal of her life.

Ranulf pushed his emotions down. He could not contemplate anything but this very moment.

Loaded with ammunition, He pinned his stare on the man he'd have behind bars before the day was out.

"Lord Worthington, on the eighth of April of our lord's year eighteen and twenty-two, you met with the local magistrate near your estate, Rose Heights, in order to formerly press charges against your niece."

Wiltshire, feeling all eyes on him, shifted uncomfortably but maintained his composure. "Yes. It was a most unfortunate affair," he answered.

And then his gaze flicked to the other imposter, the

other murderer, who was seated, oddly enough, exactly three rows in front of Beatrice. Lines of concern wrinkled the older woman's forehead—precisely as Ranulf had expected.

"Could you expand on the specifics of those charges?" Ranulf flicked his stare back to the marquess.

But Wilshire had existed as one of the entitled for nearly a decade. He folded his arms in front of him. "Since you're the one bringing it up, why don't you explain them? At my age, I don't always remember things correctly." He chuckled, and a few of those sitting around him did as well.

But nearly every other person present watched with genuine curiosity.

"Theft," Ranulf said.

Wiltshire scowled. "Yes. Nasty business; my wife's jewels"—*Beatrice's mother's jewels, actually*— "were stolen. They had been passed down for centuries and were not only valuable, but irreplaceable."

"And you have no difficulty remembering *these* details."

"None at all." The gentleman scowled, reminding Ranulf of the man's nickname. "It was a substantial loss. Are you bringing the case up because you've located them?" Wiltshire's eyes lit up at the possibility.

Ranulf ignored the question.

"Theft is not the only crime listed," Ranulf stated.

Wiltshire paused and then dipped his chin, though he then turned to Hamish. "Is this really necessary?"

The speaker nodded in simple answer. "His Lordship is the director."

The creases of Wiltshire's frown deepened before he answered Ranulf's question.

"Following the very tragic deaths of my brother and his

wife, Lady Worthington and I came forward to carry on the responsibilities of the marquessate until my brother's son came to be of age. Most unfortunately, Lady Clementine, my brother's only daughter, resented our presence. She suffered a psychological breakdown and blamed the marchioness and me for the death of her parents. We have no doubt that it was she who took the jewels. They disappeared the same night she did, the same night she kidnapped young Lord Cedric." *Jasper.*

"The heir apparent to the Worthington title," Ranulf pointed out.

"He was a frail boy," Wiltshire answered.

"You must have been beside yourself with worry."

"I was!"

"I imagine you organized an extensive search party," Ranulf said.

"Indeed."

"And yet, there is no record documenting this search, which I imagine would have been high-profile, seeing as the boy was not only frail, but the rightful heir to the marquessate."

"It was a difficult time, Sexton." Wiltshire's tone turned defensive. "We were in mourning."

"But you didn't waste time petitioning the crown for Lord Cedric to be declared legally dead on..." Ranulf glanced down at his file again. "The ninth of April of the year eighteen and twenty-two." *The very next day."*

"The boy was practically on his deathbed when Lady Clementine kidnapped him. He was suffering the same symptoms his parents experienced shortly before their passing. It was the most prudent course of action, considering I would be performing the duties of my brother's title.

If you'll check your notes, you'll see the local physician was confident the boy could not have lived."

Ranulf reached into his pocket and extracted the miniatures. "This is the boy?" He walked partway up the aisle, close enough that Beatrice's uncle could confirm the identity of the subject.

"It is. He greatly resembles me, actually." He shook his head mournfully. "I'd have done anything to save that dear, poor boy."

Holding up the other miniature, Ranulf continued. "And the young girl depicted in this miniature is his older sister—Lady Clementine?"

The marquess nodded, and then scowled. "Have you located her?

"You believe she could lead you to your nephew's body?" Ranulf asked.

Wiltshire nodded. "And the jewels as well. She deserves to rot in jail for what she's done."

Internally, Ranulf seethed. The way Wiltshire spoke of his niece was so cold, almost vicious if not for his apparent lack of passion—as if she truly *deserved* any of what he and his wife had done to her.

Outwardly, of course, Ranulf remained calm and professional, as was expected of him. "Indeed?" he asked. "But weren't they, in actuality, her own mother's jewels? Were they not bequeathed to her when she achieved her majority?"

The marchioness burst to her feet, creating a stir as she did so. "Not all of them! And she had not reached her majority. As the Marchioness of Worthington, they ought to have come to me." She pursed her lips and, for an instant, Ranulf felt as though he was getting a glimpse of pure evil.

He waited silently.

Lady Worthington then lifted her chin. "Clementine was worse than a thief. She not only stole my jewels, but she killed her parents—spooned rat poisoning into their tea, and then later, into her poor brother's morning oats."

"Hush, my lady," the marquess reprimanded his wife with a stern glance.

"I will not. You've always been too weak to do what needs to be done, Titus. Why don't you stand up to this impertinent gentleman?" Without waiting for an answer from her husband, she turned her stare back to Ranulf. "That girl accused his lordship and me of killing them, but it was *her* all along. The housekeeper even caught her putting it in their tea on one occasion—but she claimed it was an accident."

Here, Ranulf stepped in with his bluff. "I have a documented statement from a Mrs. Sarah Martle, housekeeper at Rose Heights at the time. In her statement, she claims it was *you*, my lady, who made use of the rat poison. She states that she once caught you adding it to your sister-in-law's tea."

In the frantic hours leading up to today's meeting, Stork had located Mrs. Martle. Unfortunately, she'd been long dead and buried in a small graveyard just outside of Garden Cove. His gamble was that Beatrice's aunt and uncle would not have cared to check.

Wiltshire and his wife stared at one another, no longer comfortable with where Ranulf's questions were going.

"It's not unusual for a servant who's been sacked to conjure up lies about her former employer." Wiltshire belatedly responded, visibly working to regain his composure, even as his wife was practically trembling with rage.

"What if those lies, as you suggest, are corroborated by the Marquess of Worthington?"

Wiltshire's eyes narrowed in confusion.

Until Lord Worthington himself ambled in—the *real* marquess—a boy on the cusp of manhood, who was a younger, not at all turtle-like, version of his uncle. His eyes were perhaps the most notable difference, the same vibrant blue color as his sister's. "I saw my aunt do it." He spoke clearly and with conviction. "I didn't realize at first, but after she left the kitchen, I checked. It wasn't sugar she'd been spooning into Mother's tea. It was the rat poison." The young man shook his head. "I stopped drinking tea after I saw that. I didn't think it could make its way into my oats."

"Will you please state your legal name?" In case there were any doubts.

"I am Cedric Jasper Wiltshire, the eight Marquess of Worthington."

"But this certificate says you are dead." Ranulf spoke matter of factly.

"Well it's wrong." Ranulf almost smiled at the young man's vehemence—definitely Beatrice's brother.

"But you did fall ill, did you not, shortly after your mother's passing?"

"I did." The young man nodded. "The sickness was the same as our parents'. Arsenic, as I've learned, which is the primary ingredient in rat poison, causes all the symptoms that were observed in our parents." He held up one hand, marred with spots of obvious discoloration. "I have scars left over from the sores. If Bea hadn't insisted we leave, I wouldn't be here today."

"Bea. You mean Lady Clementine? Your sister?"

"Yes."

"And where was she when you took ill?"

"She knew what they'd done, so they had locked her in the attic."

"They?"

"Uncle Titus, and Aunt Ursula."

Lady Worthington's face transformed through a myriad of emotions before, having apparently come to some sort of decision, she raised her arm and pointed a shaking finger at her husband. "He told me to do it!" she cried.

The witnesses in the chamber gasped in near unison and then fell silent.

"Will the secretary note that Mrs. Titus Wiltshire is pointing at her husband, Mr. Titus Wiltshire?" Ranulf allowed himself a slow exhale.

He met the young Marquess' eyes. "That will be all, my lord."

Cedric Jasper Wiltshire nodded and then took the only vacant seat—Ranulf's.

But there was one more matter to clear up.

He turned from Beatrice's brother to the board. "Esteemed colleagues, Mr. and Mrs. Titus Wiltshire's testimonies cast enough doubt that I propose the warrant I have here"—he lifted the decade-old form— "charging Lady Clementine Beatrice Wiltshire with theft and kidnapping, be declared void."

~

BEATRICE CLASPED her hands beneath her chin and pushed the cloak away from her face. "Jasper!"

He looked so grown-up! Was it possible that he'd grown even taller since she'd last seen him at Christmas?

In the ensuing confusion, Jasper met her stare, raised his brows, and then shrugged.

Beatrice nearly burst into tears.

Ranulf had brought him here. Ranulf had arranged all of this.

She vaguely noticed that her uncle had turned white as a sheet. The entire chamber, it seemed, had broken into discussion at the same time.

It was Ranulf who pounded the gavel this time. "Order!" He commanded the chamber as though he'd done it all his life.

It immediately fell silent.

"Is there a second?" he asked.

"I second it," the Duke of Bedwell spoke up.

"It has been moved and seconded. Is there any further discussion?"

Not even the sound of a pin dropping.

"We will now vote on the motion that the warrant against Lady Clementine be declared void. All in favor, say *'aye'*."

The response came in a resounding collection of voices.

*"Aye!"*

"All opposed, say *'nay'*."

*"Nay,"* called a single voice. A feeble attempt by her uncle.

"The motion has passed."

Beatrice had been so captivated by the drama being played out that it wasn't until she felt a cold shiver ghost down her spine. Her aunt was staring at her with narrowed eyes.

"Arrest her!" The woman had apparently not been paying attention, or else she had become damn near delusional in her state of denial. "This is what she wanted all along!"

"Enough," Ranulf ordered. And then his voice fell to a deadly calm. "You, Mrs. Wiltshire, have done enough."

Aunt Ursula opened her mouth as though she still intended to argue with him, closed it, and then, turning back to Beatrice, opened it again. "You were supposed to be next. But you wouldn't eat the sugar!" She turned back to her husband. "I told you she'd ruin everything, but you insisted we needn't go after her. And now, look! Everything is ruined!

"Guards?" At Ranulf's request, four uniformed gentlemen who'd been manning the entrances rushed forward to detain the marchioness.

Beatrice's uncle, meanwhile, clutching his chest and slumped bonelessly in his chair, apparently wasn't considered as much of a threat as his wife.

Once again, Ranulf pounded the gavel, wisely adjourning the meeting.

"Miss Wiltshire!" Beatrice heard over the din. It had been so long since she'd had to respond to her real name that she almost missed it. "The Gazette would like you to answer a few questions." But before the reporter could get to her, Beatrice pushed her way through the crowd to get to her brother, who was also being besieged with questions.

"Don't worry about them." She threw herself in her brother's arms. "Ranulf will take care of them. And why are you so much taller than me now?" When this had all started, so many years ago, her brother had been small enough that she'd had to kneel to properly embrace him. She could recall, with perfect clarity, the way he'd pressed his face into her neck, how his hair had brushed against her cheek and chin before she had left him alone for the first time at Eton.

She would ask him all her other questions later, but for now, she'd simply hold onto him. For the first time in years, they needn't hide.

Jasper stiffened in embarrassment, however, so she loosened her hold and glanced over to where Ranulf appeared to have taken to his new position quite well. Beside him, the Duke of Bedwell was flipping through stacks of papers, while a few of the other board members read over their shoulders, nodding—as though they'd suspected her uncle's deceit all along.

Then, as though he could feel her watching him, Ranulf flicked his gaze in her direction.

And winked.

# I DON'T WANT IT TO END

Riding back to Abraham House in the same carriage Beatrice had arrived in, Jasper explained that it had been Lord Sexton's assistant, Mr. Stork, who'd met with him at Eton and then arranged for the breakneck journey to London. And after providing his deposition to Lord Sexton, dearest Jasper was now convinced that he too, wished to become an investigator. "Lord Sexton is a marquess, and he does it, so why can't I?"

"I think you'll do anything you want to," Beatrice replied. Jasper always received very high marks, and Beatrice had no doubt in his abilities.

But for that moment, she simply enjoyed sitting beside her little brother, clasping one of his hands in both of hers.

She experienced none of the fear she'd become accustomed to when they were together. And listening to Jasper enthuse about the events of the past twenty-four hours with a level of excitement one could only achieve at the age of eight and ten, Beatrice sat back and smiled.

All of this had been done without her knowledge, and

although she was a little annoyed that she'd been kept in the dark, she was also grateful she hadn't been a part of it.

Because, had she known the risks involved, she would have been even more terrified.

But for now, she and Jasper could lay claim to not only their past, but also their futures.

Later that afternoon, after introducing Jasper to Lady Edith and Daisy—and even Dora, brother and sister were left alone to stroll through the garden. There was so much to say—revisiting the decisions Beatrice had made over the years, the memory of their loss—but mostly they simply marveled that it was over.

And yet, once they were truly alone, her brother's eyes, the same blue as her own, became unusually bright. When his shoulders began to shake, she took him in her arms.

She'd not expected to be free today.

She'd not expected to see him again for months.

And for all of ten seconds, her brother sobbed. When he drew away, looking quite embarrassed, it was Beatrice's turn to cry. Witnessing their aunt and uncle coming to justice had been satisfying, but the release of all her pent-up fears was nearly too much to bear. And, yes, justice seemed apparent, but there was nothing that could bring their parents back to them or replace the years they'd lost while in hiding.

If one person in a position of authority had listened to her, her aunt and uncle would have faced consequences years ago. There would have been no need for her and Jasper to live under false names, nor would she have been afraid all this time. She might have been a better friend.

Then again, she might never have met Ranulf.

She sniffed, determined that this would be the last time she'd think in terms of *'if only.'*

Beatrice withdrew her handkerchief from her sleeve and stepped away from her brother.

"I thought I'd find the two of you out here."

Would her heart always leap at the sound of his voice?

Wiping her eyes, Beatrice turned a watery smile toward her…

What was he now? The need for a make-believe betrothed was over. He was her hero. Her friend, but also her lover.

And to her, he would always be *her beloved*.

Glancing between the marquess and Beatrice with all-too-knowing eyes for one so young, Jasper took a step backward and tugged at his cravat. "It's rather warm out here. I'm going inside to see if Lady Abraham has more of that delicious lemonade. You'll excuse me, won't you, sis?" He took a second to seek Beatrice's approval.

She drank in the sight of him before dipping her chin. "Of course." He would have to return to Eton soon, having already missed out on two days of his studies.

And even though they no longer needed to worry about the warrant, or Lord or Lady Worthington, she'd always worry about *him*. He was her little brother—the only family she had left.

Neither she nor Ranulf spoke until Jasper disappeared inside.

"I don't know how to thank you," she began. She wanted to step into his arms, but according to that stupid contract she and Primm had written out, he must announce the end of their engagement now that the vote was over.

"You don't need to thank me." He took a step closer but not quite close enough to touch her.

"About last night—"

"About this damned betroth—"

They both went to speak at the same time. Beatrice was well-nigh holding her breath. "You go first." She wished she could read his thoughts better—how was it possible that she'd fallen for the most inscrutable man in all of England?

"No. Ladies first," he insisted.

Beatrice licked her lips. She could confirm the end of their charade and remind him of his commitment to solve the mystery at the school. That's what Primm would do, wasn't it?

But she wasn't Primm.

Nor was she a woman who needed to hide her identity.

She was a woman who'd... fallen in love. And after keeping most of her feelings to herself for the past decade, she refused to suffer her plight passively.

She was a fighter.

"I don't want it to end." Her voice caught.

He stilled, watching her with an unfamiliar gleam in his black eyes. "You don't want what to end?" he asked.

"Us." Beatrice held his gaze. "I don't know what it would look like, or how it would play out, but I don't want to walk away from..." She gestured between the two of them. "From this. I don't want to walk away from us."

Her voice shook as she bared her heart's desire. He took her hands in his, but she went right on talking before he could respond.

"I know we agreed this was only temporary and that I wasn't to have any expectation going forward after the vote. I just never expected so many... feelings. And I don't mean just the feelings I have… when you, when you…make love to me. I mean the feelings I have from simply being with you—from arguing with you and from agreeing with you from time to—"

Ranulf dropped onto one knee.

Still holding her hands in his, he tilted his head back, locking his gaze with hers.

"Marry me?" His voice came out strong and clear. When Beatrice stared at him in shock, he smiled. "I beg of you to make me the happiest of men?" Was that pleading in his eyes? "I didn't think it possible, but I've fallen in love with you. And I've fallen so hard that the only thing that can save me now is to spend the rest of my life… catching you?" The corners of his mouth tipped up ever so slightly. "You own my heart, and if I'm not mistaken I have at least a part of yours. Please, put me out of my misery and tell me I'm not wrong."

"You aren't wrong." Beatrice could hardly contain the bubbles dancing inside her, spreading from her heart to her belly, and out to all her limbs. There was certainly no stopping the smile that took over her mouth. "And you don't only have a part of it, you have all of it! Yes, oh, my dear, dear Ranulf. I'll marry you."

Neither of them moved for the next several seconds. They simply stared into each other's eyes, as though they were both overwhelmed at their good luck.

But then Ranulf was off the ground, taking her in his arms and swinging her around. When he lowered her onto her feet again, his mouth caught hers, sealing their decision in the best possible way.

"When?" he asked.

"I don't suppose an announcement is necessary," Beatrice barely got the words out. Both emotion and his kisses nearly stole her breath completely.

"Because we're already betrothed." He leaned back to meet her gaze, contemplating the circumstances of their unusual courtship. "So we don't really have to wait."

Beatrice smoothed her palms over his chest. "I ought to be frightened. Everything is going too well. I'm *too* happy." This wasn't the sort of thing she was used to admitting to anyone.

Ranulf didn't laugh or brush away her concerns. "The future is never a certainty." He covered her hands with one of his, pressing it tighter to his chest.

Beatrice had suffered losses in her past, but so had Ranulf.

"It isn't," she agreed. "I suppose that's why we should embrace the present." Living in the present meant being brave. It meant not hiding while one's life passed them by. It meant taking risks on the off chance that life can be so much better.

"A special license?" Ranulf cocked a brow.

Marriage. It was something she'd not envisioned for her future since before her mother's passing.

"That sounds perfect." She didn't need to know where they would live, or what they would do. Such details, in that moment, felt small and insignificant.

Because surrounded by Edith's fairy garden, she felt suddenly free. Free and *alive.*

And in love!

Ranulf was a marquess, yes, but he was *her* marquess.

She smiled. He only seemed arrogant and unyielding *sometimes*. Furthermore, at the heart of his character, he'd shown determination and loyalty and… love. He'd proven that he was so much more than any title bestowed by man. She could hardly wait to begin living her life with him. She even looked forward to working on all those puzzles he'd take on...

"We'll be the perfect team." His words confirmed her own thoughts on the matter, that their marriage would consist of more than just managing a household and attending parties thrown by the Ton.

"I'd like that."

Ranulf pulled her against him, his desire more than evident as it pressed against her belly. One hand slid between them, capturing her breast, teasing it, teasing both of them because exposed as they were in the garden, this could go no farther.

"Later," Beatrice didn't realize she'd spoken aloud until he agreed.

"But not much later." He groaned. "Where should we go for a honeymoon?" Ranulf loosened his embrace, exercising some manner of self-control.

Beatrice rolled her lips together and met his stare. "We have to go to the school," she reminded him. "Otherwise Primm will never forgive me."

He didn't look quite as pained as she'd expected. This man, she was learning, wasn't the sort to shy away from a challenge.

"But while we're there, I'm not letting you out of my sight." She knew he was thinking of the broken window incident. "And we certainly aren't sleeping in that damned little dormitory," he added.

Beatrice was perfectly fine with that. Just as Ranulf leaned down to steal one more kiss, Edith called to them to come inside so they could join the celebrations she'd planned.

But first, Beatrice pressed up onto her toes and whispered near his ear. "You'll have plenty of time to catch up on your sleep before then."

Ranulf's brows shot up, that wicked light shining brightly. "And why is that?"

As she went to slap at him playfully, he caught her hand, trapping it and raising it to his mouth to kiss the backs of her fingers.

"Rest assured, you needn't concern yourself in that area."

He squeezed her hand as she led him back to the house. Not until they reached the door did she realize she was practically skipping.

"You two look happy enough." Edith stared at them curiously.

"It's because we're getting married." Beatrice spoke without thinking.

"Oh really?" Edith glanced between the two of them, shaking her head. "So this betrothal business wasn't all for show?" It was obvious she was joking by the laughter that followed her question. But as they followed his sister inside, Ranulf dipped his chin and sent rippling joy dancing over Beatrice's skin as he whispered.

"It was never make-believe for me, love. It's always been real."

# EPILOGUE

Apparently, obtaining a special license didn't mean a couple could marry that same day—not after the groom's sister got wind of the idea, anyhow.

So Jasper missed more school, and Beatrice and Ranulf played the part of an engaged couple a little longer.

Only this time, neither of them were playing.

The same night they'd become engaged, the Duchess of Bedwell had changed her King's Society Celebration into a last-minute pre-wedding ball. It had been as well-attended as if it were the height of the season and lasted well into the night.

And when Ranulf caught Beatrice's gaze from across the room, sending her a smoldering glance filled with promise, it was real. When he bowed and asked her to dance, it was real. And when he whispered words into her ear as he led her around the floor in a waltz, she didn't hide her shiver of anticipation.

It was all real.

And early the next morning, Ranulf and Beatrice had

married in a private ceremony at an out-of-the-way church. They had done so secretly, with one of his brothers and Miss Pepperspring as witnesses, and not a single guest.

If left up to Edith, they'd have suffered through a grand society wedding at St. George's on Hanover. But they had a promise to keep. There had been no time for a full-fledged *Ton* wedding.

"Are you sad?" Ranulf smoothed his chin over Beatrice's hair, his arms around her as their carriage rolled out of London. Saying goodbye to Jasper had not been easy for her.

She had also bid farewell to her chaperone. Daisy Pepperspring had apparently made a favorable impression with his sister's children, and Edith had begged the young woman to stay on as governess.

Beatrice shifted and sat up to stare at him. "But why would I be sad?" Her lovely eyes were a little red, however, proof that she had been crying.

Ranulf shifted as well, turning sideways so that he mostly faced her, but not so much that their hands and legs weren't touching.

"Your brother." Perhaps he should not have reminded her, but he wanted to know how she was feeling, to be sure that she did not have any regrets.

He wanted to know everything about her. No more secrets.

Her eyes did seem to shine a little brighter at his words, but not with tortured tears—they shone with happiness, pride, and a little sadness.

"Saying goodbye to Jasper will likely always make me a little sad, but not enough to keep me that way. It is enough to know that he is safe, happy, and can go on with his life."

"And what of Miss Pepperspring?"

"She would have been a wonderful teacher." Beatrice grimaced. "Although Primm is not going to be very happy to lose another one."

"Two." Ranulf raised a brow and squeezed her hand. "She is losing two more teachers." Which led him to yet another reason she might be feeling a little melancholy. "You will not be able to stay on at the school," he reminded her.

She studied him for a few seconds before answering this time. "I like to teach, and I will miss my students." She grimaced. "Most of them anyway—not Allison Meadowbrook or the Metcalf girls, perhaps. But I am excited to be your wife—and to start our life together—you are going to allow me to help solve your mysteries, are you not?"

Ranulf smiled. "As long as you do as I say."

*"As long as I do as you say?"* She narrowed her gaze at him. "Such as… changing out your linens?" She cocked one delicately arched brow.

And then, staring into his eyes, she licked her lips.

In a nimble move, of which Ranulf was rather proud, he had his wife turned and facing him on his lap in less than three seconds.

The friction between them was delicious, and she would be in no doubt as to where this was leading.

"Change my linens? Oh no, my dear wife, I have other things in mind for you."

She moved her hips in an attempt to turn the tables on him.

And it worked.

But he wasn't quite willing to end his line of questioning.

"You were not disappointed to have such a rushed wedding?" He held her gaze. She had been raised a lady, and now that she could reclaim her true identity, she might have raised her expectations.

She tilted her head thoughtfully. "I think it was for the best, even if we hadn't promised Primm we'd return immediately after the vote."

But then her eyes clouded—not by much, but he noticed.

"But…?" he prompted.

"I think that having a large wedding would have been a sad reminder of the absence of my parents. My father would have liked you."

"And your mother?"

"Eventually." Her smile turned teasing, resulting in a slow, deep, and lingering kiss.

They might be in a carriage, but this was their wedding day, and they would savor one another.

It was Beatrice who ended the kiss, leaning away from him. "Do you believe in fate?"

It was not at all what he expected.

"No." He didn't have to think hard about his answer.

"But I cannot help but wonder if all of this happened for a reason." Her little nose wrinkled at some thought or another. "What if I had never met you?"

"I hadn't thought my wife was a romantic."

"Nor had I imaged my marquess was one."

"And you were right," Ranulf nipped at the side of her neck.

"No," she exhaled. "I was not. You are perhaps the most romantic gentleman I ever could have imagined."

Ranulf stopped and scowled. "Surely not."

"All the more so because you hide it under those scowls.

But what else am I to think, when my lover risks his neck climbing a trellis so he can enter my window?"

It had been a rather grand gesture. Ranulf smirked.

"That was strategy." He grasped her gown and slowly gathered the fabric, lifting the hem so he could touch her properly.

"And then, you find my brother, you essentially solve all my troubles… If that isn't romantic, then I don't know what is." Her exhale was a soft, satisfied sigh.

"And this?" Ranulf found himself less patient than he'd wanted to be, lifting her so she could help him unfasten his falls and so he could lift the fabric of her gown even higher.

Settling himself at her entrance where she was already deliciously wet.

She lowered herself back onto his lap, allowing his cock to settle between them, nestled along her delicate folds. A slow hiss escaped between his teeth.

"Lady Bedwell told me her mother advised her to think about England while her husband attended to her."

"I'm sorry to inform you, wife." Ranulf's hands unfastened the back of her gown, at the same time his teeth caught at her bodice. "That you are not going to have time to think about England or anything else while your husband… attends to you." Fumbling only a little, he relieved her of the top half of her gown, settling it around her waist, exposing her perfect little breasts.

But as his hands roved over her back, over slim ridges… He frowned. What the devil?

"Ignore them," she said.

The scars. She'd mentioned being punished by her uncle but hadn't comprehended the extent of what that villain had done.

Ranulf kissed her bare shoulder. "I can't ignore anything about you. You are my everything."

"Oh, Ranulf…" He loved hearing her name on her lips. It was the soft sigh that ended this game of anticipation. He lifted her onto him, but paused as she gazed down at him.

And as they joined, he thanked his lucky stars that he'd found this woman.

"Perhaps," he exhaled.

"Perhaps?

"Perhaps you are right." They began moving together and he forgot his train of thought as she surrounded him with unadulterated pleasure.

"About what?" She gasped, moving with him, her inner muscles clenching and unclenching.

"Perhaps I am a little romantic," he finished. "But fate isn't what brought you to me."

"Then what was it?"

"The culmination of all my very best decisions."

"Oh, Ranulf." But she laughed. "Of course it was."

# BONUS EPILOGUE

Augusta Primm drew her dressing gown a little tighter around her waist as she stepped outside.

There had been no attacks for three weeks now, so she'd decided against delaying the beginning of the term.

Nerves pricked the back of her neck every time she contemplated her decision. If there were any signs of trouble, she'd send the girls home without delay.

Aside from that, she had little choice but to rely on the Marquess of Sexton to track down whoever had set out to ruin her.

The vote was to have taken place earlier that day, so he and Beatrice ought to be arriving any day now.

She closed the door behind her.

Augusta was not accustomed to ambiguity. She'd grown to be a woman who knew her mind—a woman who had learned that no good came from second-guessing herself. Second-guessing led to regrets. Regrets, if allowed to fester, worked like poison.

Tilting her head back, she stared up at the night sky.

The moon was barely a sliver of light, but millions and millions of stars flickered and glowed reassuringly.

She was but a speck in the vast universe—as was the school. This wonderous place she'd somehow brought to life.

And for all the sacrifices she'd made, it was *her* speck.

She wasn't about to lose it without putting up a fight.

"You shouldn't be out here alone."

The voice did not startle her—even if it did send shivers down her spine. She couldn't help but remember the first time she'd heard it.

Butterflies had taken flight in her chest and her knees had turned weak. *A very long time ago.*

"I'm not alone," she answered and then turned. *Just lonely.* The thought snuck up on her with the stealth of a lion.

Rowan Stewart stood in the shadows, one shoulder slouched against the brick of her residence, his ankles crossed, looking utterly unconcerned. All she could make out was the outline of his formidable physique.

He pushed away from the building and stepped into the dim light provided by all those stars. She could make out the shape of his head, every chiseled angle, his short-cropped hair hiding nothing. He tilted his head back and stared up at the sky. He had always been a stargazer.

He was her one regret.

Her heart squeezed and she clenched her fists, pressing them into her belly.

Because he was here, now. And her resistance was wearing thin.

But she'd made a choice years ago. They'd been young, and in love. They hadn't realized their love was doomed.

And now…

She was Miss Primm. The school came first. It was all she could ever have.

She swallowed hard and moved to go inside.

"Goodnight, Mr. Stewart," she said.

He stared at her and for a moment she didn't think he'd respond.

But then, he did.

"Goodnight sweetheart."

—The End—

**Schooled By The Bastard** is book seven, the long-awaited conclusion of my series:

**Miss Primm's Secret School For Budding Bluestockings**

## MISS PRIMM'S SECRET SCHOOL FOR BUDDING BLUESTOCKINGS

A NEW ANNABELLE ANDERS SERIES

**TRAPPED WITH THE DUKE**

Miss Colette Jones

**EDUCATED BY THE EARL**

Miss Victoria Shipley

**PRETENDING TO BE A DEBUTANTE**

Lady Priscilla

**RESCUED BY THE RAKE**

Miss Chloe Fortune

**ADVISING THE VISCOUNT**

Miss Addy

**MAKE BELIEVE WITH THE MARQUESS**

Miss Beatrice Wolcott

**SCHOOLED BY THE BASTARD**

Miss Primm

January 2023

# ABOUT THE AUTHOR

Married to the same man for over 25 years, I am a mother to three children and two Miniature Wiener dogs.

After owning a business and experiencing considerable success, my husband and I got caught in the financial crisis and lost everything in 2008; our business, our home, even our car.

At this point, I put my B.A. in Poly Sci to use and took work as a waitress and bartender (Insert irony). Unwilling to give up on a professional life, I simultaneously went back to college and obtained a degree in EnergyManagement.

And then the energy market dropped off.

And then my dog died.

I can only be grateful for this series of unfortunate events, for, with nothing to lose and completely demoralized, I sat down and began to write the romance novels which had until then, existed only my imagination. After publishing over twenty novels now, with one having been nominated for RWA's Distinguished ™RITA Award in 2019, I am happy to tell you that I have finally found my place in life.

Thank you so much for being a part of my journey!

To find out more about my books, and also to download a free novella, get all the info at my website!

www.annabelleanders.com

# GET A FREE BOOK

Sign up for the news letter and download a book from Annabelle,

For **FREE!**

Sign up at **www.annabelleanders.com**

I love keeping in touch with readers and would be thrilled to hear from you! Join or follow me at any (or all!) of the social media links below!

Bookbub

Website

Goodreads

Facebook Author Page

Facebook Reader Group: A Regency House Party

Made in the USA
Columbia, SC
06 October 2022

68955342R00200